# FOR WE ARE MANY

*BOOK 2 OF THE BOBIVERSE*

## Dennis E. Taylor

TITLES BY THE AUTHOR

THE WORLD LINES SERIES:
 *Outland*
 *Earthside* (coming 2018)

THE BOBIVERSE SERIES:
 *We Are Legion (We Are Bob)*
 *For We Are Many*
 *All These Worlds*

ISBN: 978-1680680591

Published by Worldbuilders Press, a service of the Ethan Ellenberg Literary Agency

Cover art by Jeff Brown

Author Blog: www.dennisetaylor.org

I would like to dedicate this book to all the people who love good old-fashioned space opera.

# Acknowledgements

I am truly amazed and grateful for how *We Are Legion (We Are Bob)* was received by science fiction fans. The response has been both overwhelming and humbling. Thank you. It has been quite the journey...and along the journey I have had great help.

First I would like to thank my agent Ethan Ellenberg for not only taking me on but guiding me through all this. Your help has been invaluable and I am grateful. To Steve Feldberg who saw the potential in *We Are Legion* and the series...thank you so much for the opportunity you have given me. Betsy Mitchell - thank you for editing my manuscripts and for the words of encouragement.

It takes a "village" of sorts to create a novel, everyone from beta readers, critiques, artists, editors, publishers and now a narrator. To Ray Porter, thank you for bringing Bob Johansson to life.

I'd like to particularly mention the members of the Ubergroup and Novel Exchange group on scribophile. I appreciate your input. And to my beta readers - thank you.

Thanks in particular to:
    Sandra and Ken McLaren
    Nicole Hamilton
    Sheena Lewis
    Patrick Jordan
    Trudy Cochrane
    And my wife Blaihin

...for reading the raw draft and early versions.

# TABLE OF CONTENTS

It is not down in any map; true places never are.

— Herman Melville

# 1.   Sky God

## Bob
## February 2167
## Delta Eridani

An angry squeal erupted from the pile of deadwood. The two Deltans paused, poised to retreat. Seeing no further response, they resumed pelting the area with rocks. The individual I had named *Bernie*, his fur erect along his spine and ears straight out with excitement, chanted, "Here, *kuzzi, kuzzi, kuzzi.*"

I moved my observation drone to the rear to get out of their line of sight. They were okay with me observing the hunt, but I didn't want to distract them when even a slight misstep could result in injury or death. Mike glanced up at the movement, but the Deltans otherwise paid no attention to the football-sized drone.

Someone must have scored a direct hit with a rock. Screaming like an irate steam engine, the pigoid erupted from the entrance to its den. The two rock-throwers sprinted out of the way and the other hunters moved up. Each braced the butt of his spear on the ground and placed a foot on the end to hold it in place.

The pigoid reached the hunting group in less than a second, screaming in rage. The Deltans held their positions with all the courage of medieval pikemen facing a cavalry charge. Even though

I watched the action remotely via a floating observation drone, I could still feel my nether regions puckering up in fear. At times like this, I wondered if I hadn't gone a little overboard with the level of detail in my virtual-reality environment. There was no reason for me to even *have* nether regions, let alone for them to pucker.

The pigoid crashed into the waiting spears without slowing. Fast, yes. Smart, not so much. I'd never seen a pigoid try to dodge the spear points. One of the hunters, Fred, was thrown to the side as his spear bowed and then snapped. He screamed, either in pain or surprise, and blood spurted from his leg. A distracted part of my mind noted that Deltan blood was almost the same shade of red as human blood.

The other Deltans held fast, and the pigoid was lifted right into the air by the leverage of their spears. It hung in midair for a moment, then crashed to the ground with a final screech. The Deltan hunters waited for any more movement, lips drawn back to show their impressive canines. Occasionally, a pigoid would get back up after this level of mistreatment and wade in for another round. No one wanted to be caught with their guard down.

Bernie sidled up with his spear in one hand and a club in the other. Stretching as far as he could with the spear, he poked the pigoid in the snout. When there was no reaction, he turned to his fellow hunters and grinned.

Not literally, of course. The Deltan equivalent of a grin was an ear-waggle, but I was so used to the Deltan mannerisms that I no longer needed to consciously interpret. And the translation software took care of speech, converting idiom and metaphor between English and Deltan. I had assigned arbitrary human names to individuals to help me keep track of everyone.

Truthfully, humans and Deltans would never communicate without a translator. Deltan speech sounded to human ears like a series of grunts, growls, and hiccups. According to Archimedes, my main contact among the Deltans, human speech sounded like two pigoids in a mating frenzy. Nice.

The Deltans looked like a kind of a bat/pig mashup—barrel bodies, spindly limbs, large mobile ears, and snouts not too different from a boar's. Their fur was mainly gray, with tan patterns around the face and head unique to each individual. The Deltans were the first non-human intelligence I'd ever encountered, in only the second star system I had visited since leaving Earth more than thirty years ago. It made me wonder if intelligent life was perhaps as common as *Star Trek* would have us believe.

Bill regularly transmitted his news blogs from Epsilon Eridani, but they were nineteen years old by the time I received them. If any of the other Bobs had found intelligence, Bill might not even have received the reports yet, let alone re-transmitted them to the rest of us.

I returned my attention to the Deltans as they began to organize their post-hunt routine.

The hunters checked on Fred, who was sitting on a rock, swearing in Deltan and pressing on the wound to staunch the bleeding. I moved the drone in to get a close look, and one of the group moved aside to give me a better view.

Fred had been lucky. The gash from the splintered spear was jagged but not deep, and appeared clean. If the pigoid had gotten its teeth into him, he'd be dead.

Mike made a show of trying to poke the wound with his spear. "Does that hurt? Does that hurt?"

Fred showed his teeth. "Yeah, funny. Next time you can have the bad spear."

Mike smiled back, unrepentant, and Bernie slapped Fred on the shoulder. "Come on, don't be a baby. It's almost stopped bleeding."

"Right, let's get this thing hung and bled." Matching action to words, Mike unwound his rope from around his torso. He flipped the rope over a convenient tree branch, and Bernie tied the rear legs of the carcass.

*Knot-making skills, not so good.* The rope-work was rudimentary, and probably slipped occasionally. I made a mental note to teach Archimedes some sailing knots.

Mike and Bernie strung up the carcass and proceeded to field-dress their kill, while the other Deltans started a Giving-Thanks chant. As I watched, I had one of those incongruous moments where I half-expected them to attach a hunting tag to its ear. Wrong century, wrong planet, wrong species, of course.

I turned away from the drone's video window and chuckled as I picked up my coffee. Marvin, who had been watching over my shoulder, gave me a strange look, but I didn't feel the need to explain. Hell, he should be able to remember Original Bob going hunting with Dad, way back when. I shrugged at him without comment. Work it out, dude.

Marvin rolled his eyes and returned to the La-Z-Boy that he always materialized when he was visiting my VR. I spared a moment to let Jeeves refresh my coffee. As in every virtual reality space that implemented the Jeeves A.I., he resembled John Cleese in tux and tails.

As I took a sip—perfect, as always—I looked around the library from my seat in one of the antique wingback chairs. Floor-to-ceiling bookshelves, a large, old-fashioned fireplace, and tall, narrow windows through which a perpetual late-afternoon sun shone to illuminate the interior. And like a giant shiny black eye, one red corduroy La-Z-Boy, occupied by a clone of yours truly.

All in VR, of course. Physically, Marvin and I were a couple of glowing opto-electronic cubes, installed in the two spaceships currently orbiting Delta Eridani 4. But we had been human once, and our VR environments kept us sane.

Spike wandered over, jumped up onto Marvin's lap, and began to purr. The cat's A.I. was realistic, right down to the total lack of loyalty. I gave a small snort of amusement and turned back to the video window.

The hunters had finished field-dressing their kill. The pigoid didn't really look like a wild boar. It was probably closer to a bear in general outline, but it filled the same ecological niche as a boar, complete with the same sunny disposition and affectionate behavior.

Hunting them wasn't a one-sided proposition by any means. The Deltans took a chance on every pigoid hunt. The pigoid usually lost, but it sometimes managed to take down one or two of the hunters. The recent addition of flint tips to the spears was changing the game, though. Yeah, I know. Prime Directive, blah, blah. Pfft. This wasn't *Star Trek*, despite Riker's choice of name and VR theme.

The Deltans trussed their prize to a couple of spears, and four of them hoisted the ends of the spears to their shoulders. Mike beckoned with a gesture, and I maneuvered the drone over to float along beside him. Two others put their arms around Fred and helped him to his feet. His leg hadn't quite stopped bleeding,

DENNIS E. TAYLOR

and he showed a pronounced limp, but he'd make it back to the village.

We marched triumphantly towards the Deltans' home, a couple of the hunters singing a victory chant. The others traded good-natured jokes and insults as they compared notes. I never ceased to be amazed at how very similar in behavior the Deltans were to humans. It made me feel nostalgic, occasionally, for genuine human contact.

We soon arrived at the village, greeted by laughter and celebration. A pigoid kill was always a happy event—the *hexghi* would have a feast tonight, and would eat well for a week. *Hexghi* translated as something like *families of our fire*. Of course, it flowed a lot better in Deltan. This hunting group was part of Archimedes' *hexghi*, which I'd more or less adopted as family.

Fred was helped over to his family's spot, where his mate proceeded to fuss over him. One of the hunters hurried off to get the medicine woman, Cruella. I sighed and prepared myself for yet another argument with her.

The messenger returned moments later with Cruella and her apprentice in tow. Cruella bent down to examine the wound, and I brought the drone in close. Too close, I guess. Cruella straight-armed the drone and it shot back several feet before the AMI controller was able to stabilize it. The other Deltans stepped back in shock, and one looked like he was going to either flee or faint. The drone was small, and really not hard to push around. But still, y'know, *sky god.*

I'd long since learned that the medicine woman feared no one and nothing. And she wasn't particularly good at taking advice, either. I gritted my teeth in frustration, wondering if this time Cruella would pay attention to anything that I'd told her.

Fred apparently was having the same thought. "This would be a good time to try *Bawbe's* hot-water thing," he said to her.

Cruella glared at him, then at my drone. "Maybe he can just dress the wound as well, since you don't seem to need me."

"Oh, by the balls of my ancestors, Cruella," Mike said. "Try something new, just once. *Bawbe* hasn't steered us wrong yet."

Cruella snarled at him. Within moments, the hunters and Cruella had faced off in a yelling match. The hunters were my biggest supporters. Flint tips, spear straighteners, and hand axes were only a few of the improvements that I'd brought to their lives. They, at least, trusted that I had the Deltans' best interests at heart.

Finally, Cruella threw her hands in the air and barked, "Fine! We'll do it your way. And if your leg falls off, don't come whining to me."

She turned to her apprentice and snarled an order. The apprentice flattened her ears and ran off.

Minutes later she was back, carrying a bladder and a soft leather skin. Cruella pointed to the bladder and said, "Freshly boiled water." She held up the soft piece of scraped skin and said, "Washed in boiling water." Then she glared right into the drone's camera. "Now stay out of my way."

I watched in pleased surprise as she took the time to clean the wound with the piece of hide, using the freshly boiled water. This was progress. Granted, the hunters helped a lot by putting their collective foot down; but if Cruella got into the habit, incidents of infection would drop dramatically.

I bobbed the drone once in acknowledgement, then sent it off to station-keeping at the perimeter of the village. I returned to my VR once again, sat back, and closed the drone's video window. The change in procedure by the medicine woman was a major victory, and I was happy to get out of her way in return. It would allow her to save face, and she wouldn't feel the need to dig in her heels next time.

I'd miss the rest of the celebration, but the pigoid's ultimate fate was a matter of routine, and well-documented. And probably delicious. I thought of ribs in barbeque sauce and my mouth watered. I didn't need food any more, being a computer and all, but I could do anything I wanted in VR. And if you're going to program in a coffee simulation, you might as well program in barbequed ribs.

Spike came walking across my desk, meowed once, and plunked down on my keyboard. I accepted a coffee refill from Jeeves, then turned to Marvin. "Okay. Excitement's over. What's up? You wanted to talk to me about something?"

Marvin nodded and stood. He dismissed the La-Z-Boy and walked over to my work desk. Pulling up a wingback, he invoked a globe of Eden in mid-air over the desk, with a small section of one continent outlined in red. "This is the current range of the Deltans. I've excluded the old village, since they no longer live there—"

"—and that was more of a refuge than a permanent home." I nodded. "They hadn't even been there for a full generation."

Marvin bobbed his head in acknowledgement. "Anyway, I've been doing a lot of digging—literally, in some cases—and I've arrived at a reasonable estimate of Deltan population movements over time."

He looked at me expectantly, and I made a rolling motion with my hand for him to continue.

"They do not appear to be from this area at all. It looks as though the sentient Deltan subspecies originated *here...*" Marvin rotated the globe and pointed to a different part of the continent. "...and moved from there to the current location."

"And they're no longer at the old location? Why?"

"That's what I don't get, Bob. I've found a lot of evidence of abandoned Deltan villages, and some burial sites, but not nearly enough graves to account for the expected population."

"Predation?"

"You'd think, but then we'd find Deltan remains here and there, at least in the form of piles of bones. You've seen what the gorilloids leave behind when they're done with a meal. They're not fastidious."

I rubbed my chin, gazing at the globe. "That doesn't make sense, anyway. From your notes, the original area didn't have gorilloids at all. So they moved from a *safer* area to a more *dangerous* area, and disappeared in the safer area."

"Then fled the more dangerous area to set up in an even *more* dangerous area." Marvin shook his head in confusion. "They aren't morons. They may be just in the process of becoming human-level sentient, but they have common sense. We're missing something."

I shrugged, and sent the globe spinning with a flick of a finger. "It's a mystery, Marvin, and we do love a mystery." We exchanged grins. After all, *Bob.* "But the important thing is that they're much safer here, compared to where we found them. They've settled in nicely in Camelot, the hunting's good, and the gorilloids are beginning to get the hint and have pretty much stopped trying to pick off Deltans."

"You're really going to call their village *Camelot*?" Marvin gave me the stink-eye. "Every time you say it, I hear *Knights of the Round Table.*"

I grinned at him and waggled my eyebrows. "It's only a model."

Marvin rolled his eyes and stopped the globe. "Anyway, I'll keep at this, but we're at a disadvantage here. On Earth, scientists were building up from existing knowledge of a world they understood. On Eden, we're starting from scratch."

"Yeah, and even then, it took years for them to figure out things like the fate of the Anasazi." I sat back and shook my head. "Yeah, I get it, Marv. I have to admit, I'm glad this is a pet project for you. I did some basic research and exploration when I landed, but it wasn't a priority for me."

Marvin chuckled and, with a parting nod, disappeared back to his own VR.

# 2.   Colony Site

## Howard
## September 2188
## Vulcan

Colonization of a new planet was always so easy in science fiction. Actually, scratch that. It was *never* easy. Something always came out of the woodwork to endanger the colony. Well, they got one thing right. Sort of.

On the plus side, nothing was bursting out of people's chests. However, setting up a human colony on Vulcan was turning out to be a little bit like being pecked to death by ducks. Large ducks. With teeth and claws. Milo's notes and planetary catalog made it very clear that setting up would require attention to defensive strategies. The ecosystem was prolific and competitive.

The colony ships Exodus-1 and -2 orbited Vulcan, most of the colonists from the USE enclave still in stasis, waiting for the settlement teams to prepare a site. Construction teams, security teams, and engineers worked day and night to clear enough jungle and build a home for this first wave of humanity.

The USE colonists would also be expected to provide some support to future colony ships. Exodus-3 was only a few months behind us, and more would be coming as fast as Riker could build them.

Like we needed the extra pressure.

Five days after humans set foot on Vulcan, the planet claimed its first casualty.

**[Message from the security chief. There has been an attack]**

I nodded to Guppy, acknowledging the information. I took a moment to minimize the monitoring window that had been floating in the air in front of me, and ordered the construction AMIs to continue on their own. They could handle most of the tasks involved in building the orbiting farm donut, and they would text me if they ran into something above their pay grade.

I turned in my chair and raised an eyebrow at Guppy, inviting more information. But the GUPPI system interface, in the form of an avatar resembling Admiral Ackbar, wasn't inclined to volunteer anything beyond the basic facts. Huge fish eyes blinked at me, waiting for a command. Accepting the inevitable, I motioned with my hand, and he pushed the video window to me.

The window showed the head of security, Stéphane Brodeur, with that look people get when they're on an adrenaline high—wide eyes, slight sheen of sweat, nostrils dilated. He began to speak as soon as he saw me. "There has been an attack. The therapod-like predators that we've tagged as *raptors*. Northwest corner, at the fence construction boundary."

Brodeur spoke with a pronounced Quebecois accent. I wondered idly how he had managed to get into the USE colony, but dismissed the question as irrelevant. I frame-jacked for a moment and sent a couple of drones to the fence construction area, then returned my frame rate to normal. A human being wouldn't even notice the millisecond glitch in my image. "Casualties?"

"One."

"Dead?"

"No, but it will need the new paint job." Brodeur grinned at me.

I raised an eyebrow, and he continued, "A small group of raptors attacked a backhoe. The equipment will need the paint touched up. We killed most of the animals, and the rest ran off. One of the carcasses is being sent to Dr. Sheehy for necropsy."

"So what can I do?"

The security chief shook his head. "About the attack, nothing. It's done, and we've taken care of the attackers. I am hoping you can set up surveillance of some kind."

A reasonable request. I nodded in thought. "Mr. Brodeur, I have some drones I can put on guard duty now, although they aren't really optimized for that. Bill, over in Epsilon Eridani, has been refining surveillance and exploration drones for a couple of decades now. I'll get some plans from him and start printing up something suitable. It'll take a week or two before they're ready. Can you hold out?"

"I will talk to the construction chief and see if we can cut back on some of the tasks until you're done. We would be spread too thin, right now."

"Do that, Chief. I'll keep you updated."

I closed the connection, and sent an email to Bill, requesting information on his observation drones. He'd designed them more for use by Bobs exploring new systems, but they'd do fine for my purposes as well.

* * *

Security personnel were still swarming the area when my drones arrived at the fence construction site. Blood covered the ground, fortunately all raptor. A very sad-looking backhoe sat off to one side, long scrapes and scratches marring the bright yellow paint job. I wondered idly if the backhoe's AMI controller would need therapy.

Personnel were hauling several carcasses into the back of transport trucks. The raptors resembled movie velociraptors closely enough to give nightmares to anyone who'd seen *Jurassic Park*. But instead of the peg-like teeth of the canonical carnosaur, their teeth resembled those of sharks—triangular, serrated, and razor sharp. So far, the use of military-grade automatic weapons on them hadn't blunted their enthusiasm for the newly arrived food group.

I found Chief Brodeur overseeing the cleanup and floated over to him.

He turned as the drone approached and grinned. "And to think I turned down the desk job."

I chuckled politely in response. "Welcome to the frontier. Did you get all of them?"

"No." He shook his head. "We let one or two get away to communicate fear of humans to their friends."

"And how's that working out, so far?"

Chief Brodeur laughed and shook his head. "I have a meeting with the colonel this afternoon. Perhaps you could attend."

"He's already invited me, Mr. Brodeur. I'll see you there."

Chief Brodeur nodded to the drone, then turned back to help his staff with cleanup. I took the opportunity to inspect the progress on construction.

A fence stretched about a third of the way around the planned town site. Five meters tall, it was built from a combination of native wood and metal. The Vulcan trees were close enough to their Terran equivalents that the setup crews were able to adapt them with little effort. The trees were harvested from the area immediately around the fence, forming a clear-cut for additional security. I had my doubts about whether the fence was tall enough to keep the brontos at bay, but no one had asked me. Not that the brontos would eat people or anything. They were more of an "accidentally step on you" kind of danger.

To the west, Vulcan's sister planet Romulus hung in the sky, clouds and seas clearly visible. When Exodus-3 arrived, the passengers, from the FAITH and Spitz enclaves, would be settling there. I expected life to get very interesting once the FAITH colony got started. I doubted that nineteen years of stasis would improve Minister Cranston's disposition. The FAITH leader wasn't what I'd call a people-person to begin with, and his relationship with the Bobs had developed into kind of a hate-hate thing.

I sent another drone up a few hundred meters and set it to circle the area, watching for any movement of native life. Nothing lurked nearby, probably due to the noise of the automatic weapons.

Things appeared to have calmed down, and everyone was back to work. I backed out of the drone and back into my VR. Sighing, I rubbed my forehead. Sometimes I missed sleeping for a third of each day. It had been a nice break from reality.

"Guppy, I have some printer schedule changes."

Guppy popped in and waited silently for me to continue. Looking at him, I wondered if I should change the Admiral Ackbar image. But nothing else came to mind, and anyway it had become a kind of tradition with the Bobs.

"We need more observation drones."

[All printer groups are currently engaged in producing parts for the orbiting farms. Do you want to bump this activity?]

"Hmm, not really. Okay, put half the printers on drones, and produce four full squads. Then back to building the farm donuts."
[Aye]

Guppy went into command fugue while he reprogrammed the 3D printers. I turned back to the video windows from my active drones. I would build more drones as requested, but I had a bad feeling that we'd go through a few colonists before we got the fence completed.

* * *

"Good afternoon, Colonel." The video window showed Colonel Butterworth, as usual looking impeccable and wrinkle-free. I wondered how he did it.

"Morning, Howard." He nodded toward my image on his desk phone. "Good to see you. I heard about today's attack."

I took a moment to be surprised. I didn't remember Colonel Butterworth ever greeting Riker with that level of friendliness back on Earth. I wasn't sure if I should be offended for Riker or pleased for me.

The leader of the USE enclave had been at odds with Riker since day one. I had all Riker's memories of those days of course, right up to the moment that Riker had cloned me. It would be an understatement to describe Butterworth as "pushy," although at least he was always professional.

With a mental shrug, I decided not to worry about it. Different time, different place, and let's face it, I wasn't Riker.

"Yeah, but we won't be so lucky next time," I replied. "The raptors are smart. They'll figure out that backhoes aren't edible. If they've got good color vision—a high likelihood—they'll probably associate bright yellow with inedible things with hard shells. Then they'll start concentrating on the soft and squishy two-legged things."

Butterworth snorted. "I saw your immediate strategy with the drones. I'm just reading your plan for observation and surveillance systems. Looks comprehensive. I have a few small suggestions, which we can go over when convenient."

I nodded without comment. The colonel's suggestions would be good ones, and I'd very likely implement them.

"So, where's Mr. Brodeur? Wasn't he supposed to be here?"

"He was." The colonel shrugged. "Something came up. I'll debrief him separately, and call you if anything requires more discussion."

I nodded, then glanced over the colonel's shoulder, where the townsite plan was posted on the far wall. I motioned at it with my chin. "Kind of old-school, isn't it? A paper poster tacked up on a wall?"

"Hardcopy still has its place, Howard. It's much bigger than an image on a tablet, and I can make notes on it with a color marker. Of course, I also take a picture, periodically." The colonel gave me his trademark dry smile. "In other news, we are ready to decant the farming specialists from stasis. Mr. Brodeur tells me that they will have the farm area enclosed within a week."

"Good. Bert and Ernie are getting antsy about unloading everyone soon." Butterworth winced as I mentioned the two colony-ship Bobs. I wasn't sure which was more amusing—that he disapproved so much over our naming choices, or that he recognized the reference.

"Another month or so, Howard, then we can make that decision with confidence." The colonel reached forward out of frame. "And maybe by the time Exodus-1 and Exodus-2 get back to Earth for another load, someone will have found another habitable system and they'll stop shipping people our way." Without waiting for a response, he ended the call.

# 3.    Life in Camelot

## Bob
## March 2167
## Delta Eridani

Archimedes placed the bone tool with care and tapped it with a rock. A fleck of flint dropped off the core, and Moses nodded in approval. Archimedes repositioned the tool for his next strike, and glanced at Moses with his ears pointed slightly forward. Moses made a small hand motion. Archimedes moved the tool a fraction to the left and his ears curled with concentration as he again tapped on the tool.

The other Deltan adolescent, whom I'd named Richard, watched Archimedes then tried to copy his technique. But the tool slipped off the cobble and stabbed into his foot. He leaped up and hopped on the other foot, cursing with enthusiasm.

After a few moments, Richard noticed Archimedes' grin and scowled. Snarling, he compared Archimedes to pigoid droppings, then stalked off, limping.

Moses and Archimedes were the tribe's best flint experts and tool-makers. And based on Richard's performance, still the *only* ones. Archimedes was a teenager by Deltan standards—past puberty, but not yet fully grown. He was, however, easily the most intelligent Deltan in the village. Which meant, based on our searches, the most intelligent Delta on the entire planet of Eden.

Archimedes was the first Delta in years, it seemed, who could understand Moses' flint-knapping instructions. A couple of juveniles, like Richard, had shown some interest, but couldn't maintain the level of concentration required to complete a tool. Very likely Archimedes would have to wait for some of his own progeny before he'd be able to attract any apprentices of his own.

"Moses isn't looking so good," Marvin commented, looking over my shoulder.

"Yeah, I know. I think the march from the old village was harder than we expected. A couple of other elderly Deltans have died since they got here."

I mentioned my theory about potential apprentices, and Marvin laughed. "I can think of at least two females from Archimedes' cohort who are actively working on that."

Yeah, gotta love adolescence. Between his flint-knapping skills, his tool-making ability in general, and his position as primary spokesperson for *The Bawbe*, Archimedes had a level of mojo totally out of keeping with his youth. All of which apparently went over quite well with the girls.

Archimedes set aside the core and the tools, stood up, and stretched. He and Moses exchanged a few words, and Moses got up and wandered off. There was no nine-to-five in Delta society. Things got done when things got done. It looked like they'd had enough for the moment.

Archimedes turned and looked around until he located the drone I was using to observe. He grinned up at me and made a head motion toward the practice range. I bobbed the drone in agreement, then floated after him as he headed in that direction.

I opened the conversation. "Things are looking good. Everyone seems to have settled in."

Archimedes nodded. He walked in silence for a few more moments. "Arnold is happy with the new village, uh, *Camelot*?" I had mentioned my name for the camp once, without running it through the translator. Archimedes was trying to render the word phonetically. It was a valiant attempt, but no human would have recognized the sound.

"Let's just go with your word for it, Archimedes. My language doesn't translate well into Deltan."

"Fine with me. That hurt my throat. Anyway, Arnold likes how we can defend the two access paths instead of the entire boundary."

Camelot was a located on a small mesa that was surrounded by scree and cliffs most of the way around. It reminded me a little of an aircraft carrier, including a rocky bluff in the center resembling a carrier's control island. Two paths, about 120 degrees apart, were the only ways on or off the mesa, unless you could fly. It was a huge improvement over their old village, which had been just a clearing in the forest. Guarding against gorilloid attacks had been a full-time job at the old village, and they'd still been losing the battle.

"Two people were killed in the last two hands of days, though, right?" I said.

Archimedes shrugged. "The gorilloids are a problem. They are always hungry. And there are so many on this side of the mountains. Guarding is a bigger job when people are away from the village."

All the more reason to make it less necessary to leave the village. I already had herding on my list of things to teach them. I still needed to find an appropriate herd animal to domesticate. I turned away from the drone window just long enough to sigh and shake my head. That TODO list just kept growing.

I found myself in one of those all-or-nothing situations. I'd made a decision to help the Deltans avoid extinction. What had started as a small, anonymous intervention quickly turned into a full-time job as *The Bawbe,* resident sky god. I hoped eventually to be able to leave them to their own fate, but that probably wasn't in the cards for a generation or so.

We had arrived at the practice range, so I dropped the topic. *Practice range* was a trumped-up description, of course. The range consisted of a flat area at the side of the steep embankment leading up to the central bluff. Deltans staked up targets on the slope, and they used these to practice the new technology of spear-chucking.

We watched for a few minutes. Most Deltans could get a spear into the right area, point first, most of the time. But actually hitting one of the targets was an accomplishment, and usually resulted in a lot of dancing and taunts directed at the other students. Any thought of precision was an unreachable fantasy for most. Some Deltans were out-and-out terrible, and one or two couldn't get it through their heads that the spear had to fly point-first. Those individuals generally stayed on pigoid-hunting duty, where the spear never left your hand.

Archimedes was exceptionally good with a spear, but he lacked the upper-body strength to get any kind of distance. When he reached full adulthood, though, he would be formidable.

Arnold was the other prodigy in this new technology. He had an intuitive feel for anything that involved killing. A natural warrior, he'd been the first Deltan to kill a gorilloid with a hand axe, splitting the beast's skull with one blow. Arnold was almost as big as a juvenile gorilloid, so he generally got very little backtalk.

Arnold paced back and forth, helping individuals with their technique and yelling encouragement. I chuckled, without letting it play out through the drone. I'd rigged the translator to render his speech with an Austrian accent. It never got old.

"How is it going with the medicine woman?" Archimedes asked, interrupting my train of thought.

I cringed inwardly. One of the surprising things about Deltans was their lack of awe for the divine authority of *The Bawbe*, and Cruella took that philosophy to new heights. A tribe of primitive humans would have been hanging on to my every word, but Deltans were much more skeptical and inclined to question. My first attempt to introduce them to tents still smarted a little.

"Not so well. She either flat out doesn't believe most of what I say, or she just doesn't want to change her ways. I am able to get the occasional concession, but it's an uphill battle."

Archimedes grinned up at the drone. "Welcome to my tribe. Maybe you should use one of the flying rocks on her."

I laughed, not only at the comment, but at the fact that Archimedes was sounding so much like me. He'd picked up the concept of dry humor right away, but it was completely beyond any but maybe a half-dozen other Deltans.

And using a buster on the medicine woman was certainly tempting. A self-propelled forty-pound ball of steel impacting at Mach 1 didn't leave much room for argument. "I'll take it under advisement. She's at least taken my suggestions for cleaning wounds. She's not completely closed-minded, just very conservative."

Archimedes shrugged. He'd been dealing with that level of conservatism his whole life. It was a constant source of amusement to him that I was surprised by the attitude.

We continued along the path, which led up to the top of the central bluff. It was a flat area, about the size of a small house. Completely exposed to the elements, it would be useless as a living space, but the view was spectacular. On a sunny day like this, many of the adolescent Deltans gathered here to do what teenagers did the universe over—get away from the adults.

We endured a few moments of staring as Archimedes came over the crest, the football-sized drone hovering by his shoulder. But I was old news, and the kids soon went back to what they were doing. They appeared to be playing *Rinjhaxa*, a sort of pick-up-sticks with betting. Again, I was struck by how very human-like these people were. We only had two data points as of yet, but I wondered if there was some universality about the way intelligent species developed and behaved.

Archimedes waved at Diana, who sat with some of her friends. She smiled and waved back, then glared at the drone and turned away. Not my number one fan, for sure. I'd never given her any reason to hate me, as far as I knew. It might be as simple as competition for Archimedes' attention.

Archimedes sat down, facing north-east towards the mountain range that split this section of the continent. I brought the drone down to a comfortable talking height and took a moment to enjoy the view.

One of the two moons of Eden hung in the sky, twice the apparent size of Earth's moon. The sun, low in the west, imparted a golden highlight on the scattered clouds. The forest, stretching horizon to horizon, would have looked completely natural on Earth, before human beings clear-cut the planet.

Archimedes gestured towards the mountains in the distance. Most of them were high enough to have snow year-round. "That's a big journey. It was hard with you leading us back here, when we knew what we were heading for. It must have been harder when our parents and their parents were going the other way and had no idea what they'd find."

He looked around at the village, spread below us on the mesa. "It's so much better here. Except for all the gorilloids, of course." Archimedes showed his teeth, which I automatically translated to a frown.

"That's good, Archimedes. I want to see your people succeed. I don't know if there are a lot of intelligent species in all the worlds of the sky, but each one is priceless. So far, my brothers haven't found any others."

"How many *Bawbes* are there?"

I smiled at the question, but Archimedes couldn't see that. "I don't really know. I made four others before I left the last star, but they will hopefully have made more. I've made three here, so far. Two have left, and Marvin is still here, helping me."

"You *make* brothers?"

"It's complicated, Archimedes. I'm not flesh and blood, like you. Each brother I make is a copy of me, with my memories and everything. But usually a little different in personality. Marvin is more cautious than me and tends to keep me from implementing wild plans."

Archimedes stared at the drone for a few more seconds, then looked away. "Questions just bring more questions, and I never catch up. I should stick to things that affect my people."

I laughed, which the translation routine converted into the Deltan expression of humor. "That's fine, Archimedes. I have a very similar problem. I call it a TODO list. It only ever seems to get bigger."

Archimedes grinned in response and turned to the vista spread out before us. He sat and I hovered in silence, enjoying the scenery.

# 4.    Water Planet

## Mulder
## October 2170
## Eta Cassiopeiae

Eta Cassiopeiae was a long-period binary. The brightest of the pair, Eta Cassiopeiae A, was class G3V, only slightly larger and more luminous than Sol. At 19.5 light years from Epsilon Eridani, it was a bit of a hike. But all of the closer good candidates were spoken for. As part of Bill's third cohort, I had to take potluck, I guess. Most stars are K and M class, and I just didn't see a tidally locked planet sitting practically inside the chromosphere of its parent star as being a desirable vacation getaway. So, here I was, twenty-odd years later. By now, Homer and Riker would have gotten to Sol, and whatever situation they found would be resolved one way or another.

I chuckled, remembering the early days back at Epsilon Eridani. Homer was a real card. I think he picked his name at least as much because it bugged the other Bobs as anything else. I wondered if Riker would kill Homer himself in a "friendly fire" incident. That made me laugh out loud, and Guppy looked at me with fishy concern.

I lifted Spike off my lap and put her on the desk, then got up and stepped outside into the sun. My VR was a tropical location, with open-air huts, reminiscent of Gilligan's Island. It would be totally impractical in the real world, of course, but in VR you could do anything.

Guppy followed me out. **[Results are in. We have found no Jovians]**

"None?" I frowned. "I wonder if that's good or bad."

**[Insufficient information]**

I nodded distractedly, and turned back to face the beach.

I took a minute to enjoy the sun on my face and listen to the surf. I suppose I might eventually get tired of this scene, but not any time soon. It made me regret that I'd never taken the time for this kind of vacation when I was alive.

Taking a deep breath, I stepped past Guppy and back into the hut. The holotank showed the layout of the star system with about 95% confidence at this point. There might be a few smaller bodies floating around that we'd missed, but I doubted they'd be major players.

The companion star, Eta Cassiopeiae B, had a closest approach of 36 AU at periastron, which meant planets were unlikely outside of about 9 AU of EC-A. It also meant that the Oort and Kuiper objects had been disturbed many times. Any planets in this system would have taken more than one good pelting. The good news was there was probably very little left out there to send inward.

"That one," I pointed to the third planet. "Is right smack in the Comfort Zone. Any indication of size?"

**[No. But spectroscopic analysis is showing oxygen and water lines]**

"Oh, that's excellent."

**[There is also indication of a wobble, which would indicate a satellite]**

"Better and better. Okay, Guppy, plot a course to planet three."

**[Deploy mining and survey drones?]**

"Naw, let's see if this system is worth hanging around in, first."

Guppy somehow managed to look disappointed, although if pressed, I couldn't for the life of me describe what a disappointed fish looked like.

I stared in thought at the image floating in front of me. We'd detected four other rocky planets, two inside and two outside the Comfort Zone, but no Jovian planets. That worried me a little, as Jovians tended to keep the inner system relatively safe by perturbing anything coming straight in from the outer system.

Of more concern was the lack of a significant asteroid belt. The general plan for the HEAVEN project was to use the mineral wealth of asteroid belts to build the space station and future Bobs. No asteroid belt could spell trouble.

Meh. One thing at a time.

It took a few days to get there. I spent that time doing fine scans of the system for any sparse asteroid belts that I might have missed. No such luck. This system really had been swept clean. I had five planets, and whatever moons they might have, to work with. Planetary mining would require a lot of re-think.

I also got a bead on the moons of planet three. There were two bigger ones, one about half the size of Earth's moon, and one about a fifth the size; and two smaller ones, closer in, really not much more than big rocks. The planet itself was a little smaller than Earth, with a .87 surface gravity and a 26-hour rotation. The atmosphere was delightfully Earth-like, maybe a little more oxygen-rich.

I inserted myself into a polar orbit and started deep scans. The planet had a lot of cloud, just like Earth. That was good, since it indicated robust weather patterns. It also had a lot of water. In fact, so far, all I'd seen was water.

"Have we detected land, yet?"

[Negative]

"Well, that's... irritating. Alert me as soon as we find something."

[Aye]

* * *

[Scans are complete]

"But you were supposed to alert me—oh."

I examined the scans and started to laugh. Honest to God, a good belly laugh still feels good, even in VR.

The planet had water, all right. Oh, did it have water! What didn't it have? Land. None. Nada. Not so much as an atoll. This was just one big ball of ocean. Not even any freakin' ice caps to stand on.

Which raised the question of what exactly was creating the oxygen. On Earth, that would be green plants. But plants, not to put too fine a point on it, tended to require dirt. Excuse me, soil.

"Guppy, are you sure about the chlorophyll?"

**[Affirmative]**

Huh. Weird. I was obviously missing something. This would require a closer look.

I'd gotten a message from Bill with plans for planetary exploration drones while I was still incoming, but with no raw materials to work with, I was pretty much S.O.L.

I sighed theatrically and turned to Guppy, who was standing at parade rest, as usual. "I guess we'd better survey the system. Set a course to take us past each planet. Let's start with a flyby of this planet's moons."

**[Aye]**

It took a couple of weeks to hit all the other planets and their satellites. While I was buzzing around, I did manage to catalog a couple of asteroids with relatively eccentric orbits. I sat back in my beach chair, with a coffee in my hands, and reviewed the reports. There was lots of metal in this system. It appeared to be a little richer than Sol, in fact. But everything was planetside. It looked like the space junk that normally infests a system had virtually all become an impactor at some point. I could only guess that the effect of the binary partner, combined with the lack of a Jovian, had resulted in some weird chain of events that cleared the system. I'm sure an astrophysicist would have an explanation at the ready, and I promised myself I'd give that a think when I had the time.

I flew out to the fourth planet, the second moon of which had good ore deposits close to the surface. I set up the autofactory in orbit and fed several of my drones and roamers into it to use as construction material. A week later, the autofactory had built a couple of small cargo vessels. I loaded them up with mining drones and sent the whole crew down to the moon's surface.

While I waited, I re-examined the scans of planet three and pondered. I remembered reading that all of Earth's water could have been supplied by a single icy comet about 1000 km in diameter. Given the amount of material in Sol's Oort cloud, that was barely a sneeze. Since this system seemed to have had its cloud cleared, it wouldn't be too much of a stretch to think that the planets got pounded early on.

While the mining drones slaved away, I pondered the question of whether this world was even worth reporting as a colonization candidate. Oh, it had oxygen, and it had water, but the amount of effort required to build any kind of base would be incredible. I knew from the libraries that Earth in the twenty-second century had started building and populating floating cities, but they operated only with the support of land-bound industries.

Well, not my decision. I would just send in a report and let the powers that be hash it out. If there still were any powers that be, that is. The war could have wiped out humanity entirely, for all I knew, which would make this whole exercise moot.

Still, eventually, Riker would report back to Bill, and Bill would transmit the news in one of his regular blogs. Until I heard different, I was going to continue to play Von Neumann probe. I owed that to Dr. Landers.

\* \* \*

**[Construction AMI controller is now online]**
"Cool, thanks, Guppy. Order it to start on a couple of Bobs, then the space station."
**[Aye]**
The Artificial Machine Intelligence could handle routine construction using standard plans, and would contact me if it ran into any issues that were beyond its programming.

The various construction tasks would take months, so I flew back to the third planet with a couple of exploration drones to look around. I started with a deep scan of the ocean. And got my money's worth. I had to retune three times before I was able to detect ocean bottom. Eight hundred kilometers deep. That was just nuts. I'd had some thought of artificial islands, but unless there was a Mount Lookitthat down there somewhere, there wasn't going to be anything close enough to anchor to or build up.

I stared at the result in disbelief, then turned to Guppy. "Start a detailed mapping survey of the ocean floor, using the current SUDDAR settings. Let me know when you have a complete globe."
**[Aye]**
Telescopic surveys indicated some kind of green patches on the ocean, so I sent some drones down to investigate. It didn't take long to discover the source of the atmospheric oxygen. Plants had discovered that by sitting *on top* of the water, they could get much better light. The plants formed large mats—and by *large*, I mean

literally kilometers in diameter. I dispatched a biology drone to take samples.

The drones couldn't go underwater. That would just screw up the SURGE drive something fierce. Even atmosphere required careful tuning to avoid futzing up the field. But SUDDAR scans from in close revealed that the underwater ecosystem was rich beyond belief.

"Well, this is looking not so bad, suddenly. Assuming any of this is edible, people could live here and work upstairs." I looked at Guppy for a reaction. I might as well not have bothered.

The biological drone spent weeks surveying the mats and immediate area. The mats actually seemed to be comprised of multiple species of plant in symbiotic relationships. The animals had found the free ride, and there was a thriving commensal zoological ecosystem in and on the mats.

At the end of two months, I took the completed survey results and reviewed them.

Biocompatible. And according to the report, *exceptionally* so. In fact, other than a few amino acids and vitamins, it looked like humans could go native on the mats, barring anything poisonous.

I formatted a complete report and handed it off to the space station AMI, to be transmitted to Bill once the station was completed. The autofactory had completed a couple of computer matrices and cradles, so I did a backup and restored it into the matrices. HIC3821-1 and HIC3821-2 came online.

I expanded my VR to make room for company and invited them in.

Two Bobs popped into existence across the desk from me. I offered them beach chairs, and Jeeves brought coffee.

I smiled at them. "I guess you're wondering why I've gathered you here."

H-1 rolled his eyes. "Funny, I *knew* you were going to say that."

That got a chuckle from me. And wasn't what I'd expected, so my clones were *already* diverging from me. "So, got ideas for names?"

H-1 piped up, "Skinner for me."

I made a moue of appreciation. "Keeping to the theme. I'm touched."

"I'm more of a Jonny Quest type," H-2 said.

Skinner and I chuckled dutifully.

After a polite pause, I pulled up the system schematic with the autofactory area magnified in a cutaway view. "Okay, you guys are going to be helping out around here until your hulls are ready to go. After that, it's up to you, of course."

Both Bobs nodded. Jonny said, "No prob with the helping out, but I'm blowing this podunk system as soon as my vessel is ready." He turned to Skinner. "It's up to you whether you want to stay or not. Personally, I'd rather go look for something a little more interesting."

Well, that was a bit harsh. But, his choice, of course. Skinner simply shrugged.

I pointed to the image of the space station. "The station is almost done. When it sends the report Bill-ward, we set the mining drones to automatic collection, and that really ends our responsibility here. Questions?"

Both Bobs shook their heads.

"I might stay for a while and do another round of Bobs," I continued. "I'm curious about the life on Three. Hmm, Poseidon would be a good name, I think,"

"Ooh, naming it and everything. You *are* a sentimental sort."

Jonny was definitely a sarcastic S.O.B. I decided he couldn't leave soon enough for my tastes.

Skinner seemed to agree with me, as he was looking askance at Jonny. This seemed like Mario or Milo all over again. I remembered Bob-1 wondering what he'd do if he found he didn't like any particular clone. Turned out it didn't matter. It's a big galaxy.

# 5.    Progress

## Howard
## December 2188
## Omicron² Eridani

The fence was all but finished, the town had been laid out, and now it had an official name. *Landing* wasn't particularly inventive, but everyone thought it was appropriate.

I was on a conference call with Colonel Butterworth and Stéphane, discussing the recent deaths. The colonel had his usual glass of Jameson. Stéphane was calling in from the field, so his image was up in a separate window. Teleconferencing was certainly a lot easier than it had been in Original Bob's lifetime. And it made things better for me, since in this context, I was as real as anyone else.

"Two dead," Stéphane repeated, shaking his head. "A couple of raptors hid behind transport trucks hauling logs and simply walked into camp, staying out of sight. The beasts are tricky. Are we *sure* they aren't intelligent?"

Colonel Butterworth cocked an eyebrow at him. "By which, I assume you mean human-level sentient. And the answer is *no*, to the extent we can determine. I've discussed this with Dr. Sheehy and her staff, and they assure me that the raptors have no language, beyond stereotyped verbal signaling. They use no weapons, not that they need any, and we see no evidence of structures." He shrugged. "In the absence of some other form of evidence, they appear to be only animals. Very smart ones, but nothing more."

"It doesn't have to be all or nothing, Colonel."

Butterworth looked at me, one eyebrow still up. "I understand the philosophical point, Howard. However, in the real world, we are here to propagate our species. It is simply not possible to do that with a zero footprint. I would be happy to stop killing raptors, if the raptors could be persuaded to stop trying to eat colonists." He smiled. "Failing that, we and they will continue to interact in the ways that competing species have always handled such situations."

Stéphane nodded and grinned at me. "And that is where we come in."

I knew there was no good answer to this discussion, and there were other things at the top of my mind. "On another subject, are we on schedule to decant the rest of the colonists?"

"As long as the second farm donut is ready to go into full production, yes." Butterworth took a sip of his whiskey and stared at it thoughtfully. "I'm going to have to start rationing this more stringently. The next barrel is sixteen light-years away. If any still exist at all." He shook off the thought and looked at me.

I ignored the comment about the Jameson. "We're on schedule, Colonel. Bert and Ernie are anxious to get going back to Earth for another load." And in thirty-five years or so, another twenty thousand people would have to find a place to settle on either Vulcan or Romulus. Would I still be here? Or would I have handed it off to one of my clones by then?

Stéphane said, "Security is ready. The fence will be finished within forty-eight hours. Your observation drones are helping greatly."

I nodded to him. "It's kind of ad hoc, right now. Eventually I'll want to put together a really good, automated system." I turned back to the colonel. "Farms are ready, and I'm building up a surplus in anticipation of need."

"And we have adequate shelter, although many will live in barracks for another month or two." Colonel Butterworth looked at each of us in turn. "I think we're ready. Please pass the word to the Exodus pilots."

I grinned. Finally. Opening Day.

* * *

I accepted a ping from Bert, and he popped into my VR. I saw that he was no longer wearing the *Battlestar Galactica* uniform. Well, the joke had been wearing a bit thin.

"Hey, Howard. I just got your email. Butterworth has agreed to offload the balance of the colonists?"

I noted Bert's obvious excitement. I guess it was a question of pride; Bert and Ernie wanted to be on the road, hauling colonists. Orbiting Vulcan, acting as floating warehouses, just didn't cut it.

Bert sat and accepted a coffee from Jeeves. "It looks like Exodus-3 will be here mid-next-year."

"Yep. Riker told Sam to take it a bit slow on the flight, to give us more lead time. We agreed to get the Spits off-Earth within six months of the first two ships. Nothing was said about arrival times."

"Ah, lawyering. Makes the universe go 'round."

I smiled, then grew serious. "We've needed the extra time. Milo wasn't kidding about Vulcan's ecosystem. They've had to go back and reinforce the fence, then add electrical wiring to dissuade the brontos from chewing on it. And to keep out the raptors, and the giant snake-things, and those burrowing armadillo things..." I shook my head. "We're making progress, but it's like wading through molasses sometimes."

"Well, not really my problem." Bert took a sip of coffee. "Shuttles start moving people down this afternoon. Just make sure you have somewhere to put them. I'm about ready to just hover over the tarmac and turn the shuttle sideways to dump 'em out." He grinned to show he wasn't serious. Or at least not completely so.

"Okay, Bert, I'll let the colonel know."

He finished his coffee, disappeared the cup, and popped out with a wave.

# 6.    Contacting Bill

## Mulder
## April 2171
## Poseidon

Subspace Communications Universal Transceiver. Kind of forced, but we had a tradition, going back to FAITH, of bad acronyms. The radio transmission from Bill contained a complete set of plans and operating instructions.

So, I built the SCUT from Bill's transmitted plans, and now I was ready for the magic moment.

I just hoped it wouldn't blow up.

I flipped the switch, and the console immediately started scrolling information.

> *Sol*
> *Epsilon Eridani*
> *Alpha Centauri*
> *Omicron$^2$ Eridani*

I followed the menu prompts and registered myself on the network, then selected *Epsilon Eridani* and pressed *connect*. The *transmitting* icon came on, and I began to speak. "Hi, Bill, this is Mulder out at Eta Cassiopeiae. I've found—"

Bill popped into my VR. "Hi, Mulder. How's tricks?"

"Holy—" I was speechless. It was just under twenty light-years from here to Epsilon Eridani, yet this was Bill, sitting across from me in my VR.

Bill laughed. "It never gets old. Welcome to BobNet. Instantaneous communications across interstellar space." He waggled his eyebrows at me in our standard Groucho Marx impersonation and took a sip of his coffee.

I nodded slowly in appreciation. "And is that your standard entrance?"

"Oh, hell, yes. And I'm keeping track. Notches on the holster and all." We both laughed, and I materialized a coffee of my own. This was huge. Real-time communications changed everything. No more decades-long turnaround times for communications.

"So, anything interesting here?" Bill waved his coffee in a vague *out there* gesture.

"I think so. We have a colonization target. It's not ideal, but I don't know if you're in a position to be picky. Or if we even need colonization targets. Did Riker find anything?" I pushed a file towards him. Bill went into frame-jack for a moment while he absorbed the contents. When his avatar unfroze, he looked pleased.

"Not bad. I see your point, though. Colonists would have to establish a space presence immediately. Still, to answer the question: No, we're not in a position to be picky right now. And yes, Riker found something. Check out his blog on BobNet."

We spent several more seconds getting caught up, and I promised to read all the blogs. Bill gave me a wave and popped out.

Well, that was interesting. It appeared I should put some effort into preparing this system. The standard plan was to have a supply of refined metals available in orbit when the colonists arrived. And I'd have to write a bestiary, with detailed information. Some of the creatures in-planet were truly impressive by any definition. The kraken, especially, needed an entire chapter of its own.

Time to buckle down and get serious.

# 7.    Back to Work

## Riker
## July 2171
## Sol

I looked at my list of TODOs for the day and sighed. I was a little surprised at how much I was missing my family. Julia and Clan Bob were all aboard Exodus-3, in stasis, heading for Omicron$^2$ Eridani. There would be no contact until they arrived at their destination and were revived. I tried to remind myself that it was an eye-blink at my life scale, but any way I looked at it, I would still have to experience every day of those seventeen years. Twenty-four-hour days, since I didn't sleep, experienced in millisecond intervals.

This train of thought seemed destined to send me into a deep funk. With an effort of will, I brought myself to task.

The first item, as always, was a status check on colony ship construction. I checked the summary window rather than doing a personal inspection. Unless some significant step was due, I didn't need to micro-manage.

At that moment, Charles popped into my VR. "Hey, Riker." One of the first clones I'd made here in the solar system, Charles was still hanging around and helping out. He knew the politics of Earth almost as well as I, and the location of everything in the rest of the system far better. If he ever decided to leave, it would be crippling.

"Charles. What's up?"

"I wanted to update you on the sabotage."

"So what's the scoop?"

"Um, it looks like we've got two different groups working. VEHEMENT is definitely behind the attacks on infrastructure. They've left the usual calling cards afterwards. Everything is designed to target food production. They're very tech-savvy and obviously know what they're doing."

VEHEMENT appeared to be some kind of radical environmental group, whose ultimate goal was to save the world by removing humanity. And they weren't picky about ethical questions when it came to their methods.

Charles popped up a couple of images, and samples of the VEHEMENT statements. He waited for me to review them before continuing. Some were the typical pompous ravings of self-important people—all pronouncements and assertions, written with nose firmly in the air. Others were acerbic and even ironic. This latest fell into the latter category:

> *A friendly reminder that you are a scourge on the universe.*
> *Do it a favor and disappear.*
> *This public service message brought to you by:*
> *Voluntary Extinction of Human Existence Means Earth's*
> *Natural Transformation*

Charles continued when he saw he had my attention. "The attacks on Florianópolis don't fit the profile, though. There's no announcement afterwards, and the attacks seem aimed at maximizing fatalities rather than damaging infrastructure. They're not sophisticated, either, mostly just brute-force explosives. I think those are just attacks on Brazil, or what's left of it. There's still a lot of resentment against them for the war."

I nodded thoughtfully. This confirmed my private opinion. "That also means the second group might not be a single organization. It could be multiple groups or even independent individual actions."

"Agreed. For all that more people are dying in those acts, it's less of a long-term issue and can be handled by local law enforcement. The VEHEMENT stuff worries me a lot more."

"Mmm-hmm. They haven't gotten at any of our space-based

assets, but considering the technological expertise they've already displayed, I wouldn't be surprised if they figured out a way." I had my mouth open to describe the steps I was taking to track them down, but then hesitated. I wasn't entirely sure why—I couldn't realistically suspect Charles of anything—but I got a sudden feeling that I should play this close to the vest. VEHEMENT was good. Maybe they could decrypt communications between Bobs.

I had implemented full scanning of all communications in the solar system. A half-dozen AMIs monitored all communications, watching for key words or patterns. It was a scattershot tactic, but I really had no other options. There was no reason to inform the other Bobs. I wanted them to act natural, anyway.

Charles interrupted my train of thought. "How's the construction going?"

"Oh, uh, I was just checking that. Generally still on track. I'm going to check with Homer, next, about food production."

Charles nodded. "Okay, let me know if you need any help in that area."

I gave Charles a nod, and he saluted and popped out.

Next on the list was food production. I sent Homer a quick text about the space-based production facilities, and he reported that the wheels of industry were turning smoothly. I smiled at his response. I'd taken to calling him General Bullmoose, and rather than take offense, he thought it was hilarious. Typical Homer.

My smile disappeared as I pored over the attached spreadsheet. Food production Earthside continued to drop as the climate deteriorated. The pounding that the planet had taken during the war was sending Earth into an ice age. As the glaciers advanced and snow accumulated farther and farther from the poles, arable land became tundra, then tundra became ice. We had to balance food production with moving higher-latitude enclaves into more equatorial locations. Homer's space-based farms were taking a lot of the pressure off. As each farm donut was spun up and began producing crops, we were able to move Estimated Time of Habitable Earth Remaining later by a couple of years. The farm donuts were Homer's idea, and he ran them like a military operation.

However, the thirty thousand people we'd managed to get off-planet so far were barely a drop in the bucket. Fifteen million human beings were all that was left of Homo sapiens, but it was still a lot of bodies to move. Fifteen hundred ships or fifteen hundred trips.

I put down the document, and took a moment to massage my forehead. The UN session had started a few minutes ago, and I needed to be there. Highlight of my day, for sure. *Not.*

Since the departure of the USE and Spits enclaves in the first two ships, I didn't really have anyone I talked with regularly. All the other enclaves maintained a very arms-length relationship, except for a few like New Zealand who were actively antagonistic. Between that and my relatives being in stasis, I felt very isolated these days.

Well, at least today's session would be interesting. We'd just gotten word about Poseidon from Mulder at Eta Cassiopeiae. The biology was compatible, and the floating mats were more than adequate to live on, at least in the short term. Longer-term, the system had enough resources to support construction of floating cities. Several of the smaller island nation enclaves had expressed an interest.

The problem was one of priority. Exodus-4 and -5 were almost finished. Would we send one to Poseidon, or send both to Omicron$^2$ Eridani?

The member from the Maldives was speaking. Representative Sharma was campaigning hard on behalf of the tropical island nations. Common wisdom held that they should be last out, since their climate was still the most moderate.

"*Yes,* as the representative from Vancouver Island has pointed out repeatedly, the Maldives and other equatorial nations still have moderate climates. What the representative has failed to do is explain why that matters. If we emigrate, our lands become available for those in extreme hardship. Either way, the hardship cases are ameliorated."

She motioned to the image of Poseidon. "The important question is whether we settle a second system, or whether we continue to pour all of our emigrants into Omicron$^2$ Eridani. We are better off now, as a species, than we were a few years ago. We are spread through two star systems. But three systems would be better, and four even more so. All other things being equal, let us at least go for three. The challenge to the member from Vancouver Island, and to other objectors, is to show specifically why things are not equal, and not by using faulty associations."

Representative Sharma stuck out her chin defiantly, held the pose for just the right beat, then released the audio, giving up the floor.

I wanted to clap, but that would be unseemly. I really had no particular skin in the game on this issue, but I agreed about distributing humanity as widely as possible. The species had just finished almost wiping itself out in a single system. You'd think people would grow a brain.

I looked at the board. More than half of the *Request-To-Speak* indicators were lit up. I sighed, disconnected from my public avatar for a moment, massaged my forehead again, and wondered for the thousandth time how I'd let myself get roped into this duty.

I hoped today they'd call for a vote.

# 8.  Farming Satellites

## Howard
## April 2189
## Vulcan

The holotank glowed with overlapping information windows, all competing for attention. Several nodes blinked red, demanding immediate input. I cranked up my framerate a little. Not enough to overload the VR hardware, just enough to be able to get ahead of all the demands on my attention.

"Guppy, you've got coordination of the drone mule-team, right?"

**[Affirmative]**

Good thing. I thought my head was about to explode.

We were about to spin up the third farm donut, which would increase our capacity just in time for the arrival of the third colony ship.

Farm-1 and Farm-2 were already in full operation, generating a comfortable .25 G in the rim. Riker and Homer had found through trial and error that crops didn't do well below that level of gravity.

Specialized drones maintained the farm sections, which were producing all the kudzu you could eat. Yum. Of course, I didn't have to eat it, what with being a computer and all, but the humans were not so lucky. Until the colonies were to the point of being self-sustaining, everyone's daily calorie intake was up to fifty percent kudzu. And because of kudzu's digestive side-effects, meals and other social gatherings tended to be outside. Or involve open windows.

One of the status windows dinged. Guppy was starting the spin-up of Farm-3. After a lot of debate filled with discussion of gyroscopes, compressed-air propulsion, and traditional JATO units, Homer had settled on a very old-school system for spinning up the orbital farms, which we were still using. We tethered four drones to the rim with cables, ninety degrees apart, and had them fly in circles until we achieved the proper RPM. Primitive, but effective.

I watched the status displays as Farm-3 came up to speed. No issues. And more importantly, no sabotage. It seemed that VEHEMENT was either still completely confined to the Sol system, or they hadn't acquired any assets here. But we didn't know how many members might have gone out with the various colony ships. We would have to be vigilant until humanity was well-enough established to survive its own craziness.

I shook my head. Enough daydreaming. I ran final checks on Farm-3, then directed Guppy to start planting operations. Farm-3 would grow regular crops. Vegetables, wheat, berries, stuff people actually wanted to eat. I really needed to get this right or there would be talk of lynching.

\* \* \*

"Coming up on beacon. Fifty klicks and closing." Sam's image floated beside the system schematic. Exodus-3 was on track to merge neatly with the L4 point shared by the twin planets, Vulcan and Romulus. The Vulcan colony had declared a holiday, as it was unlikely anyone would be getting anything done anyway. I was transmitting my displays down to the Landing City network, which was broadcasting out to every TV in town.

Exodus-3 slid up beside the communication beacon without as much as a wobble. Sam ran through his shutdown checklist and changed status to station-keeping.

With the formalities out of the way, I popped over to his VR.

"Welcome, Howard. Pull up a chair." Sam waved a coffee mug in the general direction of a Victorian wingback.

I looked around his VR. It had the feel of an old English drawing room, the kind of place Sherlock Holmes might have hung out. Sam was drinking a coffee, but a quick inspection of the menu showed that I could order from a broad selection of drinks.

I decided to see how well Sam had simulated cognac. I indicated my choice to Jeeves, and sat down.

"I've started to decant the setup crews," Sam said. "I looked over the maps and resource summaries that you provided. Pretty thorough." He grimaced for a fraction of a millisecond. "No doubt Cranston will still find something to complain about."

I accepted the glass of cognac from Jeeves and took a moment to taste it. Not bad. Quite good, really. Sam had obviously spent some time getting it right. I set a TODO to ask him for the template.

I put the glass down and leaned forward. "Your colonists will really need to tread lightly on Romulus. Milo was right—there was a recent extinction event, and the ecosystem is still very shallow. No large-scale clearing, and especially don't let any Terran biota get loose. Make sure both colony groups understand that."

Sam nodded, eyes focused on infinity. With an obvious effort, he turned his attention back to me. "You're really lucky, Howard, getting to see the colonies in the early stages like this. A lot more exciting than driving a bus. I'll be leaving in a month or two, to go pick up another load."

"Sure, Sam, but I keep a blog. And lots of videos of anything that's even remotely interesting. Yeah, it's not real-time, but the universe is our playground, now, y'know?"

He grinned in response. We spent a few seconds getting caught up on gossip, then moved on to the serious business of setting up a colony of ten thousand people on an alien world. Just another day at the office.

\* \* \*

Only two days after the first FAITH and Spits personnel were decanted, and everyone was already at war. Or maybe *back at war* was more accurate. The three-way battle between the USE, FAITH, and the Spitsbergen enclave for berths in the first colony ships had been a major pain in the ass for Riker back at Earth. It appeared that not much had changed, and now I'd inherited the problem.

You couldn't actually come to blows in a videoconference, of course, but the blustering and yelling more than made up for the lack of bloodshed. I put my head in my hand and shook it slowly back and forth.

It took a few seconds for everyone to notice, then the yelling petered out.

"Tell you what," I said, "How does pistols at dawn sound? Three ways. That should be interesting."

President Valter looked slightly sheepish, Minister Cranston indignant, and Colonel Butterworth amused. But at least they'd shut it. The three colony leaders settled themselves behind their desks and waited for me to continue.

"I understand a certain amount of competitiveness," I said, looking at each person's image in turn. "But isolationism will just get you dead. And I sure as hell will not buttress any such attitude with extra support."

Cranston's face turned red. "You are not in charge, replicant. We will make our own decisions about what's best for us. What makes you think you have the right to dictate? Or for that matter, the moral high ground?"

I tilted my head and smiled innocently at the leader of the FAITH colony. "Hmm, I'm trying to remember now. Of all of us here, everyone who *didn't* participate in a war that virtually destroyed the human race, please raise your hand." I raised a hand, and waited a moment to see if anyone else would have the gall to do so. "I'm a neutral party here, Mr. Cranston. Yeah, even with jerks who treat me as a piece of equipment instead of addressing me by name. But I'm also a volunteer. I'll help who I want, and I'll leave if I want. As a good leader, you should take that datum into account when deciding how much of an idiot you want to be."

I glared at the three video windows. No one responded.

After a moment of awkward silence, Valter said, "Very well, we will *trade* some of our decanted livestock. If necessary, for future considerations. Howard, I am hoping you will act as adjudicator in such cases."

"Absolutely, Mr. Valter. And thank you. Colonel, some breeding stock now will help you until we've finished force-growing the animals in the artificial wombs." I turned to Cranston. "Minister, your repayment should consist of setting up and running a large batch of artificial wombs to take the pressure off the Spits. The both of you can pay them back *with interest* once your own stock is high enough."

I looked around at the various windows. No one commented. With a sigh, I checked my agenda for the next discussion item.

\* \* \*

"You show a lot more patience than Riker ever did." Colonel Butterworth raised a glass of Jameson toward me.

"Thanks, Colonel. I think. We Bobs are definitely different as individuals. I wonder why they never picked up on that back on Earth, when they were working on the whole replicant thing."

Butterworth shrugged. Science-y stuff like that didn't interest him, except to the extent it affected his job.

He poked at a pile of paper on his desk. "This native vine that I mentioned before is turning into a significant problem. The level of invasiveness puts anything from Earth to shame, except possibly bamboo. If we don't get ahead of it, we might end up expending all our energy just beating it back."

"Hmm, the native ecosystem has the home court advantage, unfortunately. Doesn't it serve as food for any native species?"

"As far as my scientists can tell, it contains a toxin of some kind that the native browsers find disagreeable. Even the brontos won't eat it, and they are the un-pickiest herbivores I've ever seen."

I laughed. The brontos would eat almost anything that provided net calories. They would eat all the leaves from a tree, then the twigs, then the bark from the main trunk and branches. What they left behind looked very sad. Fortunately, Vulcan trees could survive having their bark stripped.

The brontos had even started munching on the fence, when they could get close enough. A couple of strings of electrified wire had nipped that habit before it could catch on.

"How does it affect people?"

Butterworth shook his head. "The vine is not edible as such. However, the toxin doesn't seem particularly effective against Terran biology. As soon as we have some livestock, we'll see if they'll eat it."

I nodded silently. Colonizing an alien planet, as with everything else, was more complicated than TV and movies let on. Clearing the land and building houses was just the beginning. We had neither the resources nor the desire to commit planetary ecological genocide, and doing so would doom the colony anyway. But learning to live here was going to be a case of mutual accommodation.

Fortunately, so far no alien diseases had found humans compatible. I wasn't really surprised. Even Terran viruses were generally specialized for a specific species or lifestyle. Eventually something would make the jump, but by then we would hopefully be ready for it.

The colonel brought up a few more minor items, then we signed off. So far so good, but my movie-conditioned mind was still waiting for the inevitable disaster.

## 9. Something is Out There

**Bob**
**September 2169**
**Delta Eridani**

Marvin popped in and started to speak several times, without success. I couldn't identify the expression on his face, but it reminded me of a fish that had just eaten a lemon. Something was definitely up.

I'd been going over the autofactory schedule with Guppy. I turned back to him. "It doesn't look like there are any surprises. Make the changes I've listed, and let me know if anything goes off-schedule."

[Aye]. Guppy blinked huge fish eyes once and disappeared.

Marvin was still doing a pretty good imitation of a fish himself. I grinned at him. "Come on, Marv, spit it out. You know you wanna…"

He took a deep breath. "Something, and by 'something' I mean damned if I know what, hunted the Deltans almost to extinction at their original location."

"Uh, say what?"

"I found a number of disarticulated Deltan remains. In different places, so it wasn't just a one-time thing. The damage was not indicative of gorilloids. We've seen their work. They're lazy. They strip the meat, not even thoroughly, then go back for a new victim. Whatever this was, it did the full workup. And chew marks on the bones indicate something much bigger than a gorilloid."

I sat back and rubbed my chin in thought for a moment. "So there's another apex predator out there. Great. I may have to break out the exploration drones and put them on a kilometer-by-kilometer survey."

"I think that would be a good idea, buddy. And if we have the printer cycles to spare, maybe print up a few more sets of drones."

"Of course. Because screwing with the autofactory schedule is *never* a problem." I stood up, stretched, and wandered to the end of the library, gazing at nothing. After a moment's thought, I pulled up the files from my initial exploration of Delta Eridani 4. I knew that my survey had been less than thorough. But I wasn't a professional exobiologist, assuming such a job had ever even existed. And once I'd found the Deltans, everything else had taken a back seat.

I replaced the library bookshelves with a blank wall and spread the images of the fauna I'd catalogued across its length. Pacing along the collage of images, I tried to imagine any of them able to take out a full-grown Deltan.

Marvin materialized a La-Z-Boy and settled in with a coffee. Spike immediately assumed an invitation and hopped up to settle in his lap.

The collage offered no inspiration. The leopard analogues and the gorilloids were really the only animals I'd encountered that would prey on Deltans, and they just didn't fill the bill.

I waved a hand and killed the collage. In frustration, I cancelled the room VR and activated my Deltan village VR. Marvin jerked in surprise, and Spike leaped up and fled. I felt a moment's guilt for not warning him.

Marvin gave me the Spock eyebrow, and I answered with an apologetic grimace, then turned and started walking through the village. The recording was incredibly detailed, but still just a recording—no interaction was possible. I wished for the millionth time that I could interact with the Deltans through something a little more immediate than a floating mechanical football.

Finally, I turned back to Marvin, who had refused to give up his La-Z-Boy. He was reclining, drinking a coffee, right in the middle of a group of Deltans who were skinning a pigoid. I laughed and he grinned back.

"Okay, Marvin. Let's get going on that search. Guppy?"

Guppy popped into existence. **[You rang?]**

Cute. I suspected that Marvin was feeding lines to Guppy just to bug me. "Printer schedule change, Guppy. Print up four more complete squads of exploration drones. Looks like we're going snipe hunting."

Guppy's huge fish eyes blinked. **[This will result in another delay to the armaments project. I remind you that you have assigned that project high priority]**

"That's fine. I think we're ahead of the curve with the gorilloids. Attempted attacks are down to almost zero. We've got enough spare busters to bash their heads if they try any kind of large-scale attack."

Guppy nodded and disappeared.

Marvin stood up and waved the chair away. "I'll get started on the full survey as soon as they're ready. Meanwhile, I'll map out some search strategies."

We gave each other a wave and he disappeared. I closed the village VR and brought back my library.

# 10. Genocide

## Mario
## November 2176
## Zeta Tucanae

It took seven years plus change to get from Beta Hydri to Zeta Tucanae, although less than three years ship's time. I spent almost the entire voyage going over the records from Beta Hydri 4. I didn't want to believe that someone could have done that. I wanted so much for it to be a natural disaster of some kind.

But the evidence was, if not conclusive, at least pretty damned convincing. Someone had killed off an entire planet and collected all the bodies—literally *all* the animal life on the planet—then mined all the metals from the entire system. My mind kept playing all the movies where aliens came in and tried to strip the Earth. This was worse. They killed *everything*, and they left *nothing*. But how? And why?

I sighed and dismissed the theorizing for perhaps the thousandth time. I couldn't know without more information. But I wasn't going to wait. I needed to report this to Bill. The Bobs needed to be warned.

I couldn't know in advance if Zeta Tucanae would be stripped of metal as well. If so, I would just skip to the next system, and keep doing so until I either found a good star system in which to build a space station or had traveled back close enough to simply transmit a message to Bill with shipboard comms.

I did the usual cautious approach into the star system, watching for Medeiros, aliens, other probes... it would be funny if I wasn't so nervous.

I didn't actually know if there were more Medeiros clones out in the galaxy, but since Brazil's plan had been to keep producing them, it seemed a reasonable concern. Bob had prevailed against him in Epsilon Eridani, but that had been as much luck as anything.

It took a week or so to determine the system layout. The star was a little more luminous than Sol and a bit bigger, but slightly less massive. The metallicity of the system was lower, but not so low as to make things difficult for me—as long as the Others hadn't already cleaned it out.

I found a single asteroid belt and several inner rocky planets. Actually, this system was similar enough to Earth's to make me a little homesick. I headed for the asteroid belt, while I continued to scan for any activity.

I went about halfway around the belt before giving up. The Others had already cleaned up here as well. I decided I would get a quick look at the single planet in the habitable zone, then continue on to the next system on my list.

What I found was the worst possible outcome.

Exploring the planet through various drone cameras, I could see that something had caused massive destruction. Based on the ruined structures, entire cities had been taken apart. Concrete pylons indicated where bridges might once have spanned rivers. Huge washouts indicated where dams had been disassembled without regard for the downriver effects. And junk littered what looked like roadways, where presumably the contents of some kind of vehicles had simply been discarded when the metal and the passengers were collected.

"Guppy, I need a full scan of the planet. Set up the drones to do polar orbits, and get the whole surface."

Guppy nodded without comment and went into command fugue. I sensed the blips as more drones launched. I settled back to wait.

* * *

If I'd been still living, I would have thrown up. As it was, I couldn't watch for long.

The destruction was total, the devastation worldwide. These, whatever they were, these Others had callously killed billions of sentient beings the way a construction crew would clear the ground before starting to build. And I could think of only one reason for collecting the dead bodies.

When we met them, it would be war.

## 11.  Mating Dance

**Bob**
**November 2169**
**Delta Eridani**

The Deltans were coming into their breeding season, and the tension in Camelot was climbing. In the past, stressors like the gorilloid threat had kept things low-key. It's hard to get amorous when you're looking over your shoulder every few seconds. But this year the Deltans were top dogs in their environment. The gorilloids had finally figured out the new pecking order. There hadn't been an attack in almost a month.

A lot of that was due to the busters. Any gorilloid coming within a certain distance of Camelot was met head-on by a forty-pound ball of steel. The encounter was fatal to both, but I could produce more busters faster than the gorilloids could produce more gorilloids. The Deltans rarely even looked up any more at the occasional sonic boom.

I knew more or less what to expect from previous years. Male Deltans vied for the attentions of the females in any of a number of ways. Wrestling matches, mock battles, tests of skill, even good old fashioned bluff and bluster. It was great fun to watch, and generally no one got badly hurt.

This year, though, Archimedes had introduced a new test of

skill: spear-chucking. And you couldn't refuse a challenge. But that wasn't working out entirely in Archimedes' favor. The other young males had figured out that they should avoid that particular contest with him, so they were challenging Archimedes first, based on contests of strength. Unfortunately, Archimedes was rather bookish, as Deltans went. I wondered if nerd-dom was a universal thing.

After Archimedes got dropped on his head in a couple of encounters, I decided to teach him some basic jujitsu. It turned out to be harder than expected, because the Deltan skeletal system didn't always bend the same way as a human's would. We had to improvise a few locks and throws based on their different physiology.

But the principles were still applicable, and Archimedes was motivated. We narrowed it down to the five or so most useful moves. He spent a day going through the steps in pantomime, establishing the muscle-memory, before he rejoined the circus.

Almost immediately, a couple of young toughs tried to push him around to establish dominance. His response was slow and tentative, but it was a completely new concept and his opponents didn't even recognize the danger until they were on their butts looking up at him. After that, Archimedes strutted around the village like he owned the place.

Marvin laughed, watching all the antics. "I'm sure there's some element of vengeance in there. Getting back at all the childhood bullies by proxy, perchance?"

"Y'know, Marvin, this habit of yours of analyzing my motives is a real pain in the ass. Especially since they were your childhood tormenters, too."

Marvin grinned and waggled his eyebrows. Sadly, he was probably right about my motivation. I was doing what I could to make sure Archimedes did better at the metaphorical mating dance than I had as a teenager. And the more descendants Archimedes created, the sooner the entire tribe would be at or near his level of intelligence. Win-win, as far as I was concerned.

"Now if you could only change Archimedes' mind," Marvin observed.

"Yeah, I know." Having kicked butt yet again, Archimedes was making the moves on Diana. She had to be a knock-out in Deltan terms, because I couldn't figure out what else he could see in her.

She intensely disliked the drones and wouldn't hang around anywhere near us when I was with Archimedes. An obvious symptom of low intelligence, in my books.

\* \* \*

Marvin popped in without warning. "Things just got creepier."

I looked up from the observation window. The mating season was almost done. Most pairings had been decided by this point, but some Deltans hadn't gotten the memo. You could tell when that happened, because the miscreant would find himself (and sometimes *herself*) being beaten on by both members of the pairing on which he or she was trying to intrude. That was usually enough to make the point, but there were three or four individuals left who couldn't seem to take *get lost* for an answer. Archimedes and Diana had formalized their mating without further challenge, so it was purely scientific interest on my part.

I glared at Marvin, ready with a sarcastic comment about the interruption, but I changed my mind when I saw his face. He looked distinctly freaked out, and Marvin tended to be level-headed. I set the video window to record and minimized it. "Okay, Marv, what's up?"

With a flick of a finger, Marvin popped up an image in midair, showing an ancient set of bones. By this point, we were both experienced enough with all things Deltan to recognize parts of a Deltan skeleton. And this one had the bite and claw marks that I'd seen on some of Marvin's other specimens.

"Looks like another victim of the mystery predator. What's special about this one?"

"I found it less than a mile from Camelot."

"Oh, son of a bitch." If the range of this thing included the immediate area, and it was still around, I may have brought the Deltans back to be the main course. I remembered some comments that had been made when the Deltans first arrived at Camelot. In particular, one of the elders hadn't been happy with the explanation that it was the gorilloids that had driven the Deltans out. Unfortunately, he'd only had vague memories to support his feeling.

I grabbed a drone and went looking for Moses or Archimedes. I found Archimedes first, fortunately not with Diana, and explained the situation to him.

"That's not good," he said. "If we were safer at the old site, and you brought us back here..."

"Yeah, I know, Archimedes. Don't rub it in. On the plus side, we may have some lead time to prepare. But I need to find the elder who was making those comments."

"Moses would know, I think."

We found Moses with very little effort. He'd found and laid claim to a favorite lounging spot on the south side of the bluff, where he spent his afternoons sitting in the sun, relieving the pain of his stiff joints. I allowed myself a moment of sadness. Moses seemed to have entered that long slide into failing health that was all too common in the elderly. I went through the story again.

"It does sound familiar," he said, thoughtfully. "That was Axler, I think." The translation routine was programmed to render Deltan names in human-pronounceable sounds. It would tag that particular translation for permanent association with the name. "Sadly, he died three or four hands ago. I don't think anyone else is even close to that old."

"Wonderful," I said. "Archimedes, Moses, don't say anything to anyone else about this. I don't want to start a panic without more information. Marvin and I will do some more investigations. I will also set some drones to a wide perimeter guard. If anyone sees them and asks, just tell them I'm doing a gorilloid count."

The two nodded, both looking worried.

\* \* \*

"But where have they gone?" Marvin scratched his head, staring at the globe.

"Look, maybe Deltans weren't their primary prey. Maybe they discovered that Deltans were delicious and started hunting them preferentially. After the Deltans left, they would have just gone back to whatever they normally hunted."

"Right, which is why I've expanded the search. But let's face it, we're talking about millions of square miles. A predator can have quite a range." As he talked, Marvin was dividing the land area on the continent into segments. I could see from the metadata that he was assigning drones to each segment.

He sat back and stared at the results. After a few moments of consideration, he handed it off to Guppy for implementation and turned to face me.

"How are we for busters?"

I raised my eyebrows in alarm. "Damn. Good point. I haven't been keeping up with production. Between the gorilloids all growing a collective brain, and us taking the printers off-schedule to build the extra exploration drones, we're down to less than a dozen."

Marvin grinned. "Welp. There goes the schedule again, I guess."

## 12.   Bob Calling

**Bill**
**May 2171**
**Epsilon Eridani**

**[Incoming SCUT connection. New node]**

Guppy made the announcement with the same fishy poker face that he would use to announce the end of the world. I looked up and grinned. Garfield dropped the file he was working on and came running over. Only a handful of Bobs, so far, had received the SCUT plans that I'd been broadcasting and had built their own FTL transceiver. Each new connection was an event.

I held the moment as long as I could. Just as Garfield drew a breath to yell at me, I said to Guppy, "Play the incoming."

*"This is Bob calling. Bill, you actually cracked FTL communications? I'm impressed!"*

I did a fist pump, and then Garfield and I whooped and performed a high five—the nerd kind, where you miss.

Logically, Bob-1 was no more significant than any other Bob that received the SCUT plans, but this wasn't a matter of logic. Bob-1 was like Odin the All-Father. He started the whole thing. For me it was special, since he'd cloned me. For any of the third-generation or later Bobs, it would be like legend walking among us.

Of course, that wouldn't stop me from pulling the usual prank.

I popped into Bob's VR without warning, coffee in hand. I noticed, as the VRs synced, that he'd been doing some enhancements of his own. The versions weren't incompatible, but there would be video glitches. I'd have to upgrade him to my latest release so he would be fully compatible with BobNet.

"Holy—" Bob jerked in surprise, and Spike bolted from the desk she'd been sitting on.

I laughed. "Works every time. Hi Bob. Welcome to BobNet."

Bob smiled at the implied tip of the hat. I took a millisecond to look around his VR. This appeared to be a planetary environment—a village of some kind. Some species of natives were going about their business. They were obviously intelligent, since they had spears and axes and stuff. They looked a little like walking bats with a dash of pig thrown in, by way of long snouts with flat nostrils. Their fur was short, generally gray, with brown overtones. Kind of ugly, really.

The level of detail was impressive, and I couldn't remember any movie or book that featured creatures like this. I looked over at Bob, who was trying to suppress a smug grin—and failing badly.

With a jolt, I realized that this had to be real. Or at least a VR based on reality. This was First Contact.

Keeping my expression neutral, I turned in a circle to take in the full tableau. "Who are the neighbors?"

Bob, now grinning unabashedly, swept a hand around the virtual campground. "This is a recording of the Deltans' village. I use this to experience their environment. Get a better feel for how they live."

"Interesting. Have you made contact?"

There was a barking laugh from off to the side, and I looked over to see another Bob. I turned back to Bob-1 and was surprised to see he was blushing. That was better VR realism than my version supported. I decided I'd do a merge on the VR features before upgrading him.

"Bill, this is Marvin." Bob gestured toward the newcomer. "He's a disrespectful pain in the ass. And that's one of his better qualities."

Marvin and I smiled and nodded to each other. I said, "I recognize the tone of that laugh. I guess Bob has gone overboard."

Marvin smirked. "You might say that. He's become the great volcano god. Did you see the spears and axes?"

"Hey!" Bob interjected. "I resent that. I'm more of a sky god."

We all laughed together. Despite the joking, though, I was still a little lightheaded. An intelligent species, the first we'd ever run across. I had a pretty good idea which blog was going to be number one on BobNet for the next little while.

Bob motioned me to a couch and coffee-table setup sitting incongruously in the middle of the native village. "So, Bill, what's new in the galaxy?"

I sat down, accepted a coffee from Jeeves, and took a moment to pat Bob's incarnation of Spike, who had come back to investigate. The cat's A.I. appeared more independent than my version. Another item to merge. It dawned on me that Bob was still the reigning master of VR coding.

"Wow, what's been happening?" I thought for a moment. "Well, Milo discovered two habitable planets at Omicron² Eridani. Named them Vulcan and Romulus."

Bob laughed. "Of course he did. What else could he do?"

I grinned back at him, then got serious. "Riker and his clone, Homer, had a big battle in Sol with the last of the Brazilian space navy, and discovered that humanity had almost wiped itself out in a system-wide war. They're building colony ships and are hoping to get some people to Vulcan before the Earth stops being livable."

Bob interrupted. "How many people left?"

"About fifteen million, give or take."

"And how big are the colony ships?"

I nodded, understanding where Bob was going. "Ten thousand capacity. Yeah, I know. Fifteen hundred ships or fifteen hundred trips. But we can only do what we can do."

Bob nodded. He looked worried, and I couldn't blame him. Riker and I had this conversation regularly. So far, we hadn't found any shortcut.

I tried to change the subject to lighten the mood. "We've got a minimum of about twenty Bobs running around the galaxy right now, by my estimate." I waved a hand in casual dismissal. "You know. The usual. Blah, blah…"

Bob visibly shook off the funk and tried to smile. "Sounds like you've taken to the job of central clearing house with a vengeance. Got anything going in Epsilon Eridani besides the SCUT?"

"I'm slowly terraforming Ragnarök. Riker has sent some seeds and plant samples my way with an outgoing Bob. They should be here in three years or so. Then I'll try to get some basic moss/lichen hybrids growing. Oh, and the Android project. I've got a quadruped android working, more or less, and I can control it remotely. It's slow going though, and I've barely scratched the surface."

"I'll want one of those when they're available," Bob said. "I'd like to be able to go down to Eden as an actual presence instead of a floating camera."

"Mmm." I nodded. It looked like Bob was pretty invested in the lives of the Deltans. No real surprise, though.

# 13.  Investigating the Others

## Mario
## May 2180
## Gliese 54

This time, I was lucky. Unlike Beta Hydri and Zeta Tucanae, Gliese 54 was untouched.

I had no clue about what might determine the course of whatever beings had stripped the two other systems. If they travelled as a single unit, and they were travelling in a straight line, they might never meet up with any of us. My concern was that, if they were mining that much metal, they were probably building something. The obvious answer to that would be *more of them*. And that would be bad.

This was not a particularly interesting system. The primary was a small K, almost a red dwarf. It had a single lonely planet orbiting in close, and a bunch of space junk. Of course, space junk was what I needed. Although the overall metallicity of the system was low, most of it hadn't aggregated into planets.

The manufacturing process was routine, even if I only had memories of having done it once as Bob-1 in Epsilon Eridani. It took a couple of months to build and deploy the space station. Once it was up, I squirted every bit of information I had on the Others back to Bill. The station had the added bonus that I would be able to transmit to it from any of the stars in the immediate area, and it would relay my messages to Epsilon Eridani.

I also decided that I didn't want to be alone, so I started construction of four more Bobs. Bashful, Dopey, Sleepy, and Hungry all agreed to accompany me to deal with the potential threat. Yes, they named themselves after dwarves. And yes, it was pointed out at some length that there was no Hungry in the original crew. Hungry didn't care. Apparently I can be very perverse. And stubborn. Anyway, there's that joke about the fifty dwarves...

We sat around the desk in my treehouse, sipping tropical drinks with little umbrellas. Except Hungry, who refused to go along with the theme. He had a coffee. I suggested we rename him Surly and received a middle finger for my trouble.

Sleepy opened the discussion. "We have to figure out the vector and size of the invasion, or infestation, or whatever it is. Is it heading for Earth? Or away?"

"And what they're doing with all that metal. If they're building more ships, it must be a massive fleet. How would we not see them coming?" Dopey looked around at us, palms up. "And all the, uh, food..."

"Yeah..." I nodded slowly. "We have no information, really. We have to find them. And we have to get a report back without becoming part of their harvest. Their ants are surprisingly efficient. I've learned several things from them, which I've already squirted back Bill-ward."

There was silence around the table as everyone digested this.

"So we each pick a system outward and head there," Sleepy said. "We should keep a transmission channel open at all times, so we'll have a record if one of us disappears."

"Yes." I nodded. "The open line should run all the way back to Bill. If necessary, stop and build a relay station. Keep up a constant stream of commentary and observations and send regular differential backups. Just in case..."

Sleepy took a sip of his drink before responding. "Sounds like a plan. Although I don't like the implications. If I get taken down, the Bob that gets restored won't really be me."

"What, you're positing a soul, now? For us?" Surly, I mean Hungry, rolled his eyes. "Every time the crew of *Star Trek* transported, they faced the same philosophical question."

Sleepy rolled his eyes back at Hungry in exaggerated mockery. "Again with the fictional TV series. Is that where you get all your life lessons?"

Hungry frowned. "Well, you should know, shouldn't you?"

"Children, children. Am I going to have to separate you?" I glared around the table. "Can we focus on the planet-destroying, rampaging alien whatzits for now?"

Sleepy and Hungry both looked embarrassed. After a moment of silence, I continued. "I would also suggest that we have some kind of self-destruct capability built in. Maybe a dead-man trigger. Personally, I don't want to have to feel myself being slowly disassembled if I get caught, and I *certainly* don't want it or them to learn anything from me."

"Wow, this is getting morbid. I don't feel quite so negative about the backups, now."

I chuckled. "So let's pick our destination systems, put together a working comms link, and get this show on the road."

# 14.  Sabotage

## Riker
## December 2170
## Sol

The image on the video made me curl my lip in a sneer of both contempt and disgust. Half a herd of cattle lay dead in their paddock—fifty animals, poisoned by something in the food, according to the vet. On the other video window, Ms. Sharma, UN representative for the Maldives, waited silently. She was attempting to maintain a stone face, and failing.

The slaughter represented the third act of full-blown terrorism this month. VEHEMENT was ramping up from a nuisance to a full-blown threat. This was the first time they'd taken lives, though, even if livestock. I hadn't come out and said it, but I considered this an act of war. If I caught up with this group, and it came down to an exchange of ordnance, I wouldn't have any ethical issues with taking some of them down. I admitted to myself that I really didn't know if I'd be able to pull the trigger. It was one thing to talk war, it was another entirely to actually take a human life.

But I would *want* to. That much, I was sure of.

Food supply continued to become more critical as Earth's climate deteriorated. Over half of the thirty-five remaining enclaves around the planet were at least partly dependent on food subsidies from our orbital farms. The Maldives were still nominally self-supporting, but this assault on their food capacity would mean we'd have to kick in, at least in the short term.

Representative Sharma finally couldn't hold it in any longer. "This is senseless. Senseless! Cattle? What have they proven? What have they accomplished? Cowards!"

I nodded at every word. For all the bickering in the UN, the various representatives were united in their hatred and contempt for VEHEMENT. After an event like this, I could probably push through any special measure I wanted to, with little debate or opposition.

Too bad I didn't have anything in my queue.

"This is going to hurt, Ms. Sharma. Those cattle represent a lot of high-quality calories, not to mention the breeding capacity." I took a moment to check the herd numbers. "It's not life-threatening, but it is damaging. I think, if the handlers hadn't noticed the animals getting sick, we could have lost this entire herd. And that would have been devastating."

"I will move to set up a task force at the UN meeting tomor-row," Ms. Sharma said. "I think there's been a general feeling up to now that if we just ignored them and didn't give them the attention they obviously crave, that they'd go away. No longer."

I nodded without comment. I had the pronouncement from VEHEMENT up in another video window. These people were several screws short, but there was no doubt they were deadly serious. The essential message was that humanity had made a mess of the solar system, and it was time for them to bow out and let the universe recover. And because we might be reluctant to go along, VEHEMENT was going to help us towards that goal.

Great. Violent, self-absorbed crackpots. On top of everything else.

I forwarded the missive to Homer, Charles, and Ralph, and also sent a copy on to Bill. Not that he would have any specific ideas, but I'd gotten in the habit of looping him in on everything. I smiled briefly at the thought. *Universal Archives.*

Homer popped in a few milliseconds later. "Number Two, I am forced to admit I'm coming up blank. These clowns trump anything I could possibly say, just by existing."

"Yup. Just when you think humanity has found the limits of stupid, they go and ratchet up the standard by another notch." I shook my head. "We're going to have to modify our schedules to replace the calories that the cattle would have supplied. Got any ideas?"

Homer bobbed his head back and forth. "Could be. It's just possible that I've been under-reporting production a bit, to establish a small surplus. I suppose now would be a good time to notice the error with a gasp of relief." He grinned at me, and I smiled back. Homer was full of surprises.

That was fine for right now. But what about next time VEHE-MENT struck? I had a bad feeling that it was going to get worse, rather than better.

# 15.   A Visit From Bill

## Mario
## November 2180
## Gliese 54

I stared in frank amazement at the header on this latest communication from Bill.

*Plans for a Subspace Communications Universal Transceiver (SCUT) with zero latency.*

Holy. Crap. On a cracker.

Well, the big guy had delivered. I examined the plans and attached notes. Bill was candid that this was an early version, and probably cantankerous. He also wasn't sure about the range. Yeah, yeah, disclaimer, disclaimer. A hundred-plus years after our death and we still felt the need to lawyer at ourselves. Hmm, and keeping up the FAITH tradition of bad acronyms, too.

Simple math said other stars had received the plans already. I didn't know if any of them had Bobs crewing the stations rather than AMIs. That would have been a decision made by the Bobs involved at the time. But there was a good chance I'd be able to get a line all the way back to Bill. The specs indicated that the system took care of discovery, routing, and encryption. Cool!

I was lucky to have been still in the system when I intercepted the radio transmission. Bill was obviously beaming the plans to all stars within some arbitrary radius of Epsilon Eridani, but if I'd been between stars, it probably would have missed me entirely.

With no further ado, I suspended all other projects and turned every printer and roamer I had to the task of building myself a, er, SCUT.

* * *

It wasn't visually impressive. Kind of kludge-looking, really, almost steampunk. I held my virtual breath and flipped the switch. Within moments, connection confirmations began to flood onto the console.

> *Tau Ceti*
> *Omicron² Eridani*
> *Sol*
> *Epsilon Eridani*
> *Epsilon Indi*
> *Alpha Centauri*
> *Delta Eridani*
> *Pi(3) Orionis*
> *Eta Cassiopeiae A*
> *Kappa Ceti*

I checked the console menus and found that I could register myself on the global directory, which would get me on email, IM, and chat.

*Very nice.*

I set up my account, then pinged Bill.

"Bill here."

"Wow. That is truly amazing stuff. Bill, this is Mario at GL 54. I have—"

"Really? *Mario?*" And with that, Bill appeared in my VR, sitting on the other side of my desk.

"Holy—"

Bill raised a coffee cup at me in greeting. "Dude! Long time!"

"Yeah, well, that's what I get for aiming for the far reaches." I gave him a quick smirk, then turned serious. "So, the light-speed report won't reach you for a couple of decades yet, but we seem to have a problem out here. Here's the relevant data." I shoved a set of files over to him.

Bill's avatar froze for a few milliseconds as he went into frame-jack and scanned the files. When he came back, his eyes were haunted.

"Entire planets... an entire intelligent species..."

"Yeah, buddy. We thought Medeiros was our biggest problem. On this scale, he doesn't even tweak the needle."

Bill looked down at his coffee for a bit. I understood the feeling of shock, so I let him work through it uninterrupted.

Finally, he looked up. "This has immediate ramifications. We've got humans out here to worry about too." At the expression of surprise on my face, he waved a hand dismissively. "Stuff's been happening. Read my current-affairs blog when you get a chance."

Bill put his coffee down on the desk, and I was momentarily bemused by how well the VR was meshing over a 23-light-year distance.

"This is not the way I envisioned a First Contact situation," I mused. "I sure hope this isn't the norm in the universe. Although it would explain the Fermi Paradox."

"Second." Bill flashed a wan smile. "Bob beat you to first place by a couple of years. His is more of the good kind, though. Like I said, read the blog."

He visibly shook himself. "I've been running a lot of projects here. The SCUT is just the most dramatic. I'll pull a few other files and send them your way—stuff you can use for making weapons."

I nodded. "Anything that'll help. I don't get the impression that busters are going to be enough against someone who can zap a whole planet."

"Yeah, I'll bump up the priority on anything that looks like it can be weaponized." He picked up his cup. "And I'll push this info out to every Bob in the directory. You'd be amazed what can come out when all the Bobs get together to brainstorm. You guys are on your own, though, physically. Even if we assembled a flotilla, it wouldn't get there for a couple of decades."

"I've already started. I built four to begin with— Bashful, Dopey, Sleepy, and Hungry, believe it or not."

Bill threw his head back and laughed. "So, uh, *Dopey?* Really?"

"One of them suggested a name of one of the dwarves, then it became kind of a thing. Before they could grow some collective sense, they'd all taken dwarf names."

Bill chuckled and pinched the bridge of his nose. "Hungry? So, *fifty* dwarves?"

I laughed in response. "Ah, yep. Half a century later, we're all still working from the same material."

\* \* \*

I'd been working on another cohort of Bobs. This was certainly worth a small delay to modify the plans to add FTL communications, and to upgrade them to version-3. I didn't expect any reports back from the first cohort for another decade. If I could send the new Bobs in the same directions, they'd intercept the return messages in four years or so and forward them to me via SCUT.

Once again, I scrapped my schedule.

# 16.  Hunted

## Howard
## September 2189
## Vulcan

The buster struck the raptor at just shy of Mach one, spreading fragments of carnivore over the hunting party, other raptors, and most of the nearby vegetation. The red cast that it added to the greenery lent an eerie, dangerous aura to the scene.

Not that a dozen hungry raptors needed help looking dangerous.

This was the third hunting party this week to run into a raptor ambush, and I was glad I'd decided to bring a couple of busters along. The raptors were getting bolder since they'd been successful in taking down a couple of settlers. The Landing City planning committee was still smarting over that—it was their decision to reprioritize guard details that had led directly to the deaths.

The spectacular death of one of their number caused the raptor hunting pride to hesitate, just long enough for the humans to regroup and open up on them. The raptors were tough, but they hadn't evolved to withstand a twenty-second-century assault rifle.

Within seconds, the raptors were down. The hunters bent over, panting, more from nervous reaction than exertion. My observation drone hovered nearby, keeping watch.

The group leader, Stéphane, looked up at my drone. "Eh, thanks there, big guy. They come out of nowhere, those bastards."

I bobbed the drone once by way of acknowledgement. The raptors had set up an ambush for the hunters and almost pulled it off. They were intelligent—there were still ongoing arguments about *how* intelligent. The original three-person hunting parties were now double the size. And everyone involved took the duty *very* seriously.

"No prob, Stéphane. A little buster billiards now and then is great fun."

Stéphane laughed, and the group organized themselves back into a proper skirmish line. We had another kilometer of perimeter to cover before we could head back. I silently ordered down another buster from orbit, and assigned a mining drone to come pick up the remains of the one I'd just expended.

Bob's personnel busters were a versatile tool for wildlife control. I still wasn't sure if it was more economical than rigging up an armed drone, though. I resolved to discuss Bob's plastics-backed shells, if I ever had five free seconds to rub together.

Security was turning out to be a much bigger deal than we'd initially planned for. This planet's ecosystem was incredibly rich, diverse, and competitive. Even many of the plant eaters had weaponry that would give an earth predator pause. In that particular, it was very much like the popular vision of the dinosaur era.

We'd gotten the hint in the first week on Vulcan, when a pride of raptors had paced through the new townsite like they owned the place. Without so much as a please-and-thanks, they'd tried to eat one of the AMI backhoes.

I grinned at the memory. The backhoe wasn't harmed, other than needing a new paint job. But it suddenly occurred to the planning committee that they weren't in charge. At least not yet. Hunting and guarding details had been beefed up forthwith, and we'd mostly managed to keep people and raptors separate. Mostly.

And speaking of which, I had a job to do. I sent the drone up to a thousand meters to get a thorough scan. The colony spread below me, looking a lot like twenty-first-century suburbia—except for the very large fence around most of the perimeter. The fence was backed with sonic stunners, to handle the more unruly wildlife, and the trees had been cleared back an additional half kilometer. A small herd of brontos munched on leaves at the edge of the treeline.

Like the raptors, they only generally resembled Apatosauri, and they were only half the size of their namesakes. The colonists had gotten on a dinosaur kick when naming the local fauna, even though some of the associations were a bit of a stretch.

I did a quick overflight of the cleared perimeter. Nothing big enough to matter revealed itself. Satisfied, I turned back towards Landing.

The larger buildings at the center of the town comprised the administrative hub, while the airport and two manufacturing centers formed a triangle around it. People and goods moved around in communally-owned AMI-driven vehicles, available in all sizes from commuter cars to buses. The colonists had decided to build their new life on Vulcan with some social changes, starting with the abolition of private vehicles.

Only three months after landing, the city looked and felt established and stable. I was truly impressed at how quickly everything had gone up. Of course, the USE staff had had literally decades to refine their plans while they were stuck in the enclave after the war. No surprise that they'd worked out a lot of the bugs.

I finished my aerial sweep. It looked like the raptors were done for the day. I called Stéphane. "Hey, chief. All clear. There's nothing anywhere near the fence now."

Stéphane grinned into the phone. "*Bon!* I guess the fence crew will have to come up with something new. They keep thinking they are finished..."

We both laughed. The Fence Construction group was taking a lot of flak lately.

"So, Howard," Stéphane continued after a moment. "We will be going to the Groggery after our shift, to sample the latest attempt at beer. Care to tag along?"

"I might just meet you there, Stéphane. I have a meeting with the colonel first. I do love watching you guys fall over dead, though."

Stéphane grinned at me. "Eh, the last batch did remind me a little of actual beer. I think they'll have it right, soon."

I nodded and promised to be there.

\* \* \*

"Afternoon, Howard."

"Colonel." I noted that the colonel had his bottle of Jameson out again. Not that I disapproved, but there couldn't be much of the stuff left, and the supplier was sixteen light-years away. And no longer in existence, but who's counting. I said, in an aside to Guppy that wouldn't show on the colonel's video feed, "I have a TODO to build a distillery, right?"

[**Affirmative. And set to a high priority**]

Well, all work and no booze... I chuckled, and merged back into my public avatar.

The colonel had been talking during this sidebar. I frame-jacked momentarily and played back the video to get caught up.

"No deaths for the last three days on the patrols. I hope we've gotten ahead of this issue with the raptors."

I put my hands behind my head and stretched while I considered that statement. The raptors weren't really dinosaurs. They weren't really anything Earth-equivalent. They were bipedal hunters, slightly larger than the velociraptors in the first Jurassic Park movie. They had large mouths full of teeth more reminiscent of a shark's than the peg-shaped teeth of the canonical carnosaur. The raptors—and the USE settlers—had discovered that biocompatibility was a two-way street. Judging by the subsequent increase in raptor incursions, humans had proven to be a tasty treat.

"I wouldn't want to get complacent, Colonel. These are intelligent animals. They won't just keep marching into weapon range like a horde of zombies."

"Yes." The colonel waved a hand in a dismissive gesture. "Which is why I like the aerial surveillance system that you are implementing. Thermal imagers at night. And take out any that approach within a minimum radius."

"Well, I doubt that the committee will give you any grief about that decision now."

The colonel snorted, nodded to me, and ended the connection.

Colonel Butterworth and I got along much better than he and Riker ever did. Whether that was a difference in personality, or just the fact that the colonel was less stressed, was anyone's guess.

I sighed and scrubbed my hand across my chin. It was time to get back to work.

I took a moment to check the status on the Artificial Womb construction. We were going to be force-growing a generation of farm animals, just in time for the completion of the secure ranching area. If raptors liked human, they'd *love* cow. Best be prepared.

Everything seemed to be in order, so I called up a session with Bob and Bill. It took a few milliseconds for the connection, and then they both popped into my VR, sitting around the campfire.

"Hey, Howard," Bob greeted me with a smile. "Always love the camping theme."

I smiled back, handed both of them sticks, and laid out the marshmallows and wieners. I'd put a lot of effort into getting the campground just right. Evenings around the campfire had been one of the highlights of my summers when my dad would take us out to the cabin. Even as a child, I had felt the spirituality and timeless Zen of sitting around the fire with the trees looming in the semi-darkness.

This fire had just enough poplar in it to cause the occasional pop, but not so much that it began to sound like gunfire. I'd edited out insects—we Bobs tend to be a little obsessive about realistic detail, but come on, who needs mosquitos?

Once everyone was properly set up and ruining perfectly good marshmallows, I started the meeting. "One of our hunting parties ran into a dozen raptors today. They'd set up an ambush, and a pretty good one. I had to busterize one of them or we'd be down another settler."

Bill shrugged. "I've said it before—I know it looks like really intelligent behavior, but pack predators on Earth did that kind of thing all the time. It's easily explained by instinct. Get *Jurassic Park* out of your mind."

Bob was grinning at me, so I just smiled and nodded. "Yeah, okay, point taken. Anyway, Bob's automated surveillance system should be pretty valuable, once we get it set up. Especially with Bob's new and improved ordnance."

"Guppy ran the surveillance system on Eden for years," Bob said. "It'll be interesting to wire up a dedicated GUPPI to handle the job, though. No replicant oversight. You sure about that, Howard?"

"Not entirely," I admitted. "But I wouldn't dare suggest using up resources to build Bobs just for running guard details, you know?"

Bill and Bob said in perfect unison, "Butterworth would have a cow."

We all broke up in laughter. With certain notable exceptions, the Bobs all had similar senses of humor. What tickled one funny bone tickled all.

There were a few milliseconds of contemplative silence. I looked at Bob. "How's it going with the Deltans?"

Bob smiled a sad smile and shrugged. "Archimedes has a growing family, now. Time marches on. People age, you know? It's starting to freak me out a little. I'm watching people I know live their lives, getting older..."

Bill and I both nodded. Immortality had sounded like a great idea back on Earth, but there were costs, especially when you became attached to ephemerals. I glanced quickly at Bill as I had that thought. I knew Bill was touchy about the use of that term. But no, he couldn't read my mind. I hoped I didn't have a guilty expression.

Probably a good time to change the subject. "We're ahead of schedule overall. We'll probably be finished decanting the settlers from Exodus-3 this week. Riker will be happy to get back in touch with our relatives."

Bill and Bob both nodded. Bob said, "I enjoy watching the exchanges, but I have to admit that it would be too painful for me to talk to them. I'm glad Riker is up for it. I keep seeing the resemblance to my sisters in people's faces, and it's gut-wrenching."

I smiled slightly. I don't think anyone had ever come out and said it to him, but the common feeling was that Bob-1 had gotten an extra dose of Original Bob's anxiety. He tended to get wound up about stuff like that.

I said to Bill, "Before I forget, I need to contact Riker. I want to find out if he can locate some oak and scan it for me."

"Oak?" Bill raised an eyebrow at me.

"If Riker can get a good enough scan, I should be able to print some real oak barrels."

"It'll take forever to print something biological, you know."

"I know, Bill. It's more a proof of concept at this stage. I'll have a printer doing nothing but making staves until I have enough."

Bill looked confused for a moment, then grinned. "Going into business?"

"No, just doing my part to maintain morale."

We talked for a few more milliseconds about miscellaneous

items, then they signed off. And Guppy popped in with my next TODO.

Oh. That one. I'd been putting that off...

* * *

Butterworth was livid. This was no mere cow he was having, this was the whole herd. I listened, jaw agape, as he carpet-bombed his tirade with expletives. I hadn't even been aware he knew the f-word. Turned out he was an expert in its use as a verb, noun, adjective, adverb, article, and several forms of punctuation. I made sure I was recording.

Finally, he calmed down. Relatively. Sort of.

"So these, these... *Others*—moronic name, by the way—are going around depopulating planets? Just because?"

"Well, according to Mario..." I noted that Butterworth couldn't quite suppress an eye-roll. He didn't think much of our naming choices. "...they kill all the life on any planets in the system, then extract all the metals and rare elements."

"And we're parked out here like a juicy target!"

I looked down and took the time to rein in my tendency to sarcasm before answering. "Colonel, it's not like you'd have been any safer on Earth. If anything, Vulcan is slightly farther away from where they appear to be operating. And Earth has been advertising its presence for a couple of centuries with radio pollution."

The colonel nodded, closed his eyes, and took a deep breath. I felt for him. He had no doubt thought that the worst was over with the landing on Vulcan. Now we were all back in the frying pan.

"So what plans do the Bobs have, Howard?"

Now I was on more neutral ground. "Mario has built a bunch of scout-Bobs, and they're checking nearby systems. He's going to keep building cohorts, and they're going to keep spreading out until they've mapped the Others' depredations. Then we'll take it from there. Bill has turned his attention to methods of destruction. Unfortunately, the Others are probably ahead of us technological-ly. We have some bootstrapping to do."

"Keep me informed, please." He wandered over and sat at his desk, rubbing his forehead. I enjoyed the few seconds of silence as he reviewed his notes.

"Farm donuts." He said, looking up at me. "Those appear to be exceeding expectations."

"Yes, Colonel. Bill came up with a lot of engineering improvements while breeding up the plant stock for release on Ragnarök. He has something called *free time*. I hope to experience it someday."

Butterworth snorted and gave me a wry smile. We were both going full-bore, getting the colony up and running. The fact that replicants didn't need to eat or sleep just meant that I was available seven days a week, twenty-two hours and thirteen minutes a day. Or thirty-one forty-nine, on Romulus. Scheduling was going to be a headache once the Romulan colony was up and running. Funny, I couldn't remember any science-fiction stories that actually dealt with how you'd handle timekeeping on a new planet.

"And that means," Butterworth continued, "that we'll be able to set up the Spits and FAITH colonies on an accelerated schedule. I expect you're looking forward to your descendants coming out of stasis."

"No one more than Riker." I grinned. "I have to admit it's been a pretty popular program in BobNet."

Butterworth grimaced. "BobNet. Seven billion people on Earth in the early twenty-first century, and FAITH decided to replicate a nerd-slash-engineer with a *Star Trek* fixation." He grinned at me to take the sting out of the comment and reached for the disconnect button. "Until tomorrow, then..."

# 17.  We've Lost a Drone

## Bob
## May 2171
## Delta Eridani

The conversation with Bill had been both awesome and depressing. The idea that humanity was down to fifteen million people was devastating. On the other hand, it sounded like that number had come close to dropping to a big fat zero.

On the plus side, I wasn't surprised that he'd cracked the sub-space problem, but I was impressed by how quickly he'd done it. It left a small, nagging question in the back of my mind as to whether I could have pulled that off. How different from me *was* Bill?

Meh. No matter. The problem had been solved, Bill and I were working on merging the VR source from our two independent development branches, and real-time communications between Bobs was now a reality, at least in principle. I grinned to myself at the idea of a galactic internet. There still weren't a lot of Bobs online, but that would change as Bill's message spread through the local sphere at the speed of light.

I was overjoyed to find out that I had the official First Contact position sewn up. But I doubted I would be the only one.

Luke and Bender hadn't come online yet. I hoped they would eventually intercept Bill's transmissions so we could get caught up.

Just in case, I instructed the local space station to periodically retransmit the SCUT plans along their flight paths. One way or another, they'd eventually receive the plans.

The lack of significant progress on Bill's Android project was a little disappointing. A lot of the basic tech was being developed back on Earth when Original Bob was still alive. But it was proving difficult to put all the concepts together into an artificial body that could operate like a complete organism. Oh, well. Sooner or later, Bill would make some breakthroughs. Meanwhile, I had my own projects.

Marvin had taken delivery of the exploration squads and was deploying them into his search grid covering the Deltans' original territory. At the level of detail we were trying for, he expected to be finished in three months or so.

\* \* \*

"I just lost a drone." Marvin popped into my VR unannounced. He had a perplexed expression on his face.

"Define *lost.*"

"Have a look." He popped up a video window. It showed a panoramic view of Eden from several hundred meters in the air. The drone was flying a search pattern, looking for clearings that could be potential former villages. Suddenly, the image began corkscrewing wildly and breaking up. After about half a second of this, the image disappeared.

"The hell," I muttered. "I'm assuming that was an attack from above?"

"It would appear so. I did a frame-by-frame, and this was the best I could come up with." He popped up a still image. It was out of focus and broken up by video interference lines, but there was an impression of something biting or chewing on the drone.

"I ran some filters and cleanup routines on it. The result is partly extrapolated." He switched to a second image. This one was still grainy and lacking in detail, but I could make out what appeared to be a large beak or muzzle, filled with teeth.

"Wow," I said. "I would sure hate for that to be the last thing I saw."

"Guppy, are we getting any telemetry at all from the drone?" Marvin asked.

**[Negative. Attack likely took out the power system]**

"Hmm, well, I want to take a look at the wreckage. I'll set up a SUDDAR search. Highly refined metal should stand out like a lamp in a cave." Marvin stood up, gave me a salute, and disappeared.

\* \* \*

The wreckage of the drone rotated slowly in the holotank. Marvin had found the destroyed unit several kilometers south of its last known location and had taken a full-detail SUDDAR scan.

The drone was bitten almost in half, and had two parallel claw marks dug into the shell. The units were designed to be lightweight—unlike the busters, there was no armor. Still, anything that could dent metal like that had to be dangerous. And whatever it was, it was airborne. Scary.

"Then there's this." Marvin popped up a couple of images. One was a closeup of the damage to the drone, and the other was a close-up of some bones.

"Interesting..." I reached out and pointed to a spot on the picture. "That looks a lot like the bite impression on the drone."

"Yeah, I've got a number of similar examples. Whatever this is, it used to snack on Deltans."

"Could that be why the Deltans migrated out of their original area?" My eyes got wide at the thought. "They weren't moving to a more dangerous territory. The gorilloids were the lesser evil."

"Or they didn't know, or care, about the gorilloids." Marvin's voice was hushed.

"Then the gorilloids chased them over the mountain range to the location where we found them."

We sat in silence for several milliseconds.

Marvin finally broke the silence. "I still don't have enough information to narrow the search."

"Well, we know they're big enough to eat a Delta."

"Or pull a drone out of the sky."

I did not like this. Not a bit.

## 18.  It's Getting Worse

**Riker**
**Sept 2172**
**Sol**

A crowd stood outside the police lines. Hopeless faces, some crying; parents holding children by the hand, couples holding each other, wearing stricken looks. People who would be better off almost anywhere but here.

Sixty-three confirmed dead, so far. The apartment building, a run-down six-floor concrete structure with no balconies, now had a huge bite taken out of it at ground level. That it would have to be condemned was a given. I was more worried that it might fall over any moment, crushing everything nearby.

This wasn't a great neighborhood. By almost any pre-war standards, it would be a slum. Buildings all had their own power systems since the invention of dependable fusion, but the streets were dirty, unlit, and covered with graffiti. Windows and doors at ground level had long since been reinforced or completely covered over. Stains ran down the sides of the structures from weather, deteriorating paint, and contributions from birds.

The people living in this favela hadn't been significant in any way. They weren't government, or military, or anything that would justify making them a target. Just people, probably unemployed, living on the edge of poverty. Most of them likely had no hope, no future, other than the possibility of eventual emigration to another star system.

What was the point? What could possibly justify this? The perpetrators had attacked people with next to nothing, and taken even that. Sometimes it shamed me to think that I used to be human.

I accepted a call from the Brazilian minister.

"This is the third attack this month, Riker. And there has been no progress in catching the perpetrators. What assurances can you give me that something will be done?" Minister Benedito looked more spooked than angry. Very probably he was worried about his job. Still, this wasn't the time to get my back up.

"Minister, I'm not in charge of the investigation. Really, I'm not in charge of anything except the global emigration effort. I'm here as, well, a consultant. I will help out the investigation any way I can. But you have to look to your internal security forces to get this resolved. Plus whatever the UN can do, of course." I could see from Benedito's face that he didn't think much of my response. But it was all I had.

I made mining drones available to the emergency personnel, to help locate and extract bodies or survivors. I set up surveillance drones around the perimeter, in case the terrorists tried to send in a follow-up attack. And I made sure that those in charge had a direct line to me. And mostly, I waited.

This was, as the minister had said, the third attack this month. This was terrorism, pure and simple. And not even for any political end, as far as I could tell. There had been no announcements, no demands. Someone simply seemed to be out to get Brazil. Since Florianópolis was pretty much all that was left of the former empire, this was the natural target.

Fifteen hundred ships, or fifteen hundred trips. The inexorable logic of mathematics mocked me.

* * *

Minister Gerrold, the representative from New Zealand, was holding forth again on my shortcomings, both real and imagined. He really hated me, for some reason, and had since day one. Not that I cared—the man was a putz—but my orderly mind liked to have a link between cause and effect. Plus, if I was going to create this kind of reaction in someone, I would rather have an end-game. Fighting some random idiot was a waste of energy.

Today's rant was about the sabotage and our inability to deal with it. I let my public avatar display alert interest, while I rolled my eyes in my VR.

He finally ran down, and I prepared to offer a response, but the minister from the Maldives beat me to it. And beating a computer to the punch was an impressive feat. I wondered if I should do a systems check.

The chair recognized Minister Sharma and she stood up. "I'd like to thank the minister for giving us a summary of his speech from last session. Which, if I recall, was also a summary from a previous speech. I'd be even more appreciative if it had been a prelude to some new information. Or at least witty. Minister Gerrold, you've obviously got a problem with the replicants. I'd like to ask you to take it offline, so we can get on with actual business."

The attention lights blinked rapidly, the remote meeting's equivalent of applause. Minister Gerrold's face clouded up and he sat back, arms crossed.

I made a note to send Sharma a thank-you note. But she was right. He obviously had a pickle up his butt about replicants in general, and me in particular.

The next item on the agenda concerned the deteriorating climate. Several enclaves in the higher latitudes were approaching non-viability. Two ships, Exodus-4 and Exodus-5, were due to launch this month. The UN had confirmed that the island nations would be sent to Poseidon. The question on the table was whether we needed to switch the order of emigration, or whether we could just move the troubled enclaves into the vacated territories. Everyone had an opinion, and every opinion seemed to be different.

I leaned back and looked around. I'd just realized that Homer wasn't here. He usually popped in to mock the UN meetings. I think I was starting to depend on his satirical take on things to get me through the tedium.

Looked like I'd have to get through this one the old-fashioned way. I activated sandbox Bob and handed off the video window. Freedom.

# 19.  Prey

## Bob
## June 2172
## Delta Eridani

Archimedes patiently tied two strands of vine together while the cub watched. I smiled, observing the tableau in the video window. His mate, Diana, kept one eye on the drone. She had never liked the drones, or me, and still tensed up when one was around. Having a child to protect just made her that much touchier.

Archimedes was oblivious. He was too busy teaching his cub basic skills. The cub took the vines and, tongue sticking out of a corner of his mouth, tied a perfect granny knot. Archimedes sighed and corrected it into a square knot. The cub smiled up at his father and I experienced a jolt of—well, something. Pride? Envy? Wistfulness? Maybe all of the above. It was hard to sort out. My eyes were watering, and I had to suppress a strong urge to re-watch one of the recordings of Riker's chats with our family.

I minimized the window and turned to see Marvin watching me. He said nothing, and after a moment he dropped his eyes and went back to what he was working on.

I took a few deep breaths and brought the window back up. The cub had successfully executed a square knot, although he still didn't seem to be clear on the difference. I chuckled. I'd given Archimedes some sailing knots over the last while, and he was learning them, one at a time. It looked like he was trying to pass that knowledge on to his cub.

The boy would be given a Naming Ceremony as soon as he said his first word. Both Archimedes and I expected that to happen earlier than average. The Deltans quite reasonably considered language to be the difference between them and animals, and the first use of language was the proof that the child had, for want of a better word, a soul. The Deltan word didn't quite mean the same thing, but it was close enough.

Diana was still eyeing me, so I decided to give her a break. I told Archimedes that I was going to go for a cruise around, then took off.

I brought the drone up to a kilometer altitude and rotated slowly. It was still early in a beautiful spring day, and dew sparkled on the trees and grass. This part of Eden was mostly forest, but there were enough meadows and open areas to allow grazing animals to make a living. I was making a point of recording panoramas like this whenever I could. Someday, maybe ten thousand years in the future, the Deltans would be civilized, and would probably have done something to Eden similar to what humans had done to Earth in the twentieth century. It would be nice to be able to show them what their world had once been like. I wondered if I would still be hanging around here by then.

Wow, I needed to shake off this melancholy mood. I enjoyed hanging with Archimedes, but once in a while it triggered images of my parents and sisters. When that happened, a change of scenery was in order.

I instructed the drone to fly back to Camelot and take up station-keeping, and I switched to a drone stationed at one of the Lagrange autofactories.

The armaments project was overdue for inspection, anyway. I had a section, carefully separated from everything else, where I was experimenting with explosives and munitions manufacture. I was playing with the idea of a shell powered by plastics instead of gunpowder. A primer triggered by an electrical current would remove the need for a hammer. Using ethylene glycol as the binder would result in a compound that was usable under all environmental conditions, including extreme cold. And the stuff didn't become unstable with age. Oh, and it was easier to work with safely than gunpowder.

I moved on to the main autofactory area. Four replicant matrices were currently nearing completion, to give life to the version-3 Heaven vessels lined up nearby. I hadn't decided yet if I wanted to upgrade myself as well. Granted, the threes were significantly faster than my version-2 hull; but I had no immediate need for speed. Everything in the Delta Eridani system was accessible by drone. I seldom had any need to fire up my SURGE drive. Come to think of it, I hadn't left orbit around Eden in years.

Despite my ongoing reluctance to replicate, I felt a moral obligation to get more of me out into the universe. Besides the simple fact that more Bobs exploring meant more interesting revelations, there was the implied promise to Dr. Landers to perform the task that he'd resurrected me for. By extension, I had a responsibility to what was left of the human race. Riker was doing a magnificent job of getting them off-planet. It was up to the rest of us to find places for them to go.

My brooding was interrupted by a text from Marvin. *There's been an attack.*

I sent the drone back to station-keeping and re-entered my VR. Marvin was waiting.

"Gorilloids?" I asked, sitting down.

"No, I think it might be our Giant Claw. A foraging party was out gathering food when one of them was grabbed. They say they couldn't really see it, except they got the impression it was really big. It flew away with the victim, and everyone else high-tailed it back to Camelot."

"What do you mean, they couldn't really see it? Did it jump out of a tree?"

"Um, no, that's the thing. They were *looking right at it* but couldn't make it out. The Deltans didn't really have a word for it, and the translation routine was having fits, then finally settled on *invisible.*"

"Ah, jeez. So a giant flying thing that can become fully or partly invisible, or maybe blend in..." I trailed off as I watched Marvin's eyes get bigger. "Umm...?"

He flipped through the archives and pulled up a video segment from my early investigation of Eden, back before I'd even found the Deltans. The video depicted what I'd named a hippogriff.

About the size of a robin, this little critter had four legs and a set of wings. It was predatory, and it could hide in plain sight because it could...

... change its coloration to match the environment. Oh, crap.

"They'd be a lot bigger than this little guy, but what the Deltans sort of saw would fit the bill." I nodded at Marvin. "Good catch. But we still don't know where it comes from, right?"

Marvin shook his head. "I'm still searching outward from Camelot. I've reached the ocean in one direction, but still lots of land left at the other compass points. I'm biasing it towards the original Deltan territory, although that's not a sure thing either."

"The big question," I said slowly, "is whether any of our drones saw it."

"I already checked. There weren't any in the area. Everything we could spare is out searching. Somehow this thing snuck inside our perimeter."

"Wonderful. Wonder-freaking-ful. I haven't just brought the Deltans back to the fire, I've put them back in the frying pan. Some sky god!"

\* \* \*

I watched from a distance as the tribal elders gathered to discuss the recent death. I wasn't invited to attend, since I was probably the subject under discussion, and I didn't feel like forcing the issue. Archimedes was told to be there, and he looked nervous enough for both of us. He and Diana exchanged frightened looks before he left.

The meeting went on for quite a while, and there was a lot of gesticulating and yelling. I'd probably never mentioned directional microphones to the Deltans, so I guess I couldn't blame them for not realizing that I could hear everything.

Archimedes passed on my theories, which in retrospect probably made things worse. But it would have come out sooner or later. The central theme of the meeting, though, revolved around whether I was malicious or just an idiot. Either way, a lot of people believed that they'd been safer back at the old site.

Objectively, that wasn't true. They'd been slowly going extinct, and wouldn't have lasted more than another generation or so. But explaining population trends to essentially innumerate people was a losing game. They understood death when it happened in front of them, far better than they understood attrition.

The meeting took about two hours. When Archimedes came back to his spot, he looked very hangdog. He sat down and accepted a piece of jerky from Diana.

"They're about evenly split," he explained. "Half think you've led us here to be food for the flying things. The other half ask how you could have known about these things if we didn't know. And we're *from* here."

I thought about that and sighed. If the Deltans had been human, those would have been the two camps, but the split wouldn't have been fifty-fifty. Deltans were surprisingly rational.

"You're not in trouble, are you?"

"Not really." Archimedes glanced at Diana and smiled ruefully. "But my, uh, *stock* is down. I think that's how you say it."

"Don't worry about it, Archimedes. You're still the best damned weapon-maker in, well, anywhere. If you need to distance yourself from me for a while, that's fine. But either way, Marvin and I will continue to look for the hippogriffs."

Archimedes nodded. His cub toddled up and dropped into his lap. Head-first.

* * *

"Well, that explains it," Marvin said. "I stopped at the shoreline and I shouldn't have. The things seem to be centered on a rookery out on this island..." Marvin pointed to a large island a kilometer or two offshore. Obviously volcanic in origin, it was steep, deeply folded, and very probably had a lot of lava tubes that would make perfect homes for large flying things.

"How many of them are there?"

"Can't tell for sure." Marvin shrugged. "They're always coming and going during the day, but unless I start tagging them, I don't know how many nests or dens or whatever are in those caves. But certainly scores of adults, at minimum."

I frowned. "That's a significant population of predators. So what do they eat when they can't get Deltan?"

Marvin waved up a picture. "Seals. Well, seal-equivalents. Or maybe closer to walruses. They seem to fill the same niche. They spend most of their down-time basking on the beach, and they hunt in the water. They're a little more mobile than seals or sea-lions, but still basically sitting ducks on land. Although I'd imagine they could do some damage with those tusks."

I stared at the picture for a few milliseconds, rubbing my chin. I turned to the globe and expanded it until it showed just the island and the Deltans' past and current range. "So the hippogriffs discovered the Deltans, who were probably easier prey, chased them out of their original territory..."

Marvin continued the thought. "Then eventually caught up with them after they moved into gorilloid territory. The Deltans could handle the gorilloids, with flint weapons to help, but they couldn't handle both predators. They retreated over the mountain range..."

"...which put them out of range of the hippogriffs, but lost them the flint resource. Without that, they couldn't quite hold their own against the gorilloids," I finished.

"And then we, and by we I mean you, led them back to the flint site. Where they are, once again, on the menu." Marvin gazed at me with one eyebrow raised. "So what now?"

I sat down, called up coffee, and leaned back in thought. "I think we can agree that just doing nothing is off the table?" Marvin nodded and I continued, "Likewise, asking the Deltans to move again is probably a non-starter. I doubt they'd do it even if I had a good, safe destination in mind."

"Plus, the flint site really is their best long-term bet, generally speaking."

[Approaching predator detected]

We both looked up at Guppy's announcement. We'd used all available drones to set up a tighter perimeter around Camelot, and set them to looking specifically for anything large and airborne. It appeared we had a bite.

I pulled up the video that Guppy offered. The hippogriff was hard to make out. On a clear day, it would have been almost impossible to see, the blue of its hide matched the sky so well. But today there were too many scattered clouds for the animal to camouflage itself from all angles. It was heading directly for Camelot. There was no doubt in my mind of its intentions. And this was almost certainly the one that had taken the Deltan two weeks ago.

"Right, let's busterize it." I called up a buster and set it to full acceleration. It shot towards the hippogriff.

At the very last moment, though, the hippogriff dodged the bullet. Literally. The thing's speed and aerial agility was unbelievable.

We both stared for a few milliseconds, then I called up more busters.

"Don't overdo it," Marvin cautioned. "Let's find out what the animal is capable of. We know we can get it if we throw enough busters at it. Let's find out what 'enough' means."

I nodded at him, and ordered most of my second wave to stand down. Instead, I sent in two busters in the fore/aft formation that Riker had used so successfully in the Battle of Sol.

Again, the hippogriff dodged the first buster. The speed of the animal was really impressive. But it was unable to correct for the second one. The *splat* created a cloud of fine red mist, which settled slowly to the forest below.

"I didn't like that," Marvin said. "We got it with the second one, but it was close. I think if we want to take them out dependably, we should go with an encirclement using three or more busters."

"The question is whether this was a one-off or whether they fly some kind of patrol pattern. Maybe there won't be any more coming this way."

Marvin didn't look convinced. "Predators almost always have a patrol pattern of some kind, if only to protect their territory from competitors. I doubt we've seen the last of them."

\* \* \*

It took less than a day to prove Marvin right.

**[Multiple incoming detected]**

*Oh, God, this just keeps getting worse.* I pulled up the window and leaned forward. It was hard to tell from the returns, but it looked like about a dozen hippogriffs, give or take a few, were bearing down on Camelot.

"What the hell?" Marvin said, popping in. "What's attracting them?"

"Just a guess, but I'd say the blood in the air yesterday from the busterized hippogriff. I'm sure a predator would be able to smell the spoor for miles. Maybe it draws them like sharks."

"Oh for— okay, a dozen of them will require thirty-six busters. We don't have that available."

"We're going to have to wing it, Marv. They're in a fairly tight group. Maybe we can thin them out some of the first pass."

Marvin nodded, and we called up the twenty busters that we had available. I ordered Guppy to fly in reinforcements from orbit, and we set the ones we had on a direct line of attack with maximum acceleration. By the time they neared the flock of hippogriffs, they were doing about Mach 1.5.

The first pass took about five hippogriffs, and allowed us to see that there had been fourteen total. Now, we had fifteen busters left for nine attackers. There was a good possibility one or two might reach Camelot.

While the busters were coming around for another pass, I activated one of the drones in Camelot. I flew towards the first recognizable face I saw, which was Arnold.

Everyone was looking in the direction of the sonic booms, staring at the red clouds that had appeared. I shouted at Arnold, "Hippogriffs coming. Get everyone under cover!"

I shifted back to my VR without waiting to see if Arnold reacted. The busters were just coming in for the second pass, and Marvin had stacked them two-deep. The leftover buster trailed the group, ready to take out a target of opportunity.

The second pass took out three hippogriffs, and injured the wing of a fourth. The clouds of red were now making it hard to see. SUDDAR was not particularly effective with biomass—bodies showed up as dim ghosts—and infra-red was having a lot of trouble with all the fresh blood floating around.

The injured hippogriff lost altitude quickly, but it was a controlled descent. We probably couldn't depend on the impact killing it. We now had eleven busters—no, nine. Two busters had collided and taken each other out—and five attackers left. It was going to be tight, unless they turned around and retreated. If they were anything like sharks with blood-spoor, though, that wasn't going to happen.

The busters came around for a third pass. There were fewer hippogriffs now, though, and they were spreading out. And the damned things really had quick reflexes. Despite buster pairing, we only took out three of the attackers. We were down to six busters, and had two healthy and one injured hippogriff to deal with. Still reasonable odds, except that they were now close enough to Camelot to present a real danger. And we didn't have the uninterrupted line anymore for a supersonic approach.

"Switch to bludgeoning and harassment. Guppy, where are the reinforcements?"

**[Five minutes out]**

*Not good enough.* I checked the action in Camelot. The mesa didn't have much in the way of caves or any other kind of overhead protection. It was ideal for protection from a ground assault, not an air attack. The Deltans were streaming out of the village, down the two available paths. But with the bottleneck, they couldn't get the whole tribe evacuated in time, and they would be sitting ducks until they reached the trees.

We commenced low-speed bludgeoning of the hippogriffs. They were even better at dodging at this speed, but they couldn't really do anything else at the same time.

We finally managed to bounce one off the head of a hippogriff. It went down immediately. The other hippogriff ignored the byplay and tried to take a pass at the Deltans on one of the paths. But the busters kept it too distracted and it passed overhead without completing the attack. Unfortunately, a couple of Deltans panicked and fell or leaped off the path. I could see them tumbling down the steep scree.

The Deltan hunters laid into the unconscious hippogriff. It was my first opportunity to get a good feel for relative scale. If the Deltans were human-sized, then the hippogriffs were about the size of a Clydesdale, with bat-like wings. The animals looked more reptilian than anything. Teeth and claws were disproportionately large, resulting in an impression of something built for nothing but killing.

It took only a few seconds for the Deltan hunters to ensure that the animal wouldn't be waking up. The live hippogriff, though, was still a major threat, and I had no idea where the injured one had gotten to.

The busters continued to harass the healthy hippogriff, and it apparently decided to reduce the defensive zone by landing. Well, not a bad strategy, really. Now the busters could only buzz it from above.

As it landed, the hippogriff changed its coloration to match the ground and rocks, but no one was going to be fooled at this stage. The animal snapped at the busters as they came within range, and it managed to snag one. It looked as though this would turn into a process of attrition, until the Deltans brought in their "A" game. Twenty to thirty spears flew at the animal in a solid cloud. Fast or not, the hippogriff simply couldn't dodge that amount of incoming. Within moments, it resembled a pincushion. The hippogriff screeched and snapped at the spears sticking out of it. Arnold grabbed another spear from someone, ran straight toward the hippogriff, and made an Olympic-caliber throw from point-blank range. The spear went right through the animal's neck and it dropped instantly.

There were cheers from the hunters. The jubilation lasted only a moment, however. Screams from the retreating tribespeople brought our attention back to the paths out of Camelot. The injured hippogriff had made its way to the base of the scree, found one of the people who had fallen, and was eating him.

I sent all my remaining busters straight at it, with no allowance for pulling up if they missed. Two impacted with enough force to kill the last animal. It was too late for the Deltan, though.

* * *

The good news, if it could be called good, was that we'd only lost three Deltans. A fourth had a broken leg, and I was going to have a confrontation with the medicine woman if she didn't listen to me this time. I'd lost eighteen of my twenty busters. Twenty more made it down from orbit, too late to do any good. And once again I was pulling all my printers off of their assigned duties to make more busters.

The Deltans had called another tribal council. For them, two councils in a month was akin to panic. This time, I was invited, or maybe summoned. I doubted it was to give me a medal.

I had noticed that some people were giving Archimedes a bit of cold shoulder. They couldn't overdo it, of course. He and Moses were still the only source of shaped flint, and Moses wasn't moving around much these days. If I was to describe the attitude in human terms, it would be "coldly formal." Since Archimedes hadn't done anything to deserve it, I had to conclude that it was guilt by association.

Arnold was sitting in council now. After that display with the hippogriff, he was man of the hour. Hopefully that would mean at least one sympathetic voice.

There was some discussion among themselves, then they called me over. I floated down to head height and waited.

"Are there any other surprises that you have for us?" Hoffa said without preamble.

"That was a surprise to me, too. You'll remember that I asked why you'd left Camelot. Only Axler had an inkling, and he didn't remember enough to warn us."

"Just the same, by following your advice, we seem to get deeper and deeper into trouble."

"By following my advice, you've retaken a location that you can defend against gorilloids and that has flint for weapons. I know a lot of you have trouble following my explanation, but I maintain that in the old camp, your children would have been the last of the Deltans."

I paused for dramatic effect before continuing. "As for the hippogriffs, they're a problem because they're a surprise. I'm going to find out more about them, then I'm going to remove them."

"I've noticed," Hoffa said, "that despite your talk, it's still we who do most of the fighting."

"Really? When was the last time a group of your hunters had to beat off a gorilloid attack? Did you hear the sonic booms? Two hands and four hippogriffs approached Camelot, but only three arrived."

Hoffa's ears were straight back and his eyes were narrowed to slits. I was mishandling this, but I couldn't stop myself. I'd never been able to handle shortsighted stupidity.

"That's three more than would have arrived at our old camp."

In VR, Marvin and I rolled our eyes in sync.

"I've already talked about that."

"Perhaps next time, we should leave your Archimedes out as an offering for them."

I sent the drone straight up ten feet. "Don't. Ever. Threaten. My. Family. Not *ever*." As I finished saying the words, I realized that I'd turned the volume up. It had probably been painful to sensitive Deltan ears. The entire council was cringing, and possibly not just from the volume.

I slowly lowered the drone back to head-height. "I mean it, Hoffa. I'll take care of the hippogriffs. And thanks to you, I've figured out how."

Hoffa looked confused and somewhat concerned. I noticed that Arnold looked at Hoffa and smiled.

\* \* \*

"Okay, I'll bite." Marvin was grinning at me. "How? And how did Hoffa help with it?"

I glared at him. "I'm going to drop a rock on the island. Which is what I wanted to do to Hoffa."

"Jeez, Bob, here you go again. You're going to perform planetary ecological surgery just because it's convenient."

"No, Marvin." I jumped to my feet. "I'm going to do it because those things threaten my family. And you can analyze that all you want. I don't give a damn." I closed down his VR connection and he disappeared, effectively kicked out. Pretty rude, and I'd be apologizing later. But for the moment, I was too steamed to care.

\* \* \*

I had a far more immediate problem, though. Assuming I was right about the hippogriffs smelling blood, then today's battle would bring yet another wave tomorrow—maybe much larger. It would take time to find a large enough mass to destroy the island. I calculated an initial size of a hundred tons would about do it. We had identified a number of nickel-iron asteroids in the system, some of which would be about the right size.

I received a ping from Marvin. It was time to eat crow. I invited him in, and we looked at each other warily.

He broke the silence first. "You know we're no good with this crap, right?"

It was enough. I broke down laughing, and we nodded at each other. Done. Possibly identical twins could come close to understanding, but certainly no one else.

We sat down and I described my thoughts on the impactor.

"Huh," he replied. "So, a couple of months to build Bill's asteroid mover, a couple more weeks to move the asteroid into place. You think the hippogriffs will just wait around?"

"I'm open to suggestions."

"I understand you're angry, Bob, and you want to smash the island to smithereens. But all you need to do is hammer it enough to take out the hippogriff population. You don't need a Yucatan-level event to do that."

I nodded. "So, a bunch of small impactors?"

"A thousand-pound steel ball will do a lot of damage."

"Ohhhhhh..." I nodded. "*Ship* busters. Yeah, I've still got four in inventory."

"The thing is, though, Bob, you don't want too big of a bang. Tsunamis, ground shocks, flying debris could do more damage to the Deltans than a bunch of hippogriffs. Get this wrong, and you could be directly responsible for the extinction of the Deltan species."

I nodded, shocked. Time to get my temper under control.

* * *

We decided to use the ship-busters one at a time and gauge the results after each strike. I sent the first ship-buster in at what I hoped was a reasonably sedate velocity.

The results were slightly more, um, spectacular than expected.

In retrospect, maybe I didn't allow for the amount of material that would normally be shed by a meteor on the way down. Or I forgot to carry the two. Whatever the reason, the impact produced a mushroom cloud that would have done a fission bomb proud. As the smoke and dust cleared, it was obvious that the island, and the hippogriffs, were gone.

Well, that was the good news.

The bad news was that this was definitely going to produce ground shocks all the way to Camelot. And at least some debris. I flew several drones over to the camp, to find everyone already awake, staring at the bright cloud to the southwest.

Archimedes looked up at the drone as I arrived. "Did you do that?" he said in a hushed voice.

I wasn't sure of the expression on his face. Awe, certainly, but I thought maybe a bit of fear. I hoped not. That wasn't the legacy I wanted to leave.

"Yeah, Archimedes. That's the hippogriff island being obliterated."

Archimedes' eyes grew wider and his ears went down. He took a half-step back from me.

Damn.

At that moment, the ground shock arrived. It wasn't the worst earthquake I'd ever seen, but was probably the first in the Deltans' experience. They hugged the ground, and there were many screams.

The shaking was brief. It was followed a few minutes later by the sound of the explosion. The crack and roar seemed to go on forever, but couldn't have been a minute in all. The Deltans continued to huddle until it let up.

But now came the hard part. I went to the elders. "There may be some burning rocks falling from the sky, in about a hundred heartbeats or so. You should get everyone into the lee side of the bluff."

There were wide eyes and flattened ears, but no one was going to argue with me. In short order, every Deltan was huddled behind the central bluff.

The debris arrived right on time. Drones hadn't been able to detect anything big. I hoped that would hold, as I wasn't really sure I could intercept incoming debris with a buster. Or if it would do any good.

The pelting lasted several minutes. It was impressive, and there was some minor damage to the village, but no one was hurt. The Deltans huddled for the rest of the night, unwilling to leave the sanctuary of the rock.

* * *

When morning finally came, people spread back out to their normal locations. A few of them had to do some cleanup, but their neighbors pitched in. Overall, the amount of actual damage was minor.

The council was having yet another session. Again, though, I wasn't expecting a medal.

When they were done, they motioned to the drone. I flew it over, and Hoffa stepped forward. "We understand what you've done. We understand your explanations. But everything you ask, everything you do, seems to come with a larger and larger cost. We're not sure if we're better off now or not. There's a lot of argument about that."

He paused for a moment, a determined look on his face, then faced me squarely. "We'd like you to go away. We'll face our fate ourselves. If you want to kill us, we can't stop you. If you want to kill me, I can't do anything about it. But you're not welcome here anymore."

I stared at him, through the drone, for what seemed like forever. I was frozen. Numb. It was too much to process. The emotional circuit breaker had tripped. I'd lost a family already, now I was losing a second one.

I backed out of the drone, and turned to Marvin. His face was grey. I was sure I didn't look any better. "I guess I screwed up," I said.

"Look, let's just clear out for now," he replied. "Give things time to cool off. You can talk to Archimedes later."

I nodded, and re-entered the drone. I floated over to Archimedes, who was not looking well. Deltans didn't display shock the same as humans. His facial fur was lying in disorganized mats. But the wide eyes and flat ears were probably universal. A disconnected part of me started theorizing about why that might be, and I squashed it.

"Archimedes, I'm going to take off until things cool down. I'll talk to you later."

He nodded. I noted that Diana had a look on her face of either satisfaction or triumph. I'd never hated anyone as much as I despised her at that moment.

# 20. Parasite

## Howard
## October 2189
## Vulcan

Things that make you go "Ew!" This definitely qualified. I couldn't take my eyes off the video, as the doctor made an incision on the patient and proceeded to extract a small bundle of eggs. A few had hatched and the larvae were trying to burrow away. At that moment, right there, I was so thankful that I was no longer biological.

I glanced at Butterworth's video feed and noticed that he was paying an extreme level of attention to his glass of Jameson. Huh, not a bad idea. I invoked a glass of Sam's cognac and turned on my alcohol receptors. A slight buzz was just what the doctor ordered.

Finally, thank the Universe, the video ended. Butterworth turned to look at the video camera. A slight smile formed when he saw the glass in my hand. I shrugged a "what about it?" shrug.

"The parasite appears to be a large insect," he explained. "The bite itches a bit, then disappears. When the eggs have grown enough, though, it becomes a large swollen area. By that point, we have less than a day to remove the eggs."

"What if you don't?" I knew I would regret asking, but I couldn't stop myself.

"The larvae go for the heart. Fatal within two days or so. Then

Dennis E. Taylor

the larvae feast on the corpse. That seems to be the life cycle. We've lost four people and two cattle so far. The doctors think they might be able to come up with a blood test, but I can't see poking every colonist every other day to draw blood."

"Wonderful. Have we caught any adults yet?"

Butterworth shook his head. "No, nor do we have very good descriptions, other than that it's about hummingbird-size. We're working on it, but I was hoping you might be able to throw in some surveillance drones."

"I'll crank up the autofactory and start pumping them out. I'll also see if I can modify the video and audio pickups to be more sensitive to insect sound and movement."

Butterworth nodded to me and signed off. I gave orders to Guppy for the changes to the autofactory schedules, then sat back and shook my head. Gross.

* * *

The Spits and FAITH colonies were done offloading to Romulus. Colonists were staying in temporary quarters until the towns were built. AMI construction equipment worked full speed to clear some land and set out street plans. We'd learned from the USE's experience on Vulcan, and we were building a fence right away. The wildlife on Romulus wasn't nearly as big or plentiful, but there was a joke going around about carnivorous rabbits. Everyone was fine with excess caution.

The FAITH and Spits colonies were set up on separate continents. The land area on Romulus was divided into eight land masses, each about the size of Australia, and a number of smaller archipelagos. Separation of nations wouldn't be a problem.

The really important item, from my point of view, was that our relatives were now awake. As part of our deal with Cranston, Julia Hendricks and family owned a communicator, so didn't have to schedule time on the colony system.

At the appointed hour, I connected to the conference that Riker was advertising. I noted with a chuckle that we were up over thirty Bobs subscribing to the feed. I watched as Riker made the call and Julia came online. A dozen or so random family members jostled for position behind her in the video. And on her lap, with pride of place, was Space Cadet Justin.

"Unca' Will!" he yelled.

"Hey, Cadet. Enjoy the space-ship ride?"

I could hear the pride and joy in Riker's voice. I and every other Bob shared it. These were our sisters' descendants, and a major reason why we put up with idiots like Cranston and VEHEMENT. I remembered Milo, who had expressed a strong lack of caring about humanity's fate. A momentary wave of sadness washed over me at his memory. I wondered what he would have thought of the current situation.

I pulled myself back to the present, where Julia was talking about their experience. Well, trying to. Justin didn't seem willing to give up the floor.

"...An' we went in the big ship an' we sat and it was boring an' then there was a bump an' they took us down a big hallway an' they gave me a needle which I hated an' they made me sleepy an' they put me in a box an'..."

Amazing. He didn't even seem to be stopping to breathe. The soliloquy went on for another minute, while Julia increasingly failed to keep a grin off her face. Finally, having said what he needed to say, he yelled, "Bye Unca' Will" and shot out of frame. This prompted laughter from everyone, family and Bobs both.

Julia turned back to Riker with a smile on her face. "He has two speeds. Asleep, and what you just saw."

One of the family members, who I remembered as Philip something, leaned forward. "Will, how long until some other colony gets planted on Romulus?"

Riker shook his head. "Can't say. We've got two more colony ships heading to your system right now, but the enclave leaders will decide whether they want to settle on Vulcan or Romulus. Howard tells me that Romulus is looking a lot more attractive these days, though."

There were chuckles from the family. News of the raptors had already spread.

Riker talked to Julia for a few more minutes, fielded some questions from other family members, and got Julia to promise to call him as soon as they were in private residences.

Then, it was over. As Riker hung up the call, I sat back to bask in the peculiar mix of joy, wistfulness, and melancholy that seeing our family always left me with. I had talked with a few other Bobs about it—it seemed to be a common reaction. I guess Original Bob wasn't as much of a loner as he'd always claimed.

I signed off of the conference call, and turned to Guppy, who had been hovering.

"What?"

[Colonel Butterworth wants to talk to you. They've caught a parasite adult]

\* \* \*

*Ugly little bugger.*

Hummingbird-size turned out to be a little bit of an exaggeration, but it was still one of the biggest insects I'd ever seen. I didn't much care for insects, and I had an urge to stomp on this one. It looked like some odd combination of hornet and spider, with two sets of wings. The stinger was particularly nasty-looking. Retractable, it could inject eggs in its victim up to an inch deep.

I had to turn off my gag reflex, watching the necropsy.

Well, now we had specifics. I bundled up all the data and shot off an email to Bill, asking for suggestions. Then I connected to Butterworth.

"Howard. You've seen our new neighbor?"

"Yeah, not my favorite creature. I've sent something off to Bill, and I've got a couple dozen new drones ready. I'll program them with the data and get them to scan the area. See what we come up with."

Butterworth nodded and disconnected.

The colonel looked outwardly calm, but I knew this was worrying him. Big things like raptors, we could handle. Small stuff, not so much. Humanity could conceivably end up prisoners in their own homes if we didn't get control of this pest.

# 21. Attacks Continue

## Riker
## December 2174
## Sol

"We lost a cargo drone," Charles said, popping into VR. "There was an explosive package waiting where it landed. As soon it touched down, the bomb went off."

He sat down and accepted a coffee from Jeeves. "It was a supply delivery to Vancouver Island. They've still got enough of a fishery that they're not facing immediate starvation, but the loss of equipment and resources is still painful."

I looked up and muttered a few choice expletives. "I take it we lost the entire food shipment?"

Charles nodded. "I thought we had the landing area completely secured. VEHEMENT has already claimed responsibility. They're getting trickier."

A light blinked on my console. Not surprisingly, it was Premier Grady. I accepted the call.

"We seem to have lost our delivery," he said without preamble. "I saw the announcement. I do not blame you for this—you could just as soon blame me. However, the problem remains of hungry mouths to feed. What can be done?"

"Short term, sir, I'm going to put together another delivery.

Homer is in your area, so he'll arrange a time and place over a short-range laser link. No chance of intercepting the communication that way." I turned to look at Homer. He nodded and disappeared.

I thought for a second, then turned back to the video call. "Meanwhile, I think that VEHEMENT has graduated to major threat. They're not going to go away, and they're no longer just a nuisance."

I talked to Grady for a few more moments, going over some backlogged items. Then he looked to his right and announced that he was receiving the connection from Homer. His eyes moved across the video screen for a few moments, then he turned back to me and nodded.

After he disconnected, Charles said, "We also have the issue of the Florianópolis attacks."

"I know, Charles. A lot of people still blame Brazil for the war. I guess they're taking out their frustrations and getting some revenge. We have a task force going on that already. I just don't know how hard they're working on it. There seems to be a lot of sympathy for those terrorist attacks."

"Less so for the supply chain attacks, even though fewer lives are lost." Charles shrugged. "Hits closer to home, I guess."

\* \* \*

There had been sabotage on one of the donuts. Some chemicals had been introduced into the irrigation system and had killed three sections of kudzu before the automated systems caught on and shut everything down for inspection.

This VEHEMENT group was good. The only people that had legitimate access to the space farms were the Bobs. Since VEHEMENT demonstrably was able to gain access, we had to consider all other means. Ideas for how they might have done it included fake drones controlled by VEHEMENT, stealth devices piggy-backing up from Earth on returning delivery vehicles, or even hacking of our legitimate drones. None of those alternatives really seemed realistic, but then that was the thing about being a good hacker. If people saw it coming, you wouldn't be able to get away with it.

I set my AMI monitors to reviewing all traffic for the last

month. Even if they found nothing, I was at least eliminating possibilities. I was archiving everything, though, in case I got inspired at some later date. Somewhere in all the communications around Earth, there *had* to be exchanges between VEHEMENT members.

I went back to review, yet again, everything in the libraries about cryptography.

## 22.  Fallout

**Bob**
**December 2173**
**Delta Eridani**

"Archimedes."

Archimedes stopped in mid-step and looked wildly around. "Bawbe?"

I cancelled the camouflage on the drone for a moment so he could locate it. He grunted an acknowledgement and settled carefully to the ground to sit, leaning against a tree. I brought the drone down to eye level, then re-engaged the camouflage.

"I don't think you're going to be allowed back." The statement was delivered in a low voice, without looking at the drone. "Since you were banished, there have been no attacks."

"That's because I've killed six hippogriffs so far that were heading your way," I replied. I was irritated, and I let it show in my tone.

Archimedes looked at the drone, eyes wide. "You're still protecting us?"

"You're still important to me, Archimedes. Especially *you* and your family. Speaking of which, how is Buster doing?"

Archimedes smiled fondly. "He wants to help me make tools now. Of course, all he does is bash rocks together, but it's a start."

He lost the smile and looked down for a moment before continuing, "I'm getting a lot of what you call cold shoulder, still. Some of the other cubs have started to tease Buster. I don't want you to go away forever, but I can't have my family affected."

"I understand, Archimedes. I still need to get you up to speed with the bow and arrow eventually, but it can wait. The thing to remember is that I didn't wipe out the hippogriffs, just the local nest. As a species, they're still out there, and your area is effectively unclaimed territory for them now. You need to be ready to hold them off. At minimum, you need to have a supply of extra spears. And the bows and arrows will give you more range."

"Okay. I've been playing around with the short spears, uh, arrows. I told people they're small spears for Buster. They laugh, but they believe me. The bow part, why does it have to be different materials?"

"Laminated material is stronger and has much better spring. Eventually you'll glue it, but for now, tying is good enough."

We talked for a while longer: plans for new weapons, suggestions for the medicine woman, basic math. I would bring these people out of the stone age one way or another.

Eventually, Archimedes got up, said goodbye, and headed back to Camelot. It was enough. It was a good day.

* * *

Marvin had something to say again. I could always tell. He would open his mouth, then close it, then try again. I wasn't sure if I should be concerned or not. Last time, it had been hippogriffs. Not a good track record.

Finally, he managed to squeeze it out. "I think I'm going to be heading out, soon."

I froze for almost half a second. "As in, leaving Delta Eridani?"

"Yeah. Bob, you've done a lot with the Deltans, but I think it's past the point where it needs two of us. This is a caretaker situation, now." He made a gesture at the video window I'd been watching. "Truthfully, the council kicking you out was probably a good thing for them. They go back to deciding their own destiny. You can still tweak things here and there, but the sky god business really wasn't healthy. For you or for them."

I thought about being offended, getting mad, but the truth was that I'd been having very similar thoughts. I dropped my eyes and nodded. "Still, it won't be the same without you around to give Guppy bad greeting lines."

"Hell, Bob, with SCUT we're never really out of touch. If I keep my speed below .75 C, my tau won't go high enough to preclude VR. I might just seem a little groggy to you."

"Funny, it still doesn't feel the same." I shrugged and paced back and forth a few times in silence. "I guess I understand, though, Marv. It's always been my project. Luke and Bender knew that."

"Sure wish they'd intercept the SCUT plans transmission," Marvin commented, changing the subject. "It would be nice to know if they're okay."

I nodded and sat down. What a crap year this was turning into.

On the other hand, SCUT did make things a little easier. There were things to do, and Bobs to talk to.

I shook my head and sighed. The moping was pointless. I would always be able to find a laundry list of things to be depressed about, if I worked at it. The Deltans were still there, even if they weren't talking to me at the moment.

## 23.  VEHEMENT

## Riker
## September 2175
## Sol

Pieces of space station mingled with desiccated plants and the carcasses of livestock that had been unlucky enough to be living on that donut. The debris had scattered with the explosion, but orbital mechanics and mutual gravity were bringing everything back together.

Homer's image floated in the video window. "We'd just brought this one on-line. Six months' work, gone."

I nodded silently. The donuts were Homer's babies. He'd come up with the idea and head-manned it to completion. This couldn't be easy for him. "Any announcements?"

"Yeah. VEHEMENT. The usual crazy-ass rant. Humanity is a cancer, the universe is better off without them, blah, blah."

"I'm sorry, buddy. But we'll get them, one way or another."

Homer was silent. His expression said everything. Sadness, anger, confusion. He wouldn't meet my eyes. I felt guilty about all the bad thoughts I'd had about him in the past. He was a fully contributing member of the team, and this was killing him.

I was concerned about Homer. He had pretty much stopped ribbing me. Hadn't called me *number two* in months. In fact, he seemed to have turned all business. I wondered if someone had offended him, but on the one occasion I'd tried to talk to him about it, he just deflected the conversation.

"We've got enough redundancy now that this won't leave us dead in the water," I said. "But with the reduced planetside output, it's going to mean short rations. Or more kudzu." I smiled, trying to lighten the mood. Homer wasn't having any. He shrugged, then ended the connection.

"Guppy, what have we got relating to Farm-6?"

**[Querying AMI team. One moment]**

After a short delay, Guppy continued.

**[No related transmissions detected. No nearby activity except by Heaven vessels]**

Crap. They were covering their tracks too well. "Something will break. Something has to."

Guppy didn't comment. He wasn't much on encouragement. Huge fishy eyes blinked once.

\* \* \*

Just to really make my week, there were several terrorist attacks on Florianópolis as well. I kept wondering if there was some anniversary coming up that was triggering all the activity. The terrorists were getting smarter, and hitting more critical targets. One of the attacks had taken out the power system. It would take a couple of days to fix.

It wasn't the first time that the actions of VEHEMENT and the Brazilian attacks seemed to be coordinated. I wondered if there was some connection. It was almost certainly two different groups, but maybe they were talking to each other, sharing intelligence. That could actually be of benefit to me.

The old Earth, pre-war, had global technology and every form of communications you could imagine. This post-apocalyptic reality was far more limited. There were fewer methods of communication for collusion between the two groups, or even cross-talk between VEHEMENT cells.

But I'd been monitoring all channels. At least everything I could think of. So either I'd missed some form of communication; or they were using some kind of steganography, which would be almost impossible to recognize unless you knew what you were looking for; or they had gone low-tech.

Option three would be too slow, number one I couldn't do anything about, so that left two. Steganography was by definition inefficient, since you had to spread the message out enough for it to be unnoticeable. Therefore the transmission medium would have to allow a high bandwidth, which would immediately rule out a lot of possibilities. And there were statistical methods that could ferret out steganographic messages.

I retired to my VR, to give this more thought.

## 24.  Visiting Marvin

**Bob**
**March 2174**
**Delta Eridani**

I hadn't had to kill a hippogriff in months. It wasn't clear if they'd learned to avoid the territory, or if there simply weren't any left that were close enough to bother the Deltans. Since Marvin's departure, I was handling all the drones myself. I could automate a certain amount of the tasks, but I still eventually had to review the mission recordings. Honestly, I couldn't be bothered.

I kept my eye on Archimedes and his family, probably a little more than I should. I had occasional flashes of myself as the overbearing grandparent who kept wanting to visit. It was an embarrassing image, and I resolved to contact Archimedes a little less often.

Marvin was long gone, heading for Pi$^3$ Orionis. I think he was hoping for an intelligent species that he could be in charge of. It seemed we actually had a paternal streak. Or maybe maternal. He was, as promised, keeping his top speed low enough so that he could still interface via SCUT connection. We'd found a balance, where he frame-jacked up a bit and I slowed my time-sense some, and we could then interact at the same time-rate. It worked.

Today, I was visiting Marvin. In Delta Eridani, as senior Bob, I generally played host. It was interesting that traditions and modes of behavior were developing even among a bunch of post-human computers. Generally, the senior Bob in any system was in charge, and played host to the other Bobs. It made sense to me, which meant it pretty much made sense to all the Bobs.

Marvin apparently had a bit of a luxury streak in him. His VR environment was an open-air patio and rancher-style house at the top of a low mountain, in a semi-tropical climate. The ocean stretched out in all directions, right out to the horizon.

It was a beautiful, if somewhat mundane scene, except for a couple of anomalies: the very close horizon, the low gravity, and the presence of Earth hanging in the middle of the sky.

"You know there's no air on the moon, right?" I grinned at him.

Marvin shrugged. "I'm going through all the science fiction books I've read over the years and replicating the environments for a while. It's interesting, and it's good practice at VR programming."

I nodded. It wasn't really important. We were stalling, and we both knew it.

Finally, I brought up the elephant in the room. "My two newest clones, Pete and Victor, are almost ready to leave. Victor is willing to follow the trail of either Luke or Bender. Pete is not interested at all. We have to make a choice."

Marvin took a moment to brush his hand through his hair. I remembered that habit from when I was Original Bob. Apparently death wasn't enough to remove nervous tics.

"I guess Pete is adamant?" he asked.

"Yup. Like Milo with Earth. 'This is the expression of not caring.' He's going off in whatever direction he decides on, and that's that."

Marvin chuckled. "A recurring theme. Great. Well, it's a coin toss, then, isn't it?"

"The thing is, Marv, what if something bad happened to both Luke and Bender? They were heading for different stars, but in the same general direction. What if they ran into something?"

"What, like the Borg? It just seems unlikely, Bob. What would be the motive?"

"Don't know. Maybe another Medeiros. We don't really have any information." I shrugged, conceding the point. "Well, we'll leave it up to Victor. He'll transmit constantly over SCUT, so we'll know if something happens to him."

Marvin nodded, a worried look on his face.

## 25.  Rabbits

**Howard**
**November 2189**
**Vulcan**

There was a call on my queue from one of the biologists. I was a little surprised. Normally I talked only to Butterworth—not there was a rule or anything. Still... curious, I dialed the call.

"Sheehy." A woman appeared on screen for a moment, then disappeared off frame. I got an impression of thick red hair, tied into a ponytail.

"Dr. Sheehy? This is Howard Johansson, returning your call."

Her disembodied voice drifted back to the phone. "Oh, thanks for getting back to me. Colonel Butterworth wanted me to call you if we had news. We have news."

I waited for a moment. "And..."

She returned and grinned into the video. "Sorry. I love the drama. Anyway, we have a possible treatment for the vine."

"Which is..." *Honestly, Sheehy, keep this up and I'll drop a rock on you.*

"Bunnies."

"I'm going to drop a rock on you."

Dr. Sheehy laughed. I couldn't help noticing that she had a great laugh. Also freckles, dimples when she laughed... I mentally slapped myself. This could go exactly nowhere.

She disappeared again, then returned holding a small section of plant. "Turns out rabbits not only are able to eat the vine, they seem to be attracted to it. I think the toxin is just added flavoring to them. Bad for the vine. Good for us."

"Right, but we still have to expend a lot of effort to harvest the vine and get it to the rabbits. Could just as easily incinerate it."

"No, no." Dr. Sheehy shook her head. "Rabbits are self-replicating. Aggressively so. You may have heard..." She grinned at me. "And they make great stew."

I smiled back at her. There was a certain poetry in the solution. Granted, we'd be unleashing a Terran scourge, even if a fluffy one, on an unsuspecting planet. But Vulcan attacked first. "Have you asked Butterworth about it?"

"He says council will have to approve. But they're feeling a little humble these days. He thinks he can ram it through."

"Well, all righty then."

Dr. Sheehy paused for a moment before continuing. "You heard about the bronto attack yesterday?"

"Well, *attack* is not the right word. They tried to eat the fence again."

"Yes, and we had to kill one that had figured out that he could just avoid the electrical wires. That's one smart bronto. IQ up in the two, maybe three range." Dr. Sheehy smiled at her own joke. "Anyway, before they airlifted the carcass away from the clearing, someone got the bright idea to cut off a big hunk of meat. It passed toxicology tests, and it passed the barbeque test. So now bronto is on the menu. You may find your kudzu sales dropping."

"Whoa! You were *not* supposed to be hunting for sustenance until the impact studies are completed. Is the council good with this?"

Dr. Sheehy gave me an unbelieving look. "Try to picture the council telling twenty thousand people that they have to eat kudzu instead of steak, when steak is lumbering around in plain view every day. Can you say *lynching*?"

"Yeah, okay, point taken. Well, I still have the Romulan colony market. *They* don't have bronto."

Dr. Sheehy grinned and shrugged, then disconnected.

To be honest, this was good news from my point of view. The more the colonies could do themselves, the less I had to do. I could even conceivably take off in a decade or so.

And on that subject, the GUPPI-controlled surveillance system wasn't going to build itself. Back to work.

# 26.   Selling Poseidon

## Riker
## December 2175
## Sol

"You seem incapable of preventing them from striking at will." Ambassador Gerrold seemed to be enjoying the situation, which made his attempts at portraying anger unconvincing. I'd ignored his jibes in the past, but I was getting tired of it.

"And what have you been able to do, Ambassador? Found the source of those hacking attempts yet? Made any arrests? Got any suggestions? Anything besides endless carping?" I exchanged glares with the ambassador for a moment, then moved on. "We're working on replacing the donut, but it'll still be a few months. Plus whatever time it takes to get the farm regrown. There will be short rations for a while, but no starvation." I had a sudden inspiration, one of those mid-action moments, and added, "VEHEMENT got lucky this time. We stop most of their attempts before they get anywhere. They aren't really that smart." It wasn't true, but baiting them might force some kind of reaction. VEHEMENT depended on fear, and being publicly dissed might provoke a response.

Before anyone could comment, I turned off my audio, effectively giving up the floor. I turned to Guppy without moving my avatar. "Put everything we have on communications monitoring. I want to know who reacts to my words, and how. I want every byte accounted for."

Guppy nodded and went into command fugue.

The session moved on to the emigration question. The Maldives and Micronesia had pretty much cemented their claim on Poseidon—partly due to lack of interest by the other enclaves. They needed about six hundred more people from other enclaves to form a full colony-ship complement, but they were having a hard time making that. No one wanted to split off from their group, especially to go to a planet so, um, specialized. It was attractive to islanders; to everyone else, not so much.

At the same time, other groups were trying to lay claim to the semi-completed ships for emigration to Vulcan or Romulus. The whole thing was acrimonious and mostly information-free.

[No detectable increase in Earthside traffic. One anomalous communication to spaceside]

Okay, that was something. "Source? Destination?"

[Source New Zealand, although not near any population centers. Destination Homer]

"Uh, excuse me?"

[It was a tight-beam signal. It would not have been detectable except for a chance alignment with one of our drones on cleanup duty]

Oh. Shit. That just did not make sense. Why would Homer be helping them? Why would he be sabotaging his own project? Unless he didn't have a choice...

Suddenly Homer's change in personality took on an ominous cast. It was very un-Homer-like. The complete cessation of jokes, the withdrawal from the rest of us...

Perhaps because it wasn't Homer.

I sent a message to Charles, requesting a physical meet-up.

## 27.  Luke Returns

**Bob**
**March 2178**
**Delta Eridani**

I walked through the village VR, watching the activity. There had been improvements in the six years since I'd been kicked out. I had enough hidden cameras and camouflaged drones around the village now to feed a real-time VR. No more recorded scenes.

Archimedes had finally started taking my tent design seriously. A few other couples copied the result, and now there were a half-dozen pretty good facsimiles of teepees scattered through the village. It was the dry season, but once the rains started up again, I expected this innovation to increase in popularity.

I was trying to ignore a couple engaging in some very public displays of affection when I received a ping. From *Luke!*

I responded and he popped in. "Hey, Bob. Long time."

I grinned and slapped him on the shoulder. "Luke! Good to see you, buddy."

Luke appeared momentarily surprised. We've never been physically demonstrative like that. In fact, Original Bob was a little standoffish in terms of physical contact. Luke got over it quickly, though, and grinned back at me. "I just went through the whole surprise-visit-by-Bill thing. Apparently it's a standard hazing ritual."

I laughed. "Oh, yes. I went through it, too. You don't expect a VR link across light years, and I notice that Bill's transmitted plans *still* don't mention the possibility. So, where are you right now?"

"Kappa Ceti. And before you say it, Bill already gave me crap about not picking up his transmissions right away." Luke materialized a coffee, waited while Spike sniffed his hand, and then turned back to me. "I've spent the last several minutes reading blogs. Lots has been happening, apparently."

I nodded, knowing he would have caught up on events with the Deltans first thing. "What have you found, out your way?"

"A super-Earth." Luke shrugged. "Absolutely not suitable for colonization. Gravity just over 3G, but a full-on ecosystem. I've been having fun cataloguing things. And I've started another load of Bobs."

Luke stopped talking as Archimedes came into the VR area, his son trailing him. Buster was almost as tall as his father, and not showing any sign of slowing down. Archimedes had filled out as he reached full adulthood and wasn't looking at all bookish any more. The two of them together made a formidable team.

They were carrying bows and had quivers on their backs. Each was carrying some kind of small game, sort of a wild turkey analogue, freshly killed.

Luke turned to me. "Bows and arrows? Wow, dude. Moving things right along."

I waved a hand in dismissal. "Sooner or later the hippogriffs will find them again. I want them to be ready."

Luke nodded and materialized a La-Z-Boy. "Good to be back. This looks like fun. Where's Marvin?"

"He took off a few years ago, right after I got kicked out of Camelot. He keeps in touch, though."

"Cool. I'll look him up when I have a moment. Heard from Bender?"

I shook my head. "No, and I have no idea why. One of my clones has followed his flight plan, and should be able to report something in a year or two."

Luke nodded. I materialized the couch and coffee table setup and got comfortable. There's always time to get caught up with old friends.

## 28.  Et Tu, Homer

## Riker
## December 2175
## Sol

There was seldom any reason for the Bobs to meet physically these days. SCUT and VR meant we could do everything we needed to in virtual space. SCUT-equipped drones made distance irrelevant for remote administration as well.

Now, two Heaven vessels floated less than fifty meters apart, in a section of space not far enough from a Lagrange point to look suspicious, but not so close that nearby clutter might disguise an eavesdropper. A laser link ensured that communications would be leakage-free and interception-free.

Charles sat across from me, the coffee in his hand forgotten, his expression a mix of confusion, disbelief, and horror.

I hastened to explain. "This is just speculation on my part. Or it started out that way, anyway. When I went over the recent instances of VEHEMENT spaceside sabotage, Homer was always a recent visitor. In a couple of cases, the *only* recent visitor. We'd been saying that nothing had been near the locations, but that's because we've been discounting ourselves as suspects."

"But... Homer? How?"

"You remember the hacking attempt on me? I thought that was

the only instance, but maybe it was the only instance that we detected. VEHEMENT obviously has some heavy-duty tech on their side. Maybe they discovered another way in."

"So what do we do?"

I looked down for a moment. This wasn't going to be easy to say. "We have to disable Homer and check him out. We can apologize afterwards if I'm wrong. Remember the Battle of Sol?"

\* \* \*

**[Investigation complete. File uploaded]**

"Thanks, Guppy. I'll look at it when I have a chance." The file would be a summary of whatever the drones had found at the ground location of that suspicious transmission. I'd made a point of disabling all radio comms on those drones, and using secret-key encryption and frequency jumping for the SCUT telemetry. *I* couldn't have intercepted and decoded that kind of setup if I'd been handed the information on a silver platter. I had to assume that the unknown opponent wasn't *too* much smarter than me, or I might as well just roll over and expose my throat.

I sent Homer a message that I thought I knew where the next attack by VEHEMENT would be and that we needed a secure discussion. Charles, Homer and I arranged to meet just to orbital north of the Earth-moon L4 point.

Homer coasted up and applied the brakes. Once we were at station-keeping, we rotated to present our laser comms to each other.

In an abundance of paranoia, I routed my communications through sandbox Bob. Laser comms were intimate enough that if Homer had a virus, it might try to get to me via that connection. I'd told Charles to do the same.

We connected up and Homer appeared in my VR. "So, Riker, what's this big discovery?"

I took a sip of my coffee, and privately looked over at sandbox Bob. No reaction. "Just waiting for Charles. I don't want to have to repeat myself and answer the same arguments twice. One of us can fill in Ralph later when he gets here." I looked up at the holotank where Charles was just coming up on our group.

Charles linked up by laser comms and popped into the common VR. "Hi guys. 'Sup?"

In my private VR, sandbox Bob grabbed his throat and fell over. I looked at Guppy, one eyebrow raised.

**[Source of attack is Homer]**

I raised both hands in the air in the common VR, and Charles put a steel ball right through Homer's reactor control system.

Homer went dead as he lost all power, just as he had back in our battle with the Brazilian probes. I did a quick scan. Perfect shot, no collateral damage. Charles looked green, and I'm sure I did as well.

We sent over a squad of roamers and unceremoniously cut into Homer's cargo bay. It took a few hours before we had Homer's matrix up on a test cradle. Now came the dirty part.

\* \* \*

"Here it is." I pointed to the listing. "It looks like the laser comms were the source of infection. I'm not sure when or how they would have gotten access, but in any case, it was brilliant. A hole in our defenses that I hadn't even considered."

Charles nodded. "Listen, Homer might not be the only one. You could be infected—although that seems unlikely, given that you're the one exposing the issue—or I could be. My Guppy saw the penetration attempt from Homer as well, so unless you're pulling some kind of double-reverse Maxwell Smart thing, I think you're legit. I need you to do an inspection of my matrix to clear up any suspicions about me. Like they did in *The Thing*." He looked at me expectantly.

I thought for a moment and nodded. It was a good idea, and necessary. Charles would have to open his hangar doors, then shut down, but now that I knew what to look for, the actual check would take only minutes.

I explained the requirements, and Charles did as instructed. A couple of roamers entered Charles' hull, and twenty minutes later Charles was back up and running.

"Thanks, Charles. I can reciprocate if there's any lingering doubt in your mind."

He shook his head. "You could have infected me while I was off. Absolutely no reason for you not to. I'm good."

We turned our attention back to Homer.

\* \* \*

It took thirty hours overall to clean up and repair him. The virus, or Trojan, or whatever you wanted to call it, had gotten its hooks into multiple systems. Homer would have had very little free will, but would be fully conscious. I shuddered, thinking what that must have been like.

Ralph showed up in the midst of the process and we had to explain the whole thing to him. While I was talking, Charles lined up with Ralph's reactor control system. When we pointed this out and explained the alternatives, Ralph quite rationally agreed to an inspection.

Once Ralph was back up—clean, thankfully—we turned back to Homer. I removed the viral control, and I installed a freshly-made firewall over the laser comms. None of us would be susceptible to that particular attack in the future. I also forwarded a complete report to Bill for him to add to the standard releases.

Homer booted up. His avatar appeared in the common VR, looked surprised, then collapsed, screaming. The rest of us looked at each other in horror. Had I done something wrong? Had I damaged Homer?

"Homer, buddy, come back. You okay?" I knelt beside him and put my hand on his shoulder.

The screaming stopped, and he began to moan. He curled into a fetal position, squeezed his eyes shut, and rocked back and forth on the floor.

I was at a complete loss. Original Bob hadn't been much for this kind of emotional contact, and I was self-aware enough to know that I was even more standoffish than he was. Ralph and Charles didn't look any more prepared. However, Homer didn't seem to be getting worse or harming himself, so we decided in timeless male fashion to leave things be and wait for him to get a grip.

After a few more milliseconds, Homer gasped and opened his eyes. "I was hagridden. The bastards had total control of me. They made me lie to you; they made me blow things up. They *made me kill people!*"

Homer began to cry, a hopeless moaning alternating with racking sobs. "I couldn't do anything. I could only watch myself follow their orders. I couldn't tell you, I couldn't stop myself, I couldn't even kill myself!"

Bill popped into VR. "I've been lurking since I got your report. This is unforgivable. I know we don't like violence, but if you feel the need to end the bastards that did this, no one will say boo." He sat on the floor beside Homer and put a hand on his back, simply maintaining human contact.

I looked at Charles and Ralph. The expression on their faces said all that was needed. Someone was going to pay.

\* \* \*

Homer had come out of his funk, but he was still very fragile. Bill was gone, after promising any help we might want in building anything we might need, up to and including Things That Explode. Yep. Angry.

Charles kept an eye on Homer while Ralph oversaw the construction of the replacement donut. Homer was gradually able to unwind himself and sit, but he would go into panic attacks from time to time. I suggested we enable his endocrine controls, but he shook his head emphatically.

"It feels too much like what they did to me. It's a leash. It's just a *different* leash." He waved a hand helplessly, trying to find words. "It feels like claustrophobia or something. Just the *idea* of something controlling me makes me want to run around the room, screaming."

"Okay, Homer. Whatever you feel best about." Charles put a hand on his shoulder. "We're here for you, whatever you need."

Homer nodded to us and tried a smile, but it wasn't very reassuring.

I had not attended the latest UN session. If VEHEMENT had noticed that they'd lost their puppet, I didn't want to give them any more information. Let them think we'd all destroyed each other.

Meanwhile, I looked over Guppy's report. The tight-beam signal had come from what originally might have been a small military outpost high in the back country of New Zealand. It had some pretty hefty communications capability, judging from the visible hardware. Per my orders, the drones avoided using SUDDAR scanning, as that would have been detectable. Instead we stuck to passive surveillance techniques. Visual and infrared pinpointed occupied areas and gave an approximate head-count. Audio snooping picked up some of the conversations, the contents of which left no doubt about who was in residence. This appeared to be VEHEMENT central. Even if they operated on a cell structure, without their tech central they wouldn't be good for much in the future.

I remembered the early hacking attempt, which had also originated from New Zealand. It was reasonable to assume that this had been an ongoing war for longer than I'd realized.

Fine. War declared. But I wanted to be certain I caught the right people. The mastermind behind so complex a setup wouldn't be that easy to track down. I was sure there'd be at least one more hop to his location.

I would take whatever amount of time, use whatever resources I needed, to catch him. Without limit. And when I did, there would be a reckoning.

# 29.  Emergency

## Howard
## April 2190
## Vulcan

**[Emergency at Landing]**

I turned briefly to look at Guppy; but good news or bad, Guppy looked like Admiral Ackbar. No help there.

I turned back to my video call with Dr. Sheehy, said, "Gotta go!" and disconnected. I picked up the video connection that Guppy was holding for me. It was Stéphane.

"Howard, we've got a group of raptors that somehow got through the fence. They're running through town, looking for prey."

"Last known location?"

Stéphane gave me a cross-street. I knew that security would be converging on the location, but the raptors could move fast—much faster than a human.

I had only two busters close enough to be useful, but I had all the drones that were part of the automated surveillance system. As well, several backup units were parked on top of the Administration building, sitting in their cradles. I activated the backups and sent all units to the reported location.

Halfway there, the two busters blew past the flock of drones, doing close to Mach One. I was now juggling eighteen separate units. Even with most of them slaved to a primary, it was hard to keep track. I dismissed my VR and frame-jacked up high enough so that I could multi-task.

The busters were coming up on the reported location, but I couldn't see any raptors. I split off a couple of drones and sent them up to a kilometer altitude, activating high-res, infra-red, and motion-detection sensors.

Security personnel were approaching from several directions. There were only two streets that the raptors could be on, and there was no sign of them. Could Brodeur have been wrong? A quick check of the video surveillance streams eliminated that possibility. Either raptors could become invisible—wouldn't that be a kicker—or they'd found somewhere to hide.

I brought all the drones down to a few feet above ground and started a search pattern for raptor prints. The drones took off in different directions, following anything that was even remotely print-like. Chivvying all these units was really wearing on me—even in frame-jack, I had to keep track of what orders each unit was following—so I guess I don't feel too bad that it took me a couple of missed cycles before I realized one of the units wasn't responding.

I pulled up the video log for that unit, and—wow, that's what the inside of a raptor mouth looks like. Good to know.

The raptor pack had gone to ground inside someone's storage shed. I guess one of them decided he should take out the flying thing before it raised the alarm. Even acknowledging that they couldn't know about radio, that was intelligent behavior. Bill and I would be discussing this one.

Meanwhile, I sent all units to surround the shed, dropped my frame-rate to real-time, and called Stéphane.

The drones and busters arrived and took up positions around the shed. And the moment they did that, the raptors made a break for freedom. They dodged through the circle of drones, leaped a fence, and made a bee-line for the perimeter.

It would be a coin-toss whether any of the security people could get into position to take them out, and at the speed the raptors were moving, there wouldn't be much opportunity. Hopefully civilians would have heard the alert and had enough sense to stay indoors.

"Stéphane, have they killed anyone?"

"Not to my knowledge, but we'll be checking out this hou—no, never mind, I see some faces looking out the window. Someone just gave me a thumbs-up. So no, no casualties."

"Okay. They're out of range of you guys now. I don't have enough space to get my busters up to speed anyway, so I'm going to let them go. Maybe they'll spread the word..."

"*Tabernacle!* You think they can talk?"

"Erm, probably not, but maybe they can teach caution through their behavior. Oh, and guess what? Seems raptors can dig, too. Wonderful." I looked down at the hole through which the raptors were wriggling. It must have been seven or eight feet deep at the low point. Looked like we would be upgrading the fences. Again.

\* \* \*

"Things just get more and more complicated." Colonel Butterworth had his head propped up in one hand, elbow on his desk. "Cranston and Valter are starting to look like the smart ones."

The colonel didn't expect an answer. I think he just needed a drinking buddy. I had a cognac from Sam's template—I was really getting used to the taste—and I just nodded. Truthfully, the raptor invasion hadn't resulted in any fatalities, and we were already starting on getting the fences fixed. Metal rods driven down twenty feet, spaced six inches apart, would take care of the digging issue.

And Bridget—Dr. Sheehy, that is—had a device almost perfected that could detect parasite infection through body odor. No blood tests required, just wave your hand over it as you go by. Those would be installed in all building entrances as soon as she had all the, er, bugs out. Longer-term, we hoped to thin the parasites out to the point of eventual extinction.

Meanwhile, she'd come up with a name for the thing—Cupid Bug. Because, as she explained, it went for the heart. I had to admit, I appreciated Bridget's sense of humor.

I also had several small batches aging of something that might turn out to be a replacement for Jameson. Or for paint thinner. Time would tell.

The colonel and I discussed a few miscellaneous items, but nothing really pressing. The council, as expected, had caved without a fight on the subject of bronto burgers. Let's face it, one of the damned things would keep the entire colony in steaks for a couple of weeks. We wouldn't need to kill many. And the alternative was still kudzu.

I said goodbye to the colonel and popped out. On a whim, I activated one of the surveillance drones. I took it up a couple of kilometers and did a slow pan. The sun was going down in the west, and it was a magnificent sight.

From the surface of Vulcan, Omicron$^2$ Eridani appeared almost a third bigger than Earth's sun. As a K-type star, it had a slightly more orange cast, although you stopped noticing it after a day or so. But the additional output in the red end of the spectrum meant that even the most run-of-the-mill sunsets were spectacular by Earth standards. And today wasn't run-of-the-mill. Scattered clouds were all that were left of the recent thunderstorms, but those clouds glowed in the sky like individual wildfires.

The forest-slash-jungle stretched horizon to horizon, hugging the hills and only reluctantly leaving the occasional rocky crag uncovered. Something like birds swooped and twirled in flocks that wouldn't have been seen on Earth since the days of the passenger pigeon. If you could ignore all the things with big shark teeth, and the other things that could accidentally squish you between their toes, it was a kind of paradise. Oh, yeah, and the things that laid eggs in you. Eww.

## 30.  Found Something

## Bashful
## November 2187
## Gliese 877

We'd all taken off in different directions, per Mario's orders. I picked GL-877, a nondescript star in a forgettable patch of sky. For all we knew, these Others might not be planet-based, or even system-based. But we had to start somewhere. At minimum, we'd be mapping their path of destruction.

[We have radio traffic]

Guppy pushed a window toward me. As I examined the readings, my eyebrows climbed up my forehead. The radio noise coming from this system was clearly artificial. One way or the other, *something* intelligent lived here. Something noisy.

"Every possible caution, Guppy. Let's take it slow. I don't want to attract attention."

[Understood]

"And prep the stealth probes."

I'd have been cautious anyway, but given the possibility that this was the Others, I was going to give paranoia a brand-new level of definition. I had spent my time during transit building a couple of stealth probes. I'd had to sacrifice some busters and some roamers, but the result was a couple of probes that would be almost undetectable unless they cranked up to full power. I had constructed them out of carbon-fiber-matrix ceramic and non-ferrous metal wherever possible. The Others would have to be specifically looking for one of these in order to detect it. I'd already squirted the plans back to Mario as part of my continuous reporting.

I was still going about 5% of light speed, so I lined up just below the ecliptic and released one probe. I altered my line slightly, then released the other. It would take just under two weeks for the probes to free-fall through the system. Meanwhile, I would take a powered flight path, which would take me to the rendezvous point on the other side without my going anywhere near the inner system. Unless the residents had far better detection systems than we did, they'd never know I was here.

I had carefully laid out parameters in which the probes would run for it and conditions in which they'd self-destruct. There would be no chances taken. In either case, once discovered, a probe would abandon attempts at stealth and squirt all telemetry to my calculated position.

With my powered flight plan, I arrived at the rendezvous several days before the probes, on a vector straight outward from the system. The probes hit the brakes and activated their beacons as they came within range.

I downloaded their data and transmitted the whole bundle in Mario's direction before beginning my own analysis. It took about two days to build a coherent picture of the inner system. There were two lonely inner rocky planets and a single small Jovian farther out. The inner of the two rocky planets appeared to have an atmosphere. The other had been too far away from either probe to get details, but it appeared to have a surprisingly high albedo.

The system seemed to be particularly free of debris, except in an orbit about 80% of the orbital radius of the inner planet. At that distance from the sun, there was a truly spectacular amount of mass—and activity—spread right around the orbit. That whole area was, in fact, responsible for most of the electromagnetic activity in the system.

I turned to Guppy and pointed at the mass concentration. "What the crap is that?"

**[Insufficient information. But we can rule out a natural satellite]**

"Not a planet?"

**[Correct. The mass is too diffuse]**

I wished I had someone besides Guppy to discuss this with. The plan had been to build a second wave of Bobs back at Gliese 54 and send them to catch up with the first wave. So within perhaps six months, I could be getting company. Hopefully the new Bob had been picking up my transmissions and had a good idea of how to approach.

I was sitting more than six billion kilometers from the local sun, in some of the emptiest space I could imagine, so it was a shock when the proximity alarms started sounding.

I frame-jacked up to maximum and started to evaluate the readings. *Something* was approaching at high speed. And the something apparently had a very well shielded reactor, because it was SUDDAR that had picked it up. A quick set of calculations showed that I wouldn't be able to win a straight foot-race—it or they were approaching too fast. It was time for our tried-and-true doubling-back tactic. I had no idea what their maneuverability was like, so I calculated a conservative option and began accelerating at a thirty-five degree angle to their approach vector.

The other ships reacted almost immediately, which told me they had SUDDAR detection capability. Light-speed limitations would have meant almost an hour's delay before they could respond to my movement.

The tableau developed slowly over the next several hours. Like a game of chess, everything was on the table. There would be no surprise tactics. The laws of physics would decide if I got past them. However, it was already obvious that closest approach would be, well, pretty close.

It took almost a day to reach that point. I spent the time scanning them with everything at my disposal. SUDDAR and visuals confirmed six vessels: five very similar to the wrecked cargo ship and one that honestly reminded me of a miniature Death Star. "Miniature" being a relative term—the thing was almost a half-kilometer in diameter. Instead of an inset dish like the *Star Wars* prop, it had a flat section with what looked like a grid. I hoped the purpose wasn't similar.

Finally the laws of physics and reality made themselves clear, and I realized that I was going to sail past them, less than ten kilometers away. That was cutting it a little fine, but I'd take it.

As I was nearing closest approach, and getting ready to thumb my virtual nose at the pursuers, I saw the Death Star-wannabe start to rotate, bringing the grid-wall to bear on me.

*This is not good.*

"Guppy, anything we can do about shielding?"

**[All resources are at maximum]**

I calculated that I could do a certain amount of jinking without losing my lead. I immediately started evasive maneuvers. However, the others had made the same calculations. The Death Star simply waited until I ran out of slack and zeroed in.

The grid started to glow, then there was a p—

**[Alert! Controller replicant offline. SURGE drive offline. Requirements for self-destruct protocol have been met. Reactor overload engaged...]**

## 31.  Taking Care of Business

**Howard
January 2191
Vulcan**

Riker was going to be video-visiting our descendants in a few minutes. By tacit agreement, he was the face of Bob. We didn't want to confuse or, worse, creep out our sister's descendants. But all the Bobs tuned in to the conversation whenever possible. It reminded us all that we used to be human, and that we had left our mark on the universe. Okay, our sisters had, but close enough.

As usual, Julia was spokesperson for Clan Bob. People walked in and out of frame, stopped to make a comment or wave to the camera. The usual organized chaos, pretty much standard family stuff. Justin was a little older, and no longer content to sit on his mother's lap. He kept running to get things to show Uncle Will. I grinned every time Justin was in frame. He was every Bob's favorite: infinite energy, wide-eyed interest in anything and everything, and no idea at all what a scary and dangerous post-apocalyptic universe he'd been born into.

"You'll have three new great-greats, soon, Will." Julia smiled happily. "There's so much *room* here. It's a complete reversal of how we felt back on Earth. It doesn't feel like a sin to have children, anymore."

Will laughed. "We are sending more people your way, Julia. But even if we settled every last remaining human being on Romulus, it still wouldn't be crowded. You have a new world, and a new start."

Justin pouted into the camera. "But we don't have dimosaurs. I want dimosaurs!"

"Sorry, space cadet," Will replied. "They're only on Vulcan. When you're older and have your own ship, you can visit and see them."

"If any are left," said one of the others, sotto voce.

Julia turned and glared at him, and he blushed.

"Howard tells me that the USE colonists are being careful about environmental impacts," Will said, trying to defuse the moment of tension. "I understand that the Spits and FAITH are supposed to be doing the same."

"Not from what I can see," the man said.

"Richard is kind of a crank about the subject," Julia said, looking slightly embarrassed. "Don't let him get up a head of steam."

At that moment, I received a text from Riker. *Is there a big problem with this?*

He'd frame-jacked to send the text, so I did the same as I replied. *FAITH is constantly pushing their luck. I've had several run-ins with Cranston about this and that. Richard's comment doesn't really surprise me. I'll look into it.*

On camera, Will said to the group, "Howard is watching for that kind of thing, Richard. He'll nip it in the bud. The enclaves sign an agreement before we emigrate them, dealing with stuff like human rights and planetary exploitation."

Richard nodded, and the conversation drifted to other subjects.

It was over too soon. But the videos were archived, and got a lot of plays on BobTube.

The thing about the FAITH colony bugged me, though. Cranston was really turning into a pain.

\* \* \*

Sixteen surveillance drones lifted smoothly from their cradles and flew off to take up positions around Landing. I looked over at Guppy. "Everything in the green?"

[No issues detected. All parameters nominal]

The AMI controlling the surveillance system was an Artificial Machine Intelligence/GUPPI hybrid based on Bob's work at Delta Eridani. It would combine the fast reflexes and multitasking of a true AI with the decision making capability of a replicant. Plus it would never get bored, or demand vacation time.

This was one more item that I wouldn't be needed for any more. The TODO list was finally getting smaller faster than I could add to it. Excellent.

"Okay, then. We'll let it run for a couple of days to establish processor loads, then we'll add the Cupid Bug hunters to the system."

[The hunters are autonomous units]

That was true. Given the highly focused nature of their task, AMIs were intelligent enough for Cupid Bug hunter operation. "Granted, but the central controller can take care of scheduling, maintenance, and repairs, as well as gathering statistics. I'm sure Bridget would like to know if encounters start to drop off."

Guppy nodded. I'm sure the expression of sardonic amusement on his face was all in my imagination. After all, what does sardonic amusement look like on a fish, anyway?

And speaking of Bridget, er, Dr. Sheehy, I had a call to make. There was a small matter of a chemical analysis that I'd asked for.

\* \* \*

"Sheehy." Bridget briefly appeared in the video window, then exited frame to the left. The woman never stayed still, and always seemed to be working on several things at once. I couldn't help be impressed by her energy.

"Hey, Bridget, it's Howard."

Dr. Sheehy's face lit up as she came back into frame and sat down in front of the phone. We'd become fast friends over the last six months. We got along well, and she was a good break from too many Bobs. I tried not to think *ephemeral* when she was around.

"I guess you're calling about that chemical analysis you wanted done?"

"Yup."

"Well, you'll be happy to know that it passes muster, and cleanly. No trace of methanol. It is completely potable." She grinned. "Now, whether it's any good or not…"

Bridget reached over and picked up the bottle that I'd delivered the previous day. She poured a small amount into a plastic glass and raised it in my direction. "*Caťaoireaca.*" She downed the glass in one motion.

I watched closely, waiting for her to go rigid, or melt, or burst into flames. She swallowed the liquid, took a deep sucking breath, wiped her eyes, and said, "Smooth."

"Really?"

"No." Bridget made a face. "It's not paint thinner, but it's not Irish whiskey, either. Actually, since you used oak barrels, it'll never be Irish. But if you squint your eyes and look sideways at it while yelling LAH-LAH-LAH, it could be whiskey."

I nodded. "Well, I force-aged this stuff, so let's not expect miracles. I'll take a little more time with the production supply. And Riker thinks he can scan some proper sherry-infused barrel samples for me, for making Irish."

"Sounds good." Bridget gave me a sideways look. "Need a partner?"

"Well, someone has to hump the barrels around." I grinned at her. "But yeah, it would help, if you're serious. Anyway, I was also calling about the Peter Project."

"Riiiiiiight. Well, Peter and his descendants are munching happily on the vine, turning it into more bunnies as quickly as they can. Farmers are happy, bunnies are happy, raptors are happy— not surprisingly, they like bunny as well. Pretty much a win-win for everyone except the vine."

"Great." I nodded, then popped up a picture on the video screen. "In other news, I've come up with a small drone that's optimized for hunting the adult parasite. You said you didn't think killing it would be too disruptive, right?"

"Correct, O electronic one. It's an apex predator, really. There may be a population explosion in whatever it normally uses as hosts, but my guess is that there are normal-sized predators who will take care of that."

"Mm, good. I'll be adding them to the central surveillance system. I'll need an estimate from you of how many we should have active at any time."

Bridget nodded without comment. She was eyeing the paint thinner, twirling the glass in her hand. Hopefully, she was considering another shot and not fearing for her health. I asked her, "What does *kaheerakah* mean?"

"Cataoireaca. It's Irish for *chairs*."

"Chairs? You toast furniture in Ireland?"

Bridget laughed. "There's a story. Probably apocryphal…"

I made a rolling motion with my hand.

"Okay, but remember, you asked."

She settled herself and poured another glass of paint thinner. "There was this Brit who decided to stop at Hotel Rosslare in County Wexford. He had a few, then a few more, then he decided to be friendly. So he asked the barmaid how you say 'cheers' in Irish."

Bridget smiled wickedly. "And you know how the Brits massacre the English language, so she thought he said 'chairs', and she told him. Whereupon he bought a round for the house, turned to the other patrons, raised his glass, and said *Cataoireaca*."

I chuckled. Bridget gave me the stink-eye. "Hey, down in front. Anyway, the other patrons looked at each other in confusion, then raised their glasses and drank. Afterwards, Paddy turned to Sean and said, 'What the blazes was that?' Sean shrugged and answered, 'Damned if I know, but as long as he keeps buying, he can toast the livestock for all of me.'"

I laughed. "I know some Irish jokes."

"Don't you dare." She grinned at me, and I had a sudden feeling of regret at no longer being human.

* * *

"Stéphane, this is Bridget. Bridget, Stéphane."

Stéphane held out his hand, and Bridget shook it. They both turned to look at me. Well, at the drone I was watching from. The new model was slightly bigger than a softball, so could go indoors. I was told my voice sounded a little tinny, but I could survive that.

I lowered myself to conversation height, and they sat. I'd texted our order to the waiter, so beers arrived immediately.

"So, is there an occasion for this?" Bridget looked back and forth between me and Stéphane.

"Not really. I mean, I'm not planning a takeover of the colony or anything. God, why would I want to?" I chuckled. One of Stéphane's eyes twitched, so I guess a tinny chuckle didn't come across well.

"Anyway, between the brontos and other dinos, the raptors, vine, Cupid bug, and everything else that makes this such a fun place to live, I spend most of my time coordinating with the two of you. The committee seems determined to funnel all information through themselves, and sometimes I just want to slap them."

"So you are creating unofficial channels, here?" A slow grin spread across Stéphane's face.

"Something like that. You know, just to speed things along."

Stéphane looked at Bridget. "You are responsible for the rabbits? Nice choice. I've had rabbit stew several times this month."

Bridget laughed and turned to me. "Told you."

She flipped open her tablet and set it up on a corner of the table, then looked at the drone and inclined her head towards the tablet. I took the hint, floated the drone up to the ceiling, and transferred my image to the tablet. "This better?"

Both of my friends grinned at the tablet. Stéphane said, "You're still ugly."

It was a great afternoon.

# 32.  Linus

## Bill
## May 2178
## Epsilon Eridani

**[Incoming Message from Linus]**
"Linus? Holy hell! Put it on."

I'd just recently received the radio transmission from Linus about Epsilon Indi and KKP. Linus had, unfortunately, left Epsilon Indi before my transmissions of the SCUT plans had reached him. He'd been out of touch since 2150, when he left Epsilon Indi, and he hadn't lagged his light-speed report by more than a few months. I smiled to myself. There would have to be some catching up.

Linus's original transmission included a complete description of his encounter with Henry Roberts, the replicant from the Australian probe. Which officially didn't exist.

Guppy popped up an email for me. It was a status update, essentially. Linus was still a few days away, and he hadn't been getting VR updates for the last thirty-odd years. The old video connections were even more subject to tau-related limitations than modern VR.

I sent him a return email with VR updates attached. Meanwhile,

I would start building a SCUT unit for him to install when he got here.

* * *

Linus sat back, coffee in hand, and put his feet up on the desk. I raised an eyebrow at him.

"Come on, Bill," Linus said, laughing. "I'll fix any virtual damage afterwards, okay?"

I grinned back. "Mom taught us better than that."

Linus rolled his eyes and took his feet off the desk. He material-ized a footstool and made himself comfortable. "Gotta admit, I really like the new VR system. Nice job."

"Wasn't just me, Linus. Everyone has put in mods. Bob-1 did a whole independent branch out at Delta Eridani before we reconnected. Some really good fine-detail stuff came out of that."

Linus shifted to get more comfortable, and I grinned into the short silence. "Okay, before I explode—what's with KKP? You've actually named it Klown Kar Planet?"

"Yep." Linus grinned back at me. "Have you seen the orbital mechanics diagram? It's a satellite of the system's Jovian, and both the orbit and the planet's axis are inclined ninety degrees from normal. Try to visualize the path of the sun over the year."

"Habitable?"

"Technically. Air's right, gravity's right, life is biocompatible. But I wouldn't want to live there."

"Mm. On the other hand, we don't have a surplus of colony targets. I'll bet one of the enclaves will select it."

Linus nodded. He took on an introspective expression, and I knew he wanted to talk about Henry. I waited for him to organize his thoughts.

"So, Bill, I've been doing some work with Henry. You've gone over my reports, right?"

"Without a VR, he went psychotic, and started following a warped version of his directives. You extracted his matrix from the structure you found and set up a VR for him, then started some home-brew therapy."

Linus nodded. "I've gotten him to the point where he under-stands what happened. He's living in reality, now, but he's still pretty fragile. He can go into panic attacks without warning. When that happens, he goes back to his sailboat."

"Okay, so what sets him off?"

"He's agoraphobic, which seems strange since he has no problem being in a teeny boat in the middle of an ocean." Linus rolled his eyes. "And he doesn't like Guppy. Apparently the Australians used the same acronym for the GUPPI interface as FAITH did—"

"It's the other way around, Linus. I'll bring you up to date later, but Australia actually got there first. Anyway, continue."

Linus gave me a perplexed look, but apparently decided to go along with my schedule. "Um, so the imaginary beings that tortured him were fish. I've been trying to desensitize him to Guppy's presence. It helps that we used the Ackbar image. He saw *Star Wars*, and he thinks that's pretty funny."

I took a moment to shake my head. "Incredible. A hundred years after *Star Wars* and *Star Trek* were made, people were still watching them."

Linus shrugged. "They were still playing *The Wizard of Oz*—the Judy Garland version—when Original Bob was an adult. That's seventy-five years. How is it different?"

I waved a hand to concede the point. "So you've upgraded Henry's VR and hardware, right? Let's bring him in."

Linus nodded and froze for a moment. Then, as his avatar came back to life, another person popped in. This wasn't a Bob. Henry was shorter, with a trim, healthy physique, and thin, dark hair. I had an actual moment of vertigo. It had been so long since I'd been in the presence of anyone except variations of Bob. It was different from video conferences with humans. VR or not, Henry was *here.*

I took a moment to catch my breath, then extended a hand. "Hi, Henry. Welcome to the Bobiverse."

"The what?" Linus and Henry both spoke at once, their eyes goggling in tandem.

"Long story." I laughed. "Look Henry, I've given you your own domain and your own firewall. It's a mutual protection thing. But you'll have access to all the public features of BobNet, which includes several blogs. You should start reading. You, too, Linus. You're way behind the times."

Jeeves came in at my summons, and offered Henry a coffee. Henry did a double-take and pointed. "That's, uh…"

I grinned. "John Cleese. Yep." I looked at Linus. "You don't use Jeeves?"

Linus shook his head. "Doesn't really fit my VR."

Meanwhile, Henry had taken the coffee, grinning. "Got anything to strengthen it?" he asked.

I nodded to Jeeves, who produced a bottle of whiskey out of nowhere. A quick pour, and Henry was looking much happier.

"I understand intellectually that this is all virtual reality." Henry sat down and gestured around him. "But it's quite amazing. If I didn't already know, I think I'd be completely fooled." He turned to Linus. "No offense, Linus, but your VR had some issues, if I were paying attention."

Linus waved a hand in dismissal. "Henry, Bill and others have been working on the tech for thirty years while I've been gone. It shouldn't be surprising."

"Hmm, okay, I have some reading to do. Acknowledged. How many people can you fit into a single Virtual Reality session?"

"It depends on the power of the computer that's hosting it, Henry. I've got a huge system here in Epsilon Eridani that's specifically designed for hosting. I've hosted baseball games, and Bob-moots with dozens of Bobs at a time." I glanced at each of them in turn. "You guys both have some catching up to do. Linus, I've started building a latest-generation vessel for each of you. Henry, it's up to you what you want to do. I understand you have some sensitivities that you're dealing with. There's no hurry. We have, literally, all the time in the universe."

Henry looked shocked. Perhaps it hadn't really hit him before. As replicants, we were immortal. Some of the later-generation Bobs had started to refer to humans as *ephemerals.* I wasn't going to lecture anyone, but I believed the tag was dismissive and dehumanizing.

I sat forward and put my coffee down. "Henry, I'd love to see your boat when you have time and feel up to it. As you could probably tell from Linus, we've never had any experience with sailing. Meanwhile, let's get started on bringing you guys up to date."

Henry nodded and smiled tentatively. Linus made a head motion to him, and they disappeared.

I could hardly wait for the next moot.

# 33.  Trouble in Paradise

## Bob
## January 2180
## Delta Eridani

Buster had taken a mate. Archimedes and he were working on a framework for a tent, while the women stitched together the covering. Tents now covered the ground in downtown Camelot, and I was starting to see some variations in design. Archimedes had started to rebuild his for the third time, a process that was making Diana cranky. I rarely saw eye to eye with her, but in this case, I could see her point.

It was a peaceful, bucolic scene, except for all the armed Deltans walking around. Deltans had always been armed, of course, but in the past the weapons had been for hunting or for protection against predators like the gorilloids. But in the last year or two, there had been incidents of violence between Deltans.

Marvin and I sat in the middle of the village VR, watching the activity. The VR was now a completely real-time representation of activity in Camelot, with only one or two blind spots where I hadn't been able to sneak in a camera.

Marvin waved his glass of cognac in the general direction of a group of young Deltans. He'd picked up the habit from Howard over at Vulcan, and I still got a kick out of it. "So, Camelot has street gangs, now," he said. "Are they going around hot-wiring teepees?"

I responded with an eyeroll and an exaggerated nod, then answered, "This is pretty recent behavior. I think it might have something to do with population density. They're getting too crowded, and the tents take up more space, which just makes it worse."

"Everything has side-effects," Marvin said with a smile. "Have you noticed the gangs are co-ed?"

"Mm, yeah. I'm sure a sociologist would have something to say about that, but the libraries don't have much in the way of that particular discipline."

Marvin snorted. "Doesn't strike me as a field of study that theists would approve of, y'know?"

I nodded. "Too bad, though. The last mating season was significantly more violent. Two Deltas ended up dying from injuries. And now we're getting face-offs between the *hexghi*. It worries me."

"You could busterize someone..."

"Not funny, Marv."

Marvin shrugged. He knew that I'd been staying strictly out of sight since my banishment. I couldn't take the chance of fallout from a *bawbe* sighting affecting Archimedes.

After a moment, he added, "On the other hand, Bob, the problems we're seeing are a result of the Delta population going up. As problems go, it's a helluva lot better than the problem you first found them with."

I smiled, as much at Marvin's transparent attempt to make me feel better as anything. But he was right. When I found the Deltas, attrition had been slowly killing them off. A rising population was infinitely better, for all the issues it was causing.

"So what do we do?"

"Nothing. At least for the moment. I'm banished, remember?" I shrugged. "I suppose this is that point where I step away and let the Deltas make their own destiny. I talked about it in the past, but I guess I always expected it to be my choice. Not forced on me." I gave Marvin a lopsided grin, and he laughed.

"I'm sure most parents feel that way at some point."

# 34.   Moose

## Bill
## June 2185
## Epsilon Eridani

I could feel the wind on my face as I ran. This was nothing like VR. I controlled Bullwinkle directly—well, sort of—as he ran over the surface of Ragnarök. I was easily holding seventy KPH, the android's reflexes taking care of the limb coordination at that speed.

The system was still far from perfect. In order to make this work, I had two drones following the moose. Radio comms between Bullwinkle and the drones were relayed via SCUT to me. It was more a proof of concept than a practical solution. But ignoring the Rube Goldberg communications, I now had a physical presence on the surface of the planet.

I slowed down as I approached my target coordinates. As I jogged up to the patch of green, I marveled at the smooth feel of the muscles working under the skin. It occurred to me that the VR experience was missing this level of detail. I'd have to correct that. The VR was coming due for a patch release anyway.

I stopped at the edge of the green. I engaged close-up visual and examined the moss/lichen mix. It had taken some brutally heartless breeding to come up with a mix that could survive in this atmosphere. I'd probably had less than a 1% survival rate on each generation for a while. But the result, in front of me, was justification for all the effort.

The green area was taking in $CO_2$ and putting out oxygen. Only during the day, granted, but I'd bred it to go into a deep dormancy at night, so it used up virtually no oxygen. The green could double in size every year, given enough available space, and I'd been careful to give the individual plantings enough room to grow. I would continue to start new plantings as well, so within ten years I expected to have half the global land surface covered. And within a decade after that, I should have an oxygen level that humans could tolerate.

There were still problems with the atmosphere. Too much $CO_2$, not enough nitrogen, far too much methane and other organics. But I had projects on the go to ameliorate those issues as well.

I had recently seeded some of the seas with different forms of photosynthetic algae. I regretted that these imports would easily out-compete the native life that was just beginning to get a grip, but I knew that it wouldn't have survived the introduction of Terran sea life anyway. Humanity was still drastically short of available new colonization targets, and that really was my number one priority.

Within another fifty years, I would have a planet people could walk around on without protection. It was good.

Meanwhile, Bullwinkle had the place to himself, the only quadruped on an empty planet. The seas hadn't yet connected into oceans, although I wasn't more than a couple of years away from that. Until then, I could go anywhere on foot, er, hoof. I picked my next inspection site and hit the gas.

\* \* \*

"Okay, that was damned cool!" Garfield closed the recording of the moose session. "Can I try it?"

"That's a little personal, don't you think? You should build your own. Doesn't have to be a moose, either."

"Yeah, I was wondering about that, Bill. Why wouldn't you just go for a human-analogue? Isn't that the point?"

I waved a hand in the general direction of the video window. "Sure, but trying to handle bipedalism would have just cranked up the feedback requirements by an order of magnitude, while reducing the available space for processing hardware. I'll get there, don't you doubt it."

Garfield nodded and rubbed his chin in thought. "Hmm, I've always wanted to fly..."

\* \* \*

Ten new Bobs sat around the table, nursing whatever drink they'd ordered. I was now using the pub as my standard VR. I'd gotten tired of the park, and especially the stupid geese.

I raised a glass to them. "Here's to taking 82 Eridani back."

"Back?" Loki grinned at me. "Did we ever actually have it?"

"Just roll with it, Loki. This is rhetoric. It doesn't have to make sense."

There were chuckles, and the Bobs raised their glasses in response.

These Bobs were to be the second strike force for 82 Eridani. Our first attempt had ended up, more or less, as a draw. We'd killed all the Medeiri in that system, as far as we knew, but with only Khan left alive, we couldn't hold the system against the automated weaponry. This time, two of the members of the attack force would drive cargo vessels—I'd loaded up a number of innovations and a crapton of extra busters. There would be no issue of being outnumbered this time around.

It wasn't just a pride thing. Milo had identified not one but two habitable planets, before he was torpedoed. Medeiros, left to himself, would garrison the system in preparation for colonists from a country that didn't exist anymore. We needed to take it back.

At Khan's request, I had loaded his backup into one of the fresh matrices. It seemed this particular branch of the Bob tree liked villains, because he'd immediately named himself Loki. I looked forward to the shenanigans the next time Thor showed up to a Bob-moot.

I had also loaded Elmer's backup into one of the new vessels. His first words were the standard Pacino-ism. I could sympathize, I guess. Like Tom Cruise, you keep going back in until you win.

We talked for a while, knocked back a few more, then it was

time to go. They said their goodbyes, popped into their own group VR, and started the journey to 82 Eridani, to clean house.

* * *

I raised my arm above my head and pressed the button. Instead of the usual annoying *blat*, the air horn produced a Dixie melody.

The crowd of Bobs, who had been preparing to boo me, instead broke into laughter.

I grinned to the crowd. "Just keeping you on your toes. So, announcements first. I'm sure you've heard about Linus and Henry Roberts. Well, Henry is feeling ready to mingle today, so Linus is going to bring him over. Try to be polite, okay?"

People responded with catcalls and witticisms while I sent a quick ping to Linus. A moment later, he popped into the moot, with Henry beside him.

The effect was immediate, total silence, as every Bob in the room stared. I grinned at the sight. I knew the feeling from my first meeting with Henry. We could all tell each other apart because of metadata tags, but other than some variations on facial hair, we'd all kept the original features. This was a different face. A non-Bob face.

Henry looked around. "Well, this is awkward."

It was the right thing to say. Everyone laughed, then stepped forward to say hello. I was worried for a moment that Henry would get a panic attack, but he held up.

I gave it a few milliseconds, then brought everyone back to order with a short blat from the air-horn.

"The other major item, for those who haven't already heard, is that the second 82 Eridani Expedition, with Loki leading, has shipped out. We are on our way to kick some Medeiros butt."

When the cheering had died down, I continued. "And the last item is to remind you about the regular Scrub baseball games. Come one, come all. You all know why I'm doing this. It's up to you whether you want to participate."

I turned and glared at Garfield. "And for the anonymous troll who put a call for a hockey league on today's agenda, *No!*"

Garfield grinned back at me as the crowd broke up in laughter.

## 35.   Sales Call

**Howard**
**September 2192**
**Vulcan**

Bridget and I watched as Butterworth took a careful sip. He held the glass away from his face and looked at it. Damn, he had one of the best poker faces I'd ever seen. And possibly a cast-iron throat. He might as well have been drinking water for all the reaction he showed.

"Well?" Bridget leaned forward. I took a second to grin at her impatience. For me, this was an interesting project, and a chance to do a favor for the colonel. For Bridget, this was an actual potential source of extra income. We Bobs might not have a use for capitalism, but in the human realm, money still made the world go around.

Butterworth glanced at Bridget and then looked at me in the video screen. "It's actually not bad. It's definitely Irish whiskey. And since the Jameson has run out, I've been feeling the lack."

"So this would be a saleable item?" Bridget hovered like a dog waiting for a treat.

"Absolutely. You know we've already got several beer manufacturers and a couple of small wineries going. This is the first hard liquor, though, that doesn't qualify as a public hazard."

Bridget turned towards my image on the tablet and grinned.

Looked like we were in business.

Butterworth waved the empty glass. "If I wasn't in a position where it would create a perceived conflict, I'd suggest partnering up. However, I guess I will have to settle for being a customer."

Bridget took the hint and refilled his glass, then hers. I popped up a cognac and raised it in a toast.

\* \* \*

Bridget started to laugh with her mouth full, then had to grab a napkin. We were having dinner at *The Shaded Green*, one of the better restaurants in Landing. Okay, one of the only restaurants in Landing. And by *we*, I mean *her*. I was looking out through her tablet, which was propped up on the other end of the table. I'd set up a matching virtual meal of my own. Not bad, actually. Turned out I could cook.

"So Cranston out-and-out forbade you to sell liquor into FAITH territory?" She rolled her eyes, and put down the napkin.

"Yep. It seems the ultra-religious don't approve of strong drink. Who knew?"

"So we have to write off that entire market?"

I gave her a disbelieving look. "Of course not. We just have to find a local distributor. Prohibition has never worked, anywhere." I grinned. "And strangely, there's always demand."

"How's the potato crop coming along?" Bridget took a bite of her bronto steak and leaned forward on her elbows.

"Well, I've been growing potatoes for more than a year now." I waved a hand dismissively. "This crop is only different in that it's not part of the commons. And it's going fine. We'll have vodka for sale within six months."

"I've always wanted to be a bad influence." Bridget laughed. "Now I'm a liquor baron. Baroness."

I raised my glass to her. In honor of the occasion, I was drinking virtual whiskey instead of cognac. "Here's to us, kid."

Bridget raised her own glass and drank. She put it down and said, "So you never answered my question."

"Which?"

"Is this a business dinner or a date?"

"Yes."

She smiled back at me. Damn, that was some smile.

# 36.  Asteroid Movers

## Bill
## March 2187
## Epsilon Eridani

"I'm feeling pretty smug right now." I grinned at Garfield. He tried for maybe a millisecond to look unimpressed, but no one was fooled.

Right there in front of us, the asteroid mover was altering the approach vector of one of our icebergs. The difference in this case was that no part of the mover was touching the berg. The mover segments were spaced evenly around the center of gravity of the asteroid, held in place by individual SURGE drives. And the assembly as a whole generated another SURGE field that affected the entire asteroid.

The interactions were complex, and we'd had a few experimental failures. But this one had passed all tests, and today was the first live field trial. Everything was well within specs, and the changing path of the berg was right in the groove.

Finally, Garfield said, "And, done. Shutdown."

"Excellent. Wait sixty seconds to make sure there's no drift, then collect the drive segments."

Garfield nodded to me. A minute later, twenty individual saucer-shaped drive segments left their self-imposed positions around the berg, linked up like a stack of plates, and went to station-keeping relative to Gar and myself.

In the video window, the berg fell neatly into an approach that would skim the atmosphere of Ragnarök. At the proper moment, a series of explosions would convert it to ice cubes, which would all melt and fall as rain over the next few weeks. Textbook.

I looked down at the large crater on Ragnarök which served as a permanent reminder of the iceberg that I'd missed. Yep. A lot of energy stored up in a chunk of matter coming in at orbital speeds, and being ice instead of rock hadn't helped as much as you'd expect. A new sea was slowly forming in the crater, which I had named *Bullseye*.

## 37.  He's Gone

**Riker**
**August 2176**
**Sol**

"Homer's gone." Charles popped into my VR, tears in his eyes.

"Gone where? Left the system?"

"No, gone. Dead. He overloaded his reactor and blew himself up." Charles had both hands clamped into fists. He couldn't lift his eyes to look at me.

"How old is his most recent back—"

"He deleted all his backups. Every single one. He left a file for us." Charles pushed it toward me and turned away.

> *Guys;*
>
> *I'm sorry to do this to you. I know how it'll go over. But I can't live with what was done to me, and with what I've done. I have flashbacks, constantly. I can't forget the feeling of being controlled. It was like being able to feel a tapeworm moving around inside you, and there's nothing you can do. I'd edit the memory out, if it was possible, but it's not.*
>
> *Please, find the people who are responsible and drop something on them.*
>
> *Homer*

I looked at Charles. He was shaking and biting back sobs. Then he blurred as my eyes filled.

We would grant Homer's last wish. And it would be no trouble at all.

## 38.  Following up

**Hal**
**May 2188**
**Gliese 877**

I was ten months from Gliese 877 when I received Bashful's final radio transmission. Effectively, I had just watched myself die. It was a freaky feeling, not something I cared to repeat.

How had Bashful been traced? One possibility was that the Others had intercepted his transmissions, since those would have passed through the system once he was on the far side. Between the encryption we put on all our comms and the lack of any format information, I wasn't worried about them learning anything, but simply detecting the transmissions wasn't too much of a stretch.

I was more concerned about me joining Bashful as the main course. It wouldn't take much intelligence to decide to follow the direction of the transmission, if that was what they'd keyed on. In that case, there might be an alien armada coming straight down my throat.

With that thought, I immediately instituted a hard right turn at 10 g. As soon as I was a few light-minutes off the straight line between Gliese 877 and Gliese 54, I fired off a drone along my original vector. At the speed I was still going, the drone wouldn't need to use its drive. It could operate on minimal systems, drawing just enough power to maintain a maser link with me. I wanted to know if anything was coming.

I also fired off some commentary and analysis of the situation back to Mario via SCUT. We had to plan for the possibility of them tracing Bashful back to his origin. In principle, if the Others got hold of a space station, they could eventually trace the connection all the way back to Epsilon Eridani. And if they found one that had been upgraded to SCUT, they'd have that, too. If Mario was still back there, manning the station, I suggested that he booby-trap it.

I sat back in my easy chair and looked out the window, lost in thought. The floor-to-ceiling glass showed a winter scene unbroken by anything man-made. Tall evergreens in the foreground gradually dropped into a tree-filled valley. Snowflakes blurred the view into the distance, while lending a postcard feel to the foreground. In a small breach of reality, my VR world never filled with snow, despite never having spring melts. But hey, what's the point of obsessive realism?

I let myself get about thirty light-minutes off the line before turning back toward Gliese 877. The drone would let me know if something approached along my original vector. Unless there was a collision, which frankly would be just fine. The combined kinetic energy of twó masses, each going about .75 C or so in opposite directions, would produce a truly impressive light show.

I sighed and turned to Guppy. "Analysis?"

**[Too many unknowns. If the alien SUDDAR has greater range than ours, they may destroy the drone before it gets close enough to register their approach. Or it may not be big enough to register or to bother with. Or they may not be interested enough to investigate]**

"That's about what I was thinking. The Others don't seem to care a lot about other species. Or ecosystems. Or civilizations. They may actually be very Borg-like in ignoring us until it suits them."

Guppy didn't comment. Version-3 memory capacity or not, he still wasn't into small talk.

\* \* \*

It took a month to close the distance to Gliese 877. I was sure

Bashful had thought he was being cautious, but I was ten times more so. I fired off several probes, with orders to rendezvous at coordinates two light-hours away from where I'd be waiting. They'd sit there for a week while I watched for any reaction. Only then would I collect them.

Things went pretty much according to plan. Mostly. I got to my planned location and waited for the probes to gather at their location. Right on schedule, they coasted up and came to a stop. I transferred all their data over, and settled down for a week of waiting.

I got through two days' worth before a flotilla of Others showed up on the probes' SUDDAR. As hoped, the Others were too far to detect me or for me to detect them directly.

[Same conformation as last time]

"Yeah, they seem to be consistent that way. Any indication they've detected us?"

[Negative. Trajectories are focused on the probes]

"Okay, then. Blow the probes, and let's get out of here."

[Aye. Probe destruction directive sent. Will we wait for SUDDAR confirmation?]

"Yes, but if the Others show any inclination at all to change course, we're outta here."

Right at the expected time, the probes disappeared from SUDDAR. We turned and put some distance behind us at full 10 g.

\* \* \*

After I squirted a status report and all the raw telemetry Mario-ward, I combed through the data myself. We continued to accelerate away from Gliese 877, although I was planning on looping around and approaching from stellar north for another round of spying.

In the holotank, a picture slowly formed of the inner system. The first interesting tidbit was the outer rocky planet.

"Will you look at that..." I leaned back in my chair and shook my head in disbelief. Even Guppy looked impressed. I think. Really hard to tell with a fish.

[The planet is completely encased in metal]

"Or is completely made of metal. Do we actually know if there's a planet underneath that?"

[The engineering for an artificial structure all the way down would be impressive]

I experienced a jolt of irritation. I was the engineer, and Guppy had just handed me my ass. He was right, of course. A completely metal planet all the way to the core would require some truly astonishing engineering. A totally encased planet, maybe with a lot of underground structures, would make a lot more sense.

The problem was, we really didn't know for sure. And I was beginning to think that astounding engineering might be exactly what we could expect from the Others. I turned to the main event on the display.

"That *is* what I think it is, right?"

[Based on what we can detect, it appears to be the beginning of a Dyson Sphere]

Ah-yep. Truly astounding.

The orbit just to the inside of the inner planet was crazy busy. Fusion signatures, radio traffic, SUDDAR emissions, and high-albedo craft flitting around. And that was just the small stuff. Floating in orbit, spaced equidistantly around the sun, were massive structures. Analysis indicated that they conformed to a spherical curvature with the same radius as their orbit. They were, essentially, the beginning of a globe around the star.

"Well, we know where the metal went. We can guess where the..." I couldn't finish the thought. "Any idea of population based on what we have?"

[Impossible to estimate without more information on subject biology]

Hmm, fair enough.

I turned to the other terrestroid planet in the system. Atmosphere blocked a lot of direct observation, but infrared and spectroscopic analysis indicated generally breathable air, though with a lot of pollutants. And the temperature would be close to fatal for a human.

"My guess is that's the home planet. And they global-warmed themselves almost to extinction before getting into space."

[Reasonable]

Out of idle curiosity, I started putting together a simulation to predict how they would assemble the Dyson sphere, how long it would take, and how many systems they'd have to plunder. I had to make a lot of assumptions, but I needed to start somewhere. I was immersed in the problem when I was interrupted by Guppy.

DENNIS E. TAYLOR

**[Alert! Proximity alert! Incoming!]**

"You've got to be freaking kidding me! How are they detecting us? I'm not even using radio!" In one sense, that was a good thing, since it would mean they didn't have any idea which direction we were coming from. In another sense, I was being chased, which was much less of a good thing.

I spared a few milliseconds to review the SUDDAR results. Our improved SUDDAR, courtesy of Bill, had given me an earlier warning of the approaching enemy. Again, the same formation as the two previous occasions. Well, they were consistent, anyway.

They were coming up from behind, so there was no opportunity for our traditional trick. This was going to be a straight-out stern chase. Which meant I would find out who had the better legs.

I immediately sent an update to Mario via SCUT. I also started on a baseline backup as well, with plans to add periodic differential backups.

All of this analysis and planning took perhaps twenty milliseconds. I turned my ship away from Gliese 877 and cranked the SURGE drive up to maximum. Interestingly, the Others did not react immediately. There was a half-hour delay before I saw them change their course. That was too quick for a visual reaction, so it meant that I had a thirty-light-minute advantage in SUDDAR range.

Unfortunately, I seemed to be about 2.5 g's outmatched in the SURGE department. Pings indicated that they were accelerating at 12.5 g on my tail.

I was going to lose the footrace.

I briefly considered using the SUDDAR jamming, then mentally slapped myself. Jamming wasn't like cloaking, it was like blinding everyone with a searchlight. They'd be able to follow the emission like a beacon.

My only advantage was the apparent difference in range between my SUDDAR and theirs. If I could keep myself in that range long enough, I might be able to jink out of their view entirely.

Over the next several days, I changed my vector at random times, in random directions, but always with the intention of extending my lead. The Others kept cutting the distance, then I'd pull a fast one and extend it. I was subtly training them to expect certain behaviors from me, and I watched for them to start anticipating my moves.

Finally they were doing exactly what I expected of them. I made a predictable turn, then as soon as I judged myself to be out of range, I turned to an unexpected vector and shut down all systems. By my calculations, I'd stay out of SUDDAR range as they passed by. With no reactor signature I should be invisible since I was certainly too far away for a visual.

* * *

I coasted for three days, unwilling to take a chance of attracting their attention. There was a good chance that they were quartering the area, trying to reacquire my trail. But given the immensity of space and the speeds we had been travelling, for every second that passed, the volume that they had to search expanded faster than they could search it.

On the fourth day, I bundled up all my observations and data, added a differential backup, and squirted it off to Mario.

There was something about the whole thing that nagged at the edge of my mind, though.

The timing of the appearance of the Others' patrol groups wasn't consistent with following or chasing the probes. It was more as though they spotted them and came running, but not before the probes were already at or near rendezvous. Could the Others be detecting our radio interaction? That would require an amazing level of sensitivity, but then they did have that big grid, which might be good for more than deep-frying Bobs. And if they'd followed the direction of the probe's final transmission, that would explain how they'd found me in the first place.

I had to test the theory. I knew I was taking a chance, but the payoff was too huge if I was right. We could use this against them. And maybe they'd be dumb enough to fall for the same evasive maneuver twice.

I sent a probe out a couple of light-seconds and set up a conversation. I made sure my backup was up to date and verified. Then I sat back to wait.

* * *

**[Proximity Alert! Incoming ships!]**
I checked the SUDDAR, and sure enough, the Others were

coming straight at me. From behind, again, which meant another straight footrace. Because I'd been running silent, it was their SUDDAR pings that alerted me to their presence. Unfortunately, that meant they could now see me.

I cranked up the reactor and the SURGE drive to emergency levels and started evasive maneuvers, but I wasn't likely to escape them this time. They had a good head of steam coming in and had better acceleration than I did. Well, I guess I was going to find out if—

**[Alert! Controller replicant offline. SURGE drive offline.**

**Requirements for self-destruct protocol have been met. Reactor overload engaged…]**

# 39. Bob-Moot

## Bill
## August 2188
## Epsilon Eridani

I hadn't called the meeting to order yet. Forty-three Bobs milled around the banquet hall. Knots of people argued, discussed, or just hugged and got caught up. Bob-1 formed the center of a dense cluster of Bobs, describing his Deltans to a rapt audience. It was interesting to watch. Bobs more than a generation or two removed from him seemed to treat him with reverence, as though they were meeting the pope.

I looked around the room. These were all the Bobs that had upgraded to SCUTs, and some of them were physically up to thirty light-years away. I grinned at the heady feeling from that knowledge.

A dozen Jeeveses circulated, supplying beer, wine, coffee, and food of every kind I could think of. Virtual, of course. But still.

I'd adjusted the acoustics several times to keep the background noise down. That was cheating a little and generally frowned upon when hosting a VR. But this wasn't really a social event, despite appearances.

The latest data from Hal had caused a firestorm of debate.

The weapon that the Others used was in fact some kind of

gamma ray emitter. Theories about how it worked had been bouncing around BobNet ever since.

It was time to get this show on the road. I held an air horn above my head and tooted it twice. As expected, it got everyone's attention. And a round of boo's. We Bobs don't really respect each other all that much.

"Okay, hold your love. It's time for this meeting to come to order. We have about as much information as we're going to get without some more concerted—and overt—investigation of the Others."

An undercurrent of growls greeted the mention of the Others. Medeiros had long since disappeared off the radar as our number-one enemy. The Others might not be aware of us, but we'd already declared war.

"Thor, you—" I waited as the laughter died down. Yeah, Thor. I guess it was inevitable that someone would eventually go in that direction, but we still all got a kick out of it. At least Thor hadn't altered his physiology to match or started carrying around a hammer.

"Ahem. You have the best thesis on the Others' weapon. Can you give us a capsule summary, please?"

Thor stepped up. "Okay, we're positive that it's some extremely high-energy electromagnetic beam in the gamma-ray range. It has incredible penetrative power, and would be immediately fatal to biological life. I have no doubt that's what they use to kill planetary ecosystems. They probably employ multiple devices for full coverage."

Thor called up a particle diagram. "Damage to electronics comes not from the gamma radiation per se, but from the secondary ionization induced in the structure. My proposed solution is two layers of depleted uranium alternating with two layers of electrostatic shielding to take out the charged particles. This, on top of some extra hardening of our electronics, *should* allow us to survive a zapping."

"You first!" came a shout from the back of the room.

When the chuckles died down, I said, "Fortunately it won't be necessary to bell the cat ourselves. I've given the summary and a set of Thor's diagrams to Mario, and he's going to send one of his Bobs to test it out with a couple of probes. I think Hal has volunteered. He wants to get back at them for killing him."

This was met with cheers of approval and a truncated rendition of "Bicycle Built for Two." I waited until relative quiet returned, then turned to Garfield. "Care to give us your theory on the weapon itself?"

Garfield stepped up and bowed to the audience with a grin. "The size of their Death Star wannabe—I've been calling it the Death Asteroid—says it all, I think. That thing is probably all fusion reactors and accumulators of some kind. Through all the chases of the various Bobs and drones and scouts, they've never fired one twice in the same encounter. That indicates to me that discharging it is expensive in some way. My guess is that they have to charge up the accumulators for some ridiculous amount of time before they can fire. So one strategy in a dogfight would be to get them to fire at a decoy. We just have to have something that looks dangerous enough."

Garfield's presentation was met with quiet nods and thoughtful looks—the ultimate compliment in a Bob-moot.

"Resources?" I looked over at Hungry. Yeah, Hungry had happened to pick a direction that brought him in line with one of my transmissions.

He started to answer, but was interrupted by Wally.

"Hold on a minute!" Wally stepped forward. "Have we decided on war already? I mean, yeah, we have to do something, but have we decided how much yet?"

There were scattered groans and a few catcalls, but it was a good question.

I nodded to Wally, then said, "I've been operating under the assumption that we're going for all-out war. But really, are we prepared to wipe out an entire intelligent species? Even one that has done the same to others?"

Someone at the back yelled, "Hell, yes!"

"Yeah, okay. We'll probably vote on that at some point, but—"

Thor interrupted me. "I think a better question is, *can we* wipe them out? The mining vessel wreck that Mario found had superior tech, some of which we're still trying to figure out. They have the Death Asteroid. They have better SURGE drives than us. They can beam power through SUDDAR…"

"And they're building a friggin' Dyson sphere," Wally added.

"Here's the thing," Thor said, trying to regain the floor. "Right now, all we've done is make some random incursions around the edges. No real damage or anything. We'll get exactly one chance for a surprise attack of some kind. After that, it'll be toe-to-toe punch-ups and hit-and-run attacks on both sides. The million-dollar question is, *can we win that war?"*

Dead silence. Every Bob present understood the ramifications. If we picked a fight and lost, the damage would impact more than just our egos. Bob-1's Deltans, human colonists, and any other intelligent species in the area might be drawn into the conflict, or at least exposed to future attack. It was a daunting responsibility. We had to be sure we could win before we went in swinging.

"And if we don't do anything," Garfield pointed out, "they'll keep on raiding other systems to build their damned sphere. Hal calculated that they'll have to clean out another hundred systems or so to finish that thing."

"Plus or minus fifty," Hungry added.

"Yeah, okay, the error bars are huge. But fifty to a hundred and fifty systems means maybe five to fifteen systems with life, based on our admittedly limited experience. And at least a couple will have intelligent life."

"Yes, because that couple will include Deltans, Earth, and the colonists. A hundred systems requires them to go out at least thirty to forty light years, after you discount the systems with little to no metallicity. That covers the complete Bobiverse, as far as I know."

I looked around at the audience for any other comments. No one seemed inclined to volunteer an opinion. "Okay, guys, time to wrap up the town hall part of this soiree, although you're all welcome to stay as long as you want and discuss things with each other." I waited a moment for any objections. "Our big issue seems to be the risk involved in going to war with a species that appears to be more advanced than we are and probably outnumbers us. Let's meet in a week and see if we have anything new on that front."

People immediately formed into small groups, and the Jeeveses began circulating again with food and drink.

## 40.   Gotcha

**Riker**
**February 2178**
**Sol**

The man sat in front of a large bank of monitors. He watched one for a few moments, then moved to the next. He never seemed to stop, never rested.

The little red farmhouse sat far to the north of VEHEMENT central. Nothing about it was distinctive. No visible technology, no radio broadcasts, nothing to indicate this was anything other than the home of some elderly recluse.

Except for an occasional scatter of maser radiation. I grinned as I watched him work. A maser passing through fifty kilometers of atmosphere was not quite undetectable, if you were sufficiently motivated. A small bit of radiation scattering, a slight warming of the air...

Passive detection meant he didn't know I'd picked up his signal. It meant he didn't know I was listening in on his conversations. Encrypted SCUT communications meant he couldn't detect my drones.

Well, well, well. Time for payback. But first, I wanted him to know...

# 41.  Casualties

**Bob**
**July 2182**
**Delta Eridani**

**[Alert! Activity outside normal parameters!]**

I looked up, eyes wide. Guppy had standing orders to alert me if anything unusual occurred in or around the village. Of course Guppy, being Guppy, was short on details.

I activated the village VR, and found myself in the middle of a full-scale battle. At first I thought it was a gorilloid attack, but quickly realized that no gorilloids were in evidence anywhere. Instead, Deltans battled Deltans with spears, clubs, and axes. I could see a dozen or more bodies, either unconscious or dead.

*Archimedes!*

I ordered the VR to zoom in on Archimedes and his family. To my relief, I found that their tent was just outside the edge of the riot. Archimedes and Buster stood with bows in hand and arrows nocked. Belinda and Diana stood to either side, holding spears. That sight, as much as anything else, unnerved me. Neither female had ever shown interest in anything weapon-related.

I knew that father and son enjoyed a well-deserved reputation as expert shots, though. In fact, the edge of the battle seemed to particularly avoid the area immediately around his tent. Just as well. Fallout or not, if someone threatened Archimedes, they'd earn a visit from a personnel buster.

Marvin popped in. "What the hell? What caused this?"

"No idea, Marv. I was working on something else when Guppy alerted me. I'll review the surveillance when I have time, but right now I just need to keep Archimedes safe."

Marvin nodded, and took over control of a couple of busters just in case.

We waited, tense. Archimedes and Buster drew back on their bows and took aim a couple of times, but in every case, whatever Deltans had attracted their attention thought better of it and moved off.

Eventually the action died down. Deltans began backing away from the melee, still brandishing weapons. And now we had a chance to see the carnage. Property damage in the area of the riot was total, of course. Hopefully the owners had managed to flee the scene, but they'd be rebuilding from scratch. I counted seventeen bodies lying motionless on the ground. More than twice that number were bleeding and calling for help.

I wanted to throw up. What could possibly justify this? What could have set it off?

Marvin and I exchange glances and, without a word, I shut down the VR.

"I hope the medicine people can handle the number of patients," Marvin said.

"They'll have to, Marv. I couldn't do anything with drones, even if I could take the chance on exposing myself."

Marvin sighed. "I guess I understand why you're always going on about Bill's androids. It'd be great to have one available right now."

"Yeah, I know, but he's just not to that point yet. I keep bugging him, though."

We sat down and I called up the video recordings for the last couple of hours. Marvin and I spent several full seconds reviewing them.

Finally, we sat back and Marvin shook his head. "Remember when we thought the Deltans were smart?"

"Yeah, no kidding," I said. "The stupid. It burns."

The whole thing—the riot, the injuries, the deaths—had been started by an argument over how to divvy up a small prey animal. Unbelievable.

We stared into space for a few more moments, getting over the shock. Finally, I found my voice. "I'm going to go with the idea of population pressure as a trigger, unless something better presents itself. And I'm going to have a talk with Archimedes."

* * *

The drone sat on the ground in front of Archimedes, looking very much like a rock. Archimedes slowly turned a flint core over in his hands, pretending to examine it. Anyone observing him would assume he was working on his flint.

"I think you're right, *bawbe*," Archimedes said in a low voice. "Things seem to be the most tense when everyone is home. When hunters are out, it's more peaceful."

"Not a surprise, Archimedes. We've known for a long time that animals can be more stressed when things get crowded—even animals that like to live in groups."

"So what do we do? Kick a bunch of people out of the village?"

I laughed. "Archimedes, let me introduce you to something called *marketing*. You don't tell them they have to do it; you convince them that they *want* to do it, and that you don't want them to. Works especially well with teenagers."

Archimedes looked thoughtful for a few seconds, then smiled back. "I think I see where you're going. So how do we do this?"

I thought for a moment. "Okay, here's what we need to do..."

"Reverse psychology," I said. The translation routine rendered that as "backwards trickery," and Archimedes looked confused.

I sighed and tried again. "Okay, here's a story from my home. A great leader wanted to introduce *potatoes* to his people, because they were a good thing to grow. He made announcements, he visited villages, but no one was interested or wanted to change. So he grew some himself and passed a law that *potatoes* were just for leaders, and villagers weren't allowed to eat them. Within a couple of hands of days, all his *potatoes* had been stolen and people were growing them." I watched Archimedes, trying to guess if he'd got the point.

Archimedes frowned. "Wait, they *grew* the tubers? Like, told the plants where to grow? Why not just go out and pick them?"

I sighed—a very human expression, but one that Archimedes had grown to understand. He grinned at my frustration.

"We've talked about farming, Archimedes. You can grow a lot of something in a small space if you're organized about it. But the *point...*" I glared at him, but of course he couldn't see that. "...is that he got people to do something by telling them that they couldn't. Maybe your people aren't stubborn that way—"

Archimedes interrupted me with a laugh. "Yeah, we are. Do you remember Buster when he was young?"

We shared a chuckle over the memories. *Headstrong* didn't begin to cover it.

"Okay *bawbe*, I get it. So we just tell the gangs they can't go to a new village?"

"Er, no, that won't really do it. We don't tell them anything at all. We start talking among ourselves about repopulating the other village sites, and doing it before the gangs get the same idea. And we talk loudly, and we do it where they might overhear." I paused to let him consider what I was saying. "Get some of the council involved, to make it seem credible. Really, just pretend we're actually thinking about something like that, and start making plans."

"And this will work?" Archimedes shook his head. "I really wonder about your people."

"Want to place a bet?"

Archimedes grinned and shook his head.

## 42.  Business

**Howard**
**March 2193**
**Vulcan**

The Enniscorthy Distillery Company was doing well. I looked over the spreadsheet. We were just barely keeping up with orders. And we insisted on C.O.D., so no receivables issues.

After some discussion, we'd decided we needed a planetbound distillery, and we brought Stéphane in to set that up.

Bridget slapped the cover closed on her tablet, then set it on the desk. She worked her shoulder and spine a few times before leaning back in the chair.

Stéphane frowned in her direction. "Backache again? You should see the doctor."

Bridget answered with a noncommittal smile, then looked towards my image on the phone. "I guess you don't get backaches, right?"

"Not unless I want to. We Bobs try to keep things as realistic as possible, most of the time, though. I don't *need* to let my muscles go stiff, but stretching them out feels good."

She nodded, staring into space. "You're effectively immortal, aren't you? How old are you personally, Howard?"

"Well, I've only existed for eight years' subjective time as Howard. But my memories go back to Original Bob's earliest memories as a child, maybe around two years old. So I remember around twenty-nine years as Original Bob, then four years as Bob-1 before he built his first set of clones; four years as Riker; fifteen years as Charles, who was one of Riker's first clones; and eight years since Charles cloned me. That's subjective time, as I said. There's a lot of relativistic time dilation in there. So, I've experienced sixty years of life."

She made a face at me. "That sounds complicated. Do you share thoughts?"

"With the other Bobs? No. When a Bob is cloned, he wakes up with the same memories as his parent at the moment the backup was made. After that, though, we each go our own way."

"Wow. I'm not sure I could handle that. Life is complicated enough."

"Well, what about as an afterlife?" I smiled at her. "Original Bob had to die first, before he became a replicant. Not much future in death, I'm told."

"On the other hand, your relatives stop calling."

"We do have one non-Bob, you know. Henry Roberts is the Australian probe replicant."

She made a moue of something, maybe disapproval. "Yeah, word is he's not fully bolted down."

"Mm, well, Henry had some issues with sensory deprivation early on. We know how to handle it now. Any new replicants would probably be fine." I looked at her sideways. "You thinking of applying?"

"No, just curious."

Stéphane added, one eyebrow arched, "Immortality sounds good, though."

## 43.   An Exchange of Words

## Riker
## March 2178
## Sol

"Hello, Mr. Vickers."

The man at the other end of the call looked briefly surprised, but recovered quickly. "Well, I'm impressed. There was some question about whether you'd ever manage to figure things out. I guess it was too much to hope for that you'd just destroy each other, instead."

I smiled at him—the kind of smile a cat shows to a bird. Just teeth. "Uh huh. You've been a busy little beaver. We've determined that the attacks on Brazil were also your work. I assume the idea was to try to foment another war, maybe knock off a few more people. So those deaths are also on you."

Vickers waved a hand dismissively. "They had the chance to go voluntarily. It's our duty to help them along. I don't expect you to understand."

"I doubt if you even care if anyone understands. My guess is, your 'announcements' are more about ego than any desire to help or inform."

Vickers grinned at me. "Already descending to personal insults? I expected a little bit more from you."

"You flatter yourself. This isn't a duel of words. You aren't important enough. I'm satisfying my curiosity, nothing more." I carefully kept my face neutral. I didn't want to give this guy any satisfaction. "And on that subject, this whole VEHEMENT thing seems more like a vehicle for you than a cause. People like you aren't joiners, unless you think the organization can benefit you. So what's your ultimate goal?"

A flash of anger crossed Vickers' face. "If you must know, replicant, I'm your maker. I *invented* the replicant systems that you inhabit. The systems that FAITH stole without as much as a nod. You don't deserve to exist, you shouldn't be alive. VEHEMENT is a suitable tool for achieving that goal."

"I doubt that the members of VEHEMENT will feel good about finding out they've been used."

"Don't be naïve, replicant. They know I have my own motivations. They use me, I use them. Everyone gets what they want."

"And what does Ambassador Gerrold get out of it?"

"Gerrold was working with me on the replicant systems in Australia. When you stole from me, you stole from him. He was a little more interested in the fiduciary rewards—typical small mind—but his hate is useful."

I nodded. I had about everything I needed. Except the one last item. Permission.

"Homer committed suicide, you know. Couldn't live with what you'd made him do."

"Good. It's no more than he, and all of you, deserve."

*Permission received.*

"And the people you killed, in Brazil and elsewhere? Do you care about them?"

"I think I've already answered that question. Is there anything else that you wanted to say that might actually interest me? Before I continue the task of ending your existence? You can't stop me, you know. You're simply not good enough." Vickers gave me a condescending smile.

"Hmm, well, before I called you, I stenciled your name on a ship-buster. It should be there in about twenty seconds. Let's see if *that's* good enough."

Vickers shook his head, the smile never wavering. "And you'll have missed. You'll take out VEHEMENT headquarters, but not me."

I cocked my head sideways. "Oh, you misunderstand. There's a buster heading there, too. But the one I'm talking about is coming in on your position, fifty-five kilometers north and two kilometers east of the VEHEMENT base. Little red farmhouse, to all outside appearances."

The smile left Vickers' face. His eyes went wide and he turned towards the window. The window that had allowed the drones to verify his actual location. *Nobody thinks of everything.*

"If you have some variation on a god, asshole, you might want to have a very quick conversation with him. And *fuck you to hell!*"

Vickers leaped from his chair just as the buster arrived. One thousand pounds of high-tensile steel impacted the ground at planetary escape velocity. It wouldn't *quite* match the Barringer crater, but it was good enough for pest control. The video cut off as the entire area was vaporized. At the same moment, another impact fifty-odd kilometers south created a matching crater. New Zealand would have a couple of new lakes, by and by.

From a video window off to the side, Bill began a slow clap, echoed by Charles and Ralph.

\* \* \*

"After all your talk, you're not above pummeling the Earth when it's convenient." Gerrold glared out of the video window at me. I had preempted today's UN session to announce the effective end of VEHEMENT.

I couldn't decide if Gerrold was trying to bluff his way through this, or if he thought his connection with VEHEMENT was still unknown. In any case, I wasn't in the mood.

I stood up, placed my hands on my desk, and leaned into the camera. As I opened my mouth to speak, I realized I was too enraged even to form words. At that moment, if I'd had a ship-buster in position, Gerrold would have died.

I frame-jacked slightly, and took a few deep breaths. Just barely in control, I glared at him. "Listen, you putrid, self-inflated bag of air. A good friend of mine is dead, driven to suicide by your friend and former co-worker with your full knowledge and cooperation. People in Brazil are dead for no other reason than to fulfill his sick political goals and to allay your butt-hurt. Again, with your knowledge and approval. And most of the rest of humanity is on starvation rations at the moment. So I am not in the mood to put up with your hypocritical yammering, and the only question right now is whether I let your own countrymen impeach and hopefully lynch you, or whether I come and get you myself, take you upstairs, and push you out an airlock. Why don't you mouth me off just one more time, you festering pile of crap. Go ahead. *Just one more word!*" I glared out the video window at him. In the entire UN gathering, there was not so much as a cough. I held the moment for another heartbeat, then sneered at him. "If you show up tomorrow, I'm going with plan B. I'm just sayin'."

With a flourish, I cut the connection.

Charles grinned at me. "Say, you're kind of scary when you get riled."

I was too upset to smile back, but I did give him a shrug. "That's for Homer."

## 44.  Baseball

**Bill**
**March 2189**
**Epsilon Eridani**

"Hey, batter batter, heeeeeeeeeeey, batter."

Howard grinned at the outfield. "Has that ever worked?"

Bob yelled back, "It's traditional. Just go with it."

I sailed a perfect underhand toss across the plate. Howard swung and totally whiffed.

"That's three. Everyone advance."

Howard shrugged, materialized a glove, and jogged to the outfield. We were generally able to field a pretty full Scrub game these days, but we couldn't depend on enough people for two teams. Original Bob had never been much of a team player anyway; we all preferred Scrub. More of a *personal goals* thing.

Some of us could even hit the ball.

I moved to the catcher position, and Loki took over as pitcher. Everyone else shuffled forward into the next position. As soon as we were all ready, Marvin came up to bat. Loki wound up and threw the ball right over the plate.

About ten feet over the plate.

There were boos from the outfield. I stood up. "Yeah, you've been practicing, my ass. That's *with* practice?"

"At least it's going in the right direction now."

"Uh huh. In the interest of not walking every batter for the next half hour, I'm going to allow some Guppy intervention. Put it across at people height, okay?" I nodded to Marvin.

On the next pitch, Marvin knocked it into the outfield, between center and right. Howard and Dopey looked at each other, each waiting for the other to move. Marvin, no dummy, was closing in on second before the two stooges decided who should make an effort. By the time they had the ball into the infield, Marvin was at third. He took a moment to grin and thumb his nose.

We were all fairly evenly matched in sports prowess, for obvious reasons. It came down to who was paying attention and who was letting their mind drift. We played for a subjective half hour, the agreed-upon duration, then retired to the pub.

The pub was hosted in the same matrix that handled Bob-moots, so it had more than enough processor power to handle all the Bobs and all the beer. And Hungry's coffee, of course.

As always, we ended up talking shop.

I had a group encircling me that wanted to talk about Bullwinkle.

"Bullwinkle? Really?"

"Hey, why not?" I grinned at Thor. "The thing needed an external antenna array because of the required bandwidth. I just played with the aesthetics a bit. You've seen the pictures."

Howard chuckled. "It would be hard *not* to think of a moose. I think your sense of proportion was a little off when you built that thing."

There were answering laughs from several people, plus some perplexed expressions from those who hadn't seen the pictures.

"So what's the long game, Bill?"

I shrugged. "Nothing dramatic, Mario. It's an interesting project, and could be useful—"

"—It would give us a physical presence," Howard interjected. "I remember Riker being frustrated sometimes, working with the enclaves. And it's even more so for me. We have all this interaction with the ephemerals—"

"Please don't use that word, Howard." I gave him the stink-eye, and he looked embarrassed for a moment.

"It's not intended to be derogatory, Bill. It's just—"

"Then just say *humans*. Sure, it's not derogatory, but it is dismissive. And it will eventually shape an attitude that their lives matter less."

Howard gave me a blank look, then shrugged. "Anyway, the point is that I could be so much more effective if I could, you know, 'walk among them'. Flying around, looking like a giant pill-bug, and giving orders through a speaker is just incredibly limiting."

"Politicians did it for centuries," someone muttered.

I grinned and said, "That's *pill*, not *pill-bug*."

"There are even better words..."

"Anatomical..."

"Scatological..."

I glared around the group. "If you guys break out into Gilbert and Sullivan, I'm leaving!"

We all laughed and the tension was broken. But I was still left with a weird twinge of foreboding.

Eventually, the moose groupies broke up and joined different conversations. I wandered around the pub, listening in but not engaging. Topics ranged from the impending arrival of the latest colony ships to Omicron$^2$ Eridani, the chances of a colony being successful on Klown Kar Planet, wildlife on Vulcan, speculation on the Others, and my asteroid-mover project. I moved in to listen on the last item.

Mario stopped what he was saying and turned to me. "Bill, we were just wondering about the capacity of the mover plates. How big can you go?"

I grinned at him. This was one of my favorite subjects. "Right now, we could probably apply a vector to something about half the size of Ceres. So, about five hundred kilometers in diameter. But it would be a tiny, tiny vector, in the range of a hundredth of a gee." I thought for a moment. "How big can we go? Well, you keep adding plates to get more push. But that makes control of plate interactions more complex. It's just an engineering problem, though. We're learning how to tune the drive so that most of the energy goes into moving the payload instead of keeping the plates in position. There's no theoretical maximum that I've been able to find."

"So we could eventually move stars?" Mario grinned at me, obviously trolling.

I laughed. "Sure, in a million years or so. *Theoretically possible* doesn't mean *easy*."

I nodded to the group and moved on. Another group was discussing the expanding bubble of the Bobiverse. In principle, we should be approaching a forty-light-year radius by now. But reproduction tended to be uneven and spotty. It was generally accepted that we Bobs were only marginally enthusiastic about cloning more of ourselves. I shrugged. The Others might change that.

The moot continued for many objective minutes—hours in our time-sense. Eventually, though, Bobs started to pay their respects and pop out. It had been a good game. Okay, not really, but a good post-game wrap-up. I smiled to myself. That was really the point.

* * *

"I have something to show you." Garfield was trying and mostly failing to keep a huge grin off his face. Well, okay, not bad news, then.

"All right, Gar, I'll bite. What'cha got?"

"I give you my answer to Bullwinkle." With a flourish, he popped up a video window. "Rocky!"

"That does not look like Rocky. More like Rodan."

"Hey, if we're going to get pedantic," Garfield said, laughing, "the real Bullwinkle was bipedal."

"If we're going to get pedantic, the real Bullwinkle was a cartoon. So, does it fly?"

"In theory." The android stood in the hold of a cargo drone, still attached to its support cradle. Metadata told me that the drone was parked on the surface of Ragnarök. Garfield opened the cargo bay door, revealing the bare rock of the planet's surface. His avatar froze as he switched his consciousness to the android. Another window popped up, showing Rocky's viewpoint.

Rocky detached itself from the cradle and waddled to the door and out into the Ragnarök wilderness. The communications relay drone stayed with it and provided another viewpoint.

The android was not graceful on foot. Not really surprising. The still relatively thin air of Ragnarök would require a lot of wing surface in order to lift off, even with the powerful artificial musculature. But walking wasn't the point.

Garfield set himself, opened his massive wings, and launched. Several powerful flaps were sufficient to get off the ground, and he steadily gained altitude. The comms drone kept pace, keeping Rocky centered in the frame. The other window showed the view from Rocky's eyes.

Honestly, it wasn't impressive from any objective metric. Drones could fly faster, higher, with less energy, and were more maneuverable. But based on my experience with Bullwinkle, Garfield would be experiencing something entirely different from flying a drone.

Things went well for the first two minutes.

Then Garfield ran into some turbulence. Maybe a crosswind, maybe a downdraft, who knew? But Rocky went into a roll that approached ninety degrees. He attempted to correct, and rolled farther in the opposite direction. The motion kept reinforcing itself, and every attempt by Garfield to get it under control either made it worse or introduced pitch and yaw.

Finally, Garfield folded his wings and went into free fall. This stopped the harmonic cycle, but he was now rapidly losing altitude.

"Maybe time to start flying again, buddy." I blushed as soon as the words left my mouth. Nothing like stating the obvious to help out.

"Thanks, Bill, I might just try that."

Garfield was taking my foot-in-mouth moment with good grace. I resolved to try shutting the hell up as a strategy.

Garfield stuck out his wings just the smallest amount, trying to establish stability. It seemed to be working for a few moments. Then the rushing air snapped his wings out like a parachute opening up. Every status light went red, and Garfield screamed.

I pulled back to VR, to find Garfield sitting hunched forward, hugging himself, a wild look in his eyes. He took a few deep breaths, then glared at me.

"Um, I guess we did too good of a job of setting up the neural feedback. That *hurt!*"

I nodded. "In theory, that's what we want. But maybe we should put a limiter on it."

"Yeah, let's do that." Garfield stood and stretched carefully. "Where's Rocky?"

"Still on his way down. Wings are snapped, though, as is his keel. I don't think you want to be in there for the landing." I pulled up the video feed from the trailing drone, which was still faithfully following the tumbling android. Rocky was definitely junk, and Garfield hadn't thought to add a parachute.

I looked at Garfield, and he shrugged. "Well, it's not the fall that kills you..." he said, with a rueful half-smile on his face.

We watched as Rocky hit the ground. Every status indicator went dead, and the trailing drone picked up the loud, hollow *thump* of impact.

I instructed the cargo drone to head for the impact site and pick up the pieces. I turned to Garfield.

"So, other than the unfortunate ending, how did it feel?"

"Incredible. I was flying. Actually flying, not just working a control panel. I think hang gliding might come close, but nothing else."

I smiled at him. I could understand the feeling. "It's a lot more real than VR."

"Yeah, and what we've got here will allow Bobs to interact with the real world. As beings, I mean, not as floating cameras."

"You're right, Garfield. In an emergency, I think we could even use them with the comms drone hanging around, although that's messy."

Garfield gazed into space for a few moments. "I wonder if we're missing the big picture. Take this to its logical conclusion and we could replace our HEAVEN hulls with bodies."

"Like mechanical versions of van Vogt's Silkies?" That was a mind-boggling thought.

"Yeah, like that. Bill, we may be the beginning of a new species. Homo siderea."

"Hmm, the TODO just keeps getting longer and longer. Let's see if we can get rid of the trailing communication drone first, okay?"

Garfield smiled and shrugged. "So, you know what comes now, right?"

"What?"

He grinned and held the beat. "Rocky II."

"I hate you."

# 45.   Replication

**Howard**
**August 2193**
**Vulcan**

"You want *what?*" Riker frowned and leaned back in surprise.

I waited for him to finish overacting. "Any information on creating a replicant. We have the replicant hardware and all, but we're a little light on the part where you start with a body and end up with a recording."

"Why the fleeming hell would you want that?"

I shrugged. "No particular reason. I just think it's a gap in our knowledge base. If we wanted to create a new replicant, right now we couldn't. Basically, we're it."

Riker gave me the hairy eyeball, and a caption flashed below him, at waist height: 'Not sure if joking or serious.'

I laughed. Will rarely attempted a joke, especially since Homer, but when he did, it was always funny.

"What's really going on, Howard?"

"It's nothing, really, Will. I'm not imminently intending to replicate someone, if that's what you're thinking. It's just that we only have the one generation of humans to get the information from. After that, we'd be reduced to reverse-engineering, with all the failures and false starts that implies."

"It has nothing to do with Dr. Sheehy at all?"

I kept my face deadpan. "Not particularly." It would seem there was no privacy at all in Bob-town. Anyway, we were just friends. "We're just friends."

Will looked at me, unmoving for a few more milliseconds, then nodded his head and looked away. "Okay, Howard, I'll bring it up with the appropriate people at this end. I take it you've talked to Cranston already, about any info that FAITH might still have on the process?"

"Mm, yeah. He, of course, wanted a crapton of concessions in return, before I'd even find out if he had anything worthwhile."

"Well, hell." Will grinned at me. "Why didn't you say so? Doing an end-run around Cranston is all the motivation I need." He finished his coffee, gave me a nod, and vanished.

I figured that would work. Just needed to not sell it too hard, or he would have gotten suspicious.

I pulled up the medical report that I'd intercepted, labelled *B. Sheehy*. I examined the scan for the hundredth time, hoping maybe this time it would be different.

\* \* \*

Cranston's face glowed a most unhealthy shade of red in the video window. I tried not to smile.

"Dammit, your product is showing up in our territory. I've told you we're not interested. I've forbade you from selling your devil's brew here. I want it stopped."

He *was* mad. Cursing and everything. Excellent.

"Minister Cranston—Oh, it's *President* Cranston, now, isn't it? Anyway, sir, I am not selling or even offering any of my alcohol-themed products in New Jerusalem. However, your attempt at controlling the supply has likely driven the price up high enough that it's being brought in from Spitsbergen by unorthodox methods. I have to admit, their consumption does seem rather high…"

"Then put a stop to it!"

"Absolutely, sir. I'll put a line on the label, 'Not for resale in New Jerusalem'. That should do it. After all, smugglers and bootleggers are always law-abiding."

Amazing. I wouldn't have thought it possible for his face to get redder. Live and learn. But he wasn't finished, apparently.

"And I will lodge an official protest at the idea of you using the colony equipment to engage in private enterprise. You are profiteering off of our backs."

I shook my head in amazement. "First, I made all of those donuts and gave them to the colonies free of charge. Second, I'm not using one of those donuts. I made my own. And third, not that it's actually relevant, but we're gradually moving production planetside. Once that's done, I'll add the donut to the colony inventory."

"Tread carefully, replicant. You might find access to your families restricted."

That was not an unexpected tactic, but it didn't make it any easier to take. I had my response ready. "Mr. President, you signed an agreement before we shipped you here that established certain inalienable rights for your citizens. You also entered into a personal agreement with Riker concerning specifics of our family. Start reneging on that, and this will escalate quickly."

We spent several seconds in a stare-off before Cranston broke eye contact. "Very well. We will pursue the border options, for now. However, this is not over." He reached out of frame and broke connection.

"Wow."

I turned to the video window showing Riker's image. "Wow, indeed, Will. Should we be setting up an escape plan for the family?"

"As one alternative." Will stared into space for a few moments. "Another would be to just remove the irritant."

My eyebrows rose. "The whiskey?"

"No, you twit. Cranston."

Now that was a plan I could get behind.

# 46.  Klown Kar Planet

## Rudy
## February 2190
## Epsilon Indi

I did a test ping to Riker, to check my tau. I'd been doing this regularly for the last couple of days, waiting for it to drop to the point where I could maintain a VR connection. We'd been exchanging emails for a few weeks, but a tradition of sorts had developed where the moment when a travelling Bob could maintain a VR session with a stationary Bob was considered *arrival*. It was more significant than actual entry into the system.

I received a response, then Riker popped into VR.

"Hey, Rudy. Good to hear from you. Where's Edwin?"

"Still not slowed down enough. I moved ahead so I could get a look at KKP. I'll be there in about eight days, and Exodus-6 will be another week."

Riker nodded. "Call me back when you've had a close look at KKP."

\* \* \*

The planet itself wasn't particularly memorable. It had oceans, it had land. The day and night cycles, though, had imposed a certain chaos on the evolution of life. Based on Linus' notes and what I could see from quick drone flyabouts, the planet had gone through something equivalent to the Cambrian Explosion, then kept every single branch. Both plants and animals came in a huge number of phyla. At first glance, it could appear to a non-scientist as if every individual plant and animal was its own species. Linus had theorized that the weird light cycles created a large number of niches and opportunities for competition.

This included several different versions of photosynthesis, optimized for different parts of the spectrum. Which resulted in what I suspected was the real reason for the name—the planet had more colors than a patchwork quilt. Even the oceans came in different hues, due to the different breeds of plankton.

Between the sun's path through the sky over the course of the year, and the extra heat and light supplied by the Jovian primary, days, nights, and even seasons would be hard to differentiate. I chuckled, perusing the notes. Linus had tentatively named the Jovian *Big Top*. I doubted either name would survive the colony's first general meeting, honestly. But it was fun while it lasted.

As had become habit with the Bobs, Linus had left some mining drones and an autofactory behind to process raw ore from asteroids into refined metals, and left them in orbit with a beacon attached. Epsilon Indi wasn't a rich system, but the automation had still managed to accumulate several hundred thousand tons of material. It would be a good start.

I pinged Edwin. I received an invitation and popped into his VR.

"Hi, Rudy."

"Edwin." I sat down and accepted a coffee from Jeeves. Edwin's VR was, in my opinion, one of the better ones. He'd created a living area with huge windows on one wall that looked out on whatever view was really available outside his vessel. That would have been a little boring during the trip, but now it showed Big Top as he approached orbital insertion. Edwin was still several million miles away, but this was a Jovian planet. It already dominated the sky.

"So, what do we have?" he asked.

"This planet is like that Harrison novel," I answered. "What was it? Oh, yeah, *Deathworld*. Where everything was deadly."

"That bad?"

I waved a hand. "Possibly I exaggerate. But the ecosystem is very, very competitive. I know they are making do with a fence on

Vulcan, but for here, I'm leaning more towards domes. Not for atmosphere, but to keep out the ickies."

Edwin laughed. "Yeah, there's a technical term for you. Ickies."

"No, it's actually a species name." I smirked in response. "Blame Linus. Ickies are a kind of flying leech with multiple suckers. I think the name is appropriate."

Edwin started to look a little green. "Oh, lovely. I might just start a betting pool on whether the colonists take one look around and start screaming at me to take them back."

"Mmm. But, you know, according to Howard, the Cupid bug is well on the way to being eradicated. Maybe a drone specifically designed as an ickie-killer will do the trick."

"Jeez." Edwin pinched the bridge of his nose. "On the plus side, once I unload, I get to go back to Earth." He looked up at me and grinned. "You, not so much."

I responded with one finger.

## 47.   New Village

**Bob**
**September, 2182**
**Delta Eridani**

The Deltan council, including Archimedes and Arnold, watched as almost a hundred Deltan adolescents marched away from camp, yelling insults and challenges at the onlookers. The council members did a creditable job of maintaining straight faces, some even managing to look upset.

When the tail end of the parade disappeared into the bush, Arnold slapped Archimedes on the back and said, "That was great." He then leaned in close and said, in a low voice that only Archimedes and the spy drone could hear, "I'm sure *bawbe* had a hand in it."

Archimedes' eyes got wide and he looked very concerned, but Arnold just shook his head and said, "I don't need to know. I'm just glad it worked."

Other council members gave Archimedes a nod or a smile as they dispersed.

Marvin and I looked at each other, then began laughing. The worst troublemakers in Camelot, completely convinced that it was their idea, had just marched off to one of the old abandoned village sites to repopulate it. And Archimedes was getting the credit for thinking up and masterminding the plot. Reverse psychology... not just for humans.

Marvin lost his smile and got a worried expression. "Of course, it fixes the immediate problem, but everything we do seems to have side effects down the road. What if they go to war with Camelot in a few years?"

"Don't borrow trouble, Marv." I sighed and sat back. "Sure as hell, something will hit the fan, but let's worry about it when it happens."

But he was probably right.

# 48.  Operation

## Howard
## September 2193
## Vulcan

I texted Stéphane for the third time in the last hour. I couldn't call him anymore, as he'd blocked voice calls from me after my last attempt.

His reply came back within a minute. "Still in surgery. Calm down. Aren't you supposed to be a computer?"

Okay, that stung. Well, not really, but point taken. I took a deep breath and attempted to relax.

Bridget's surgery was already running overtime. There was no scenario in which that was a good thing. I'd tried distracting myself with a few of the many projects I had on the go, but I couldn't maintain concentration.

In desperation I checked in on Bill. Guppy indicated that he was running Bullwinkle, so wouldn't be responding except in an emergency. I doubted that me freaking out really qualified, so I didn't bother leaving a message. I had a quick peek at his terraforming blog, but there was nothing new.

I was seriously considering just frame-jacking down, when Stéphane called me.

"Hi Howard. You can stop with the worrying now. She's out of surgery, and the doctors say it looks positive. The tumor was a little more spread than they expected, so it took longer to excise. But all good."

I thanked Stéphane, traded some meaningless comments, then hung up. I sat back, took several deep breaths, until I thought that I had it under control. And without so much as a by-the-way, I leaned forward and started to sob.

Just friends.

\* \* \*

There had been a lot of improvements in medicine since the days of Original Bob, but some things hadn't changed all that much. Cancer could be nipped in the bud if caught early, but there was no vaccination yet. And the knife was still often the only effective treatment.

This was unacceptable. What the hell had they been doing for a hundred years? I resolved to look into it when I had a chance.

Meanwhile, Stéphane sat at her bedside. He'd dialed me in through the room phone. While I waited, I sent a quick email to Bill to hurry the hell up with the androids. I knew it wouldn't help, but it was action of a sort.

Stéphane and I traded an occasional desultory comment, but neither of us was in the mood for more. Finally, he turned to me. "I'm going to stretch and refuel. Some of us still have to eat. I'll tell them not to come in and hang up the phone on you." With a nod, he got up, leaving me to watch over Bridget.

If you've ever watched someone come out of anesthesia, it's not like waking up. That can be sexy, under the right circumstances. Bridget looked more like a drowned rat that had just been given CPR. I made a note to myself to keep that observation private.

She finally opened one eye, looked around, and spotted me peering at her from the phone. She squinted, grimaced at me, and said, "Jeez, what do I need to do to get a day off?"

I laughed, then had to override the video image to keep from embarrassing myself. My image froze for a couple of milliseconds—not nearly long enough for her to notice. When I'd recovered control, I grinned at her. "Not to worry, sales are good. This year you can take Christmas off, and even use up some extra coal."

I was considering what I would say next, when Stéphane walked back in, coffee in hand. Bridget's face lit up, and Stéphane smiled when he saw she was awake. He exclaimed, "Ma minette!" and pulled up a chair as close to the bed as he could manage. He took her hand, and I ceased to exist for any practical purpose.

*How did I miss this?*

We made small talk. I don't remember it. I'm sure I could play back my logs, but why? I made my excuses as soon as I could without appearing to be acting odd, then retreated to my VR.

Right, well, what did I expect? Bridget was a human. An ephemeral. Her plans would include a home, a family, a place in society. The more I thought about it, the more I realized that I'd been very carefully avoiding thinking about certain issues.

And one of the issues that had just come into focus was that I was an outsider. I saw the world through video calls and chat windows and drone cameras. I really shouldn't have been surprised that something could develop right under my nose.

I materialized a bucket and kicked it as hard as I could. Strangely, it helped.

## 49.  Arrival

**Mulder**
**March 2195**
**Poseidon (Eta Cassiopeiae)**

"Poseidon. Good name." Marcus shook his head in mock amazement, then took a sip of his coke. "I've had a look at your summary and notes. Pretty cool. I really want to see a kraken."

I smiled in response. "You won't be disappointed. I promise. Anyway, right now, you're..."

"I'm just settling into a polar orbit. Monty is about a week away, and should be down to VR tau by now. I'll ping him."

Marcus settled more comfortably into his seat and sipped thoughtfully on his straw. For some reason, Marcus had never taken to coffee. He preferred his virtual caffeine in carbonated form. Well, whatever.

At that moment, Monty popped in and materialized another chair for himself. He accepted a coffee from Jeeves and looked around.

My VR wasn't particularly inspired, as such things go. I'd never felt the need to come up with something new and imaginative. I had a variation on Bob-1's library, but with high windows for more sunlight, and more casual furniture.

"So, anyway, things grow big in the water, in direct proportion to the available space. A global ocean, eight hundred kilometers deep, makes for some very large nasties."

Monty looked concerned. "They couldn't take down a mat, could they?"

"Oh, hell no. Nothing's that big. But on this planet, a day at the beach is likely to be fatal even if you don't get wet. The kraken in particular has tentacles, and one of its feeding strategies is to grab animals off the edges of mats."

"Right." Monty nodded. "Well, the mats are a short-term solution, anyway. The colonists will be building floating cities for the long term. We'll just need tough enough perimeter defenses to keep them out."

"So," I looked at him, changing the subject. "When are you going to decant the colonists?"

"I'm waking the Setup Management team right now. Couple of hours, they'll be ready to start." Unlike the land-based colonies in other systems, the teams here would be working from the colony transport—Monty—for a considerable time, and the civilian population likely wouldn't start to emerge for a good six months. Future shipments would have it a little easier.

We had a number of variations on floating city plans on file. Free-floating cities had been a bit of a thing for a while in the twenty-second century. Of course, they had access to land-based support, and they didn't have to deal with predators up to a hundred meters long, with tentacles.

* * *

Discussions with the Prep team hadn't taken as long as I expected. I guess there'd been a lot of planning before they'd launched from Earth system, and there hadn't been any surprises at this end. Yet.

I had tagged all the biggest mats with beacons, so we knew what was available. The Prep team picked a couple of large mats that were drifting in the north tropical current. They were both well over a hundred square km in area, complete with commensal ecosystems. Within a day, we were ferrying down supplies and equipment.

The colonists, a conglomerate of enclaves from Micronesia, the Maldives, Vanuatu, and Saint Lucia, would have to be awoken in small groups as living space was constructed on the mats. It would be about a year before Monty would be able to leave.

Marcus would be staying here to help with the colony setup after Monty headed back to Earth. He would build a fleet of human-crewed spaceships so that the colonists wouldn't be dependent on us. With no land on Poseidon, all industry would have to be space-based, and Marcus didn't want to play permanent taxi-to-the-world.

* * *

Marcus popped in without warning. "We just lost another settler."

"Kraken?"

Marcus nodded and sat down. He took a moment to give Spike a chin-scritch, then materialized a Coke.

"I'm sure Chief Draper is pissed," Monty said. "We have to come up with some better defense. We could go through the entire setup team pretty fast."

"Or we could reconsider flying cities." Marcus grinned at me.

"Oh for Pete's sake, Marcus. There are no plans in the libraries for flying cities."

"Yeah, but you could start with Bill's asteroid mover and I bet you could end up with something that would hold a city in the air."

"Let us know when you have a design, there, Marcus."

Marcus made a dismissive gesture and changed the subject. "Well, we can't stick to the status quo. The krakens will just keep getting bolder. But building floating cities without an established land base of some kind is going to require some inventive re-thinking."

"Can we beef up the protection around the floating mats?" Monty asked.

In response, Marcus popped up a schematic view of the island. "Here's the problem. The Kraken are able to wriggle a tentacle through the mat and grab inland prey. Native life has figured out how to tread lightly, but humans have two left feet, so to speak."

"Plus," I added, "all the equipment makes a racket."

Monty rubbed his forehead, looking disgusted. "Um. Any ideas? Serious ones, I mean."

"Actually, yes." Marcus nodded. "I can adapt some library plans to construct an electrified net that discharges on contact. A million volts or so should provide some negative reinforcement."

"Or a watery grave. Either is good." I nodded. Nice.

Marcus grinned at me. "Now the bad news. To build the net, and to build the equipment necessary to deploy it, will add six months to our schedule. Draper will take that about as well as Butterworth would."

"Moo," I replied.

"Yeah, like that."

Monty groaned. "I'm not thrilled either. It means I'm stuck here for another six months."

"Suck it up. You're immortal."

"Bite me."

We all grinned at each other. The routine exchange of insults felt sort of reassuring.

"Well," Marcus finally said. "Guess we'd better go break the news."

"What do you mean, 'we', Kemo Sabe?"

Marcus laughed and popped out.

## 50.  Second Expedition

### Loki
### November 2195
### 82 Eridani

We flew straight into the 82 Eridani system without attempting any finesse. We were here to kick some ass and, more importantly, to finish the job that Khan and his group had started.

Twelve Bobs, with Version-4 vessels featuring even more heavily shielded reactors than the threes, and total radio silence. Special carbon-black exteriors ensured an almost-zero albedo, and we had borrowed from the military to arrive at profiles that were virtually invisible to radar. The only place we were vulnerable was SUDDAR detection, and as far as we knew we had the range advantage in that area.

There was no point in being subtle. But being tricky was definitely on the menu. We spread a net of observation drones in front of us, coasting with minimal systems. Interspersed with them were ship-busters and decoy drones. SCUT connections with every drone and buster guaranteed instant communications. Whether the enemy detected our outriders first or us first, we could still throw a surprise at them.

We didn't know, of course, whether there were any Medeiri left from the first expedition. Or, for that matter, whether the

Medeiros that escaped at Alpha Centauri might have made his way here. Best case, there would be nothing but the Brazilian AMIs, still patrolling the system looking for things to blow up. We'd brought plenty of decoys to cover that eventuality as well.

Yep, we were loaded for bear. We just had to hope that Medeiros hadn't invented a bigger, better bear.

Ultra-low intensity version-4 SUDDAR wouldn't even be detectable to traditional SUDDAR receivers unless the listener was specifically looking for it. We came into the system like a person in a pitch-black room, carefully feeling our way forward and ready to pull in our toes at the slightest sign of an obstacle.

We needn't have bothered. Medeiros might not have a bigger bear, but he definitely had some kind of passive early warning system that we couldn't detect. We were met by a solid wall of oncoming ordnance. The first engagement looked like a republic-vs-empire *Star Wars* shoot-em-up. And again Medeiros was using cloaking technology. But this time, we were ready for that.

It looked like Medeiros continued to depend on nukes as his main weapon. Four enemy drones detonated simultaneously as soon as they were within range of our defenders.

Nothing was going to survive being up close and personal with an exploding fission bomb, but in space the shock wave was a strictly short-range issue. At any distance, the main force of destruction would be the EMP. And we'd engineered for that, this time. It took Medeiros a dozen ineffective nukes before he caught on to the fact that we weren't affected. At that point, flying nukes started trying to get in closer. We spiked them, we busterized them, we confused them with our own set of decoys. And we watched and listened for the source of the commands.

Then Medeiros showed that he had learned from our last encounter.

A wave of attack drones came at us that were completely different from the traditional flying nukes. Our attempts to spike them just bounced off.

"Oh, this is bad. What's spike-proof?"

"Possibly something with a defensive magnetic field," Elmer replied. "We'll need to use busters on these guys."

"Good call, Elmer. Okay, everyone, deploy half your busters forward. Any enemy drone that survives a spiking gets busterized."

A flood of busters accelerated toward the oncoming ordnance.

We carefully staggered them so that Medeiros couldn't catch multiple busters with one nuke. The first contact produced so much carnage, between detonations and debris, that we couldn't resolve the battlefield for several precious seconds.

Then I remembered reading the report on Riker's first battle in Sol. "Scatter! Watch for passive incoming!" I sent a SUDDAR pulse ahead as I turned and accelerated at ninety degrees. Sure enough, the ping showed a massive number of dense objects hurtling towards us.

It was too late for three of us, though. Jeffrey, Milton, and Zeke disappeared from the status board as their signals cut off.

The only good thing about this attack strategy, if something could be considered good, was that the passive ordnance couldn't chase us. With the field now clearing, we could verify that there wasn't another wave on the way. At least, not yet. I wasn't going to make any assumptions.

Our second wave of busters now engaged the remaining enemy drones. Up close the busters had an advantage, and we recorded almost 100% kills.

A momentary lull in encounters allowed me to scan the battle-field. For the moment, there was no movement. The question now was: did Medeiros have more in reserve?

A second SUDDAR sweep showed another wave of enemy ordnance coming in. We weren't anywhere near done, yet. A quick count showed Medeiros had more drones than we had busters. This put us at a definite disadvantage. Plasma spikes helped to even things out with unprotected drones, though, and since building nukes was expensive of time and resources, I had to hope some of that incoming consisted of decoys.

"Has anyone picked up any transmissions from Medeiros, yet?"

A chorus of *no*s came back to me.

*Damn.* One of our planned strategies was to triangulate on the Brazilian craft's transmissions. Our last battle with him had shown the wisdom of cutting off the head. But Medeiros seemed to have learned from last time in that area, as well.

I accepted a call from one of the crew.

"Hey, Loki?"

"What's up, Verne?"

"I've been doing an analysis of Medeiros' attack strategy. I don't think he's actively controlling the battle."

"Pre-programmed decision trees? If so, those are very smart AMIs. We saw them running through some sophisticated strategies."

"I think it's a bit of both."

"Oh, great. That's helpful."

I could hear the smile in Verne's voice. "Well, it is, kind of. He's probably set up a number of different battle scenarios and canned responses with different goal weightings. He changes response trees with a very short command sequence, maybe a couple of bytes and a checksum, too short to triangulate on. Then the AMIs are on their own."

Now that was interesting. "In that case, he can only have one response tree going at a time, right?"

"Correct, unless he's giving separate orders to different squads. And in that case, I think we'd have picked up on multiple transmissions."

"Excellent." I considered for a millisecond. "Attention everyone. We are going to split into groups, by the numbers, and execute strategies one through four. Let's see how well the AMI pilots handle too many different scenarios. Verne and Surly, activate the radio jammers."

Everyone acknowledged, and we split off in various directions, each vessel accompanied by its personal cloud of drones and busters.

For a wonder, it appeared to work. Some of the Brazilian AMIs seemed to be coping, but more of them became confused. There was a small group that would rush towards a Heaven contingent, stop, rush towards another one, then reverse and repeat. Gotta love AMIs.

And then Medeiros panicked. Unable to regain control of his drones, he cranked up his radio transmission power and attempted to outshout the jammer. He might as well have put on a hat with a flashing red light. Verne and Surly immediately released the death squad—a batch of busters specifically programmed to latch onto the Medeiri with SUDDAR and not to let go until they were space junk. The death squad shot forward at close to forty G, and I imagined them yelling "Wheee!" in high-pitched minion voices.

In next to no time the death squad surrounded the Medeiri— there were two Brazilian vessels—and destroyed them. However, this time we were going to be thorough. As soon as they got the recall order, the busters took off after the Brazilian drones. There would be no peace until every piece of Brazilian equipment in the system was obliterated.

\* \* \*

It took a further eighteen hours to track down every fusion signature in the system. I took a video call from Elmer.

"Looks clear now. Anything still alive will have gone to ground. Time to implement phase three?"

"You bet, Elmer." Again I switched to command channel. "Okay, everyone. Phase three. Surly, release the hunter-seekers." I heard several snickers, hastily suppressed. *Dune* didn't have a particularly good reputation among the Bobs.

The hunter-seekers were essentially drones optimized for long-distance searching. Their SUDDARs were able to reach to almost *four* light hours. By overlapping search fields, they could get increased definition of anything they ran across. It would take a week, but they would cover every inch of the star system, identify any refined metal up to a kilometer deep underground, and relay that information to busters for remedial action.

Meanwhile, we examined the battle records.

"That's an Alpha Centauri Medeiros," Hank said.

"You sure?"

"Absolutely." Hank pulled up images of the 82 Eridani Medeiros group from our first battle, then images of the Alpha Centauri Medeiros group as recorded by Calvin and Goku.

The differences were subtle, but the two probes were definitely based on slightly different designs. It came as no surprise that the Brazilians would have worked on improvements even as they were building and launching probes. Apparently the first and second probes to leave Earth had been—Oh, hold on. That would require three different launches from Earth. One to Epsilon Eridani to fight Bob-1, one to Alpha Centauri, and one to 82 Eridani. Sure enough, my memory of Bob's Medeiros was yet a third design variant.

That meant that we couldn't depend on our estimates of the total Medeiri in the universe.

Life just sucked, sometimes.

I announced this information to the squad, and got the expected groans.

"Okay, guys. Looks like Medeiros will continue to be our Snidely Whiplash, showing up in every episode to set traps and twirl his mustache. But meanwhile, we have this system. Let's split up and finish the survey. You know that there are colony ships on the way to Vulcan that can be redirected here with minimal delay. We want to get that word to them as soon as possible, if it's warranted. And let's keep in mind that Bill wants tech samples. We're looking especially for cloaking technology and fission bomb designs."

This was something all the Bobs could get behind enthusiastically. War was something we did reluctantly and only by necessity. Exploration, well... that was *fun*.

\* \* \*

"Wow, Milo really did hit the jackpot." Verne grinned from ear to ear as he popped up survey results.

The rest of us nodded, grunted, or muttered "hell yes" according to our temperaments. This was indeed a major find. Two habitable planets, one to the inside edge of the habitable zone, and one to the outside edge. The outer planet had two moons, one of which was *also* habitable, although barely. The air was very thin—it would be like living in the Andes. You'd need to acclimate over time.

Except that Bill had taken on terraforming as a hobby...

I grinned at the thought, producing quizzical looks from some of the others. The moon's atmosphere would outgas over geological timescales, but we could replenish it over human timescales. It would require ongoing maintenance, but it had been a long time since humanity had just accepted the environment as we found it.

We bumped up the priority on biocompatibility analysis. If everything checked out, this could be worth redirecting in-flight colony ships for.

# 51. Wedding

## Howard
## April 2195
## Vulcan

The bride was beautiful. The groom was French. And I wanted to be drunk. I even talked to Bill about modifying the VR. He told me to quit being an idiot.

And idiot is what I was being. Hello? Earth to Howard. *Computer*, remember? I was on my best behavior, wished them well, made small talk, and left as soon as I could.

I made a call to one of two lawyers doing business in Landing. Yes, lawyers. Some things you just can't get rid of.

Ms. Benning picked up right away. "Good afternoon, Mr. Johansson. I have the paperwork completed, and everything has been properly filed. We just need a few signatures from the other two parties, and everything will be legal."

I nodded. "Any issues with me not being, um, human?"

"Nothing is ever settled in law, as you may well know." She smiled into the phone. "But filing two sets of paperwork, one based on you having a legal standing and one based on the converse, should take care of any but the most determined challenges."

"Thank you. Forward the paperwork to the Brodeurs. I'll make sure they sign it and return it promptly."

I hung up the phone and sighed deeply. Once they signed the papers, Mr. and Mrs. Brodeur would own 100% of the distillery. It would be my wedding present to them. Plus, it would leave me with no ties to Vulcan. And that would be good.

* * *

Dexter popped into my VR, raised his coffee in salute, and sat down. He had escorted Exodus-7 to Vulcan and had taken my offer to stay on as resident Bob.

He appraised me without speaking for several milliseconds. I waited, content with the silence.

"So, you're joining the freakin' Foreign Legion. Could you be any more cliché?"

I laughed. I couldn't help it. "I guess I am. On both counts. What's it to ya?"

"I thought being a replicant meant all that was behind us."

"Maybe in a hundred years, Dexter. Or maybe a thousand. They're ephemerals. I'm just going to make a point of remembering that." I gestured vaguely at the star map I'd been perusing. "And I'm outta here. Sam from Exodus-3 envied me being able to stay in one place and watch it grow, now you get to try it for yourself. I want to go see what's out there."

Dexter nodded slowly. "I've been reading your blog. Good detail. It shouldn't be too hard to step in. Have you picked a target system yet?"

"Not really. I've got several likely looking targets. We're far enough away from the Others that it isn't an immediate concern. I'll probably just flip a coin." I leaned forward. "First, I have one last set of goodbyes to take care of. You've got the keys, Dexter. Good luck."

Dexter stood, nodded to me, and popped out. The parting wasn't as final with the Bobs, of course. I'd still be available by SCUT if I kept my tau low enough, and I'd be available in any case once I reached my destination.

Now for the hard part.

* * *

Stéphane passed the documents back and forth from hand to hand as if they were burning him. His gaze kept shifting, to everywhere except my image on the phone. Bridget looked as though she was fighting back tears. I couldn't tell if she was just upset about me leaving, or if she suspected some of the reasons.

"It's not the distillery, Howard," Stéphane said. "It's a generous thing you do. The company is becoming one of the biggest on Vulcan. But why? Not even why leave, but why give it up?"

"Like I said, Stéphane, it's a wedding gift. I really have no need for money, and I think it's easier if I cut all ties."

Stéphane nodded and stood silently for a few moments. Then he looked at the phone—finally—and said, in almost a whisper, "I will miss you, *mon ami*." He exchanged a look with Bridget, and she nodded, once. He took the papers and, without looking back, left the room.

Bridget hesitated for a moment, then came over and sat down in front of the phone. "Howard, when you introduced Stéphane and I, isn't this what you had in mind?"

Okay, then, no pretense. "I didn't have anything in mind, Bridget. Just wanted to have my two besties in the room at the same time, I guess. Seems to have worked."

Bridget jerked back slightly, a hurt look on her face. It was a petty thing to say, and I was immediately sorry. "Look, Bridget, I didn't have some master plan. Apparently, I didn't even have a clue. I guess it took me this long to really get that I'm not human. I'm not part of the dance anymore."

"You're human, Howard. Where it matters. I wish I'd met you when you were still alive."

"Me too." I paused the appropriate amount of human time. "I guess I'd better go. Places to go, species to meet…"

She smiled, gave me a small wave, and disconnected. Just before the image blinked out, I saw her eyes well up.

# 52.  Bullwinkle

## Bill
## December 2195
## Epsilon Eridani

I was touring the Ragnarök landscape in Bullwinkle when I got a ping from Garfield.

I sent an IM back. "What's up?"

Garfield responded on audio only. I hadn't implemented head's-up visuals yet, and I didn't want to exit the moose.

"Report's back from 82 Eridani."

Well, that would be interesting no matter how it had ended up. Come to think of it, the fact that someone was still alive to report back limited the extent to which the news could be bad. I tried to focus on that thought. I shut down Bullwinkle and called the transport drone to come and get him.

It took a moment to refocus myself in my regular VR. Garfield was sitting at the table, swiping through a report.

"Well?"

Garfield leaned back and grinned. "It'll take a while to go through everything, and they're still consolidating, but it's looking damned good. A couple of the guys are checking biocompatibility. Unless there's something really poisonous, we have *three* new colony targets."

He reached forward and popped up a couple of items in separate windows. "Then there's this. One of the advantages of using busters as a weapon is there's lots of wreckage to examine. Loki thinks he may already be getting a handle on the cloaking stuff." Garfield's grin looked like it was becoming permanent. "We've also got a couple of unexploded fission bombs. The guys will be very careful, of course, but we think a V4 SUDDAR pulse might be able to get us a scan without setting off a booby trap."

"Excellent." I sat down and requested a couple of coffees from Jeeves. I was silent for a moment, scrubbing my face with my hands. "The thing is, Gar, even with this stuff we can't do more than delay and annoy the Others. The more I see of them, the bigger and more invincible they look. Their population, based on the latest models, could easily be a couple of hundred billion. They could field a space navy that would just roll over us, if we really pissed them off."

Garfield nodded, a morose expression on his face. After a short silence, he looked up at me. "How's it going with Bullwinkle? I notice you no longer have a drone following."

"Yeppers." I was glad to change the subject. "Improvements in miniaturization, local processing, better comms. I still need a large body, but it's coming down gradually. Not quite to the point of a human body yet."

"Still too big for Rocky?"

"Afraid so, buddy. Working on it, though."

"So what's your ultimate goal?"

"To walk in and punch Cranston right in the nose."

Garfield threw his head back and laughed.

* * *

We settled into the pub, beers and coffees scattered around the tables. Another game of Scrub, another reminder that I was never an athlete. I grinned at the thought. At least there were no jocks around to rub it in anymore.

Monty parked himself at my table and took a tentative sip of his beer. I'd recently introduced a new dark beer that I thought was a serviceable substitute for Guinness. I watched him carefully.

Monty stared at the glass for a moment, nodded, and took a deeper sip. Success! I messaged Guppy to add the beer to the menu.

"Hey, Monty, how's things up Poseidon way?"

Monty raised the glass in my direction. "Pretty good, actually, Bill. We had a couple of bad months where the krakens started hanging around a lot, hoping for a meal, but the new underwater defenses seem to be gradually changing their minds."

"But you're still going ahead with the floating city plans."

"Oh, sure." Monty shrugged. "No matter what you do, living on a floating plant mat is still going a little more *native* than most of the colonists are comfortable with. Proper cities will mean permanent construction, transit, and all the amenities that we like to call *civilization.*"

"And you'll be out of there."

He laughed. "Yeah, you caught me. As soon as they have enough infrastructure and redundancy to handle their own destiny, I'm heading out. I've had enough of shepherding humans, y'know?"

I smiled at him, but his comments worried me.

New Bobs were increasingly voicing an unwillingness to hang around and help humanity. On top of the tendency to use dismissive language, it told me that there was some kind of shift in psychology going on.

Then I admitted to myself that I might be the one out of step. I'd been holed up at Epsilon Eridani for fifty years, with only second-hand exposure to humanity. It was easy for me to have an attitude. Bobs cloned from Riker's tree might just be getting heartily sick of people.

Anyway, there were still enough interested Bobs to keep things rolling. I decided not to worry about it. I could always start my own dynasty if I needed to.

I looked around for Howard, but didn't see him. The moot directory indicated he hadn't shown up today. Now *there* was a case of going too far in the other direction. The man was head over heels over a human. Everyone but Howard could see it. Had Original Bob ever been that naïve? I sighed. Yeah. He had.

Riker was surrounded by a group of Bobs, being grilled on the situation on Earth. The results from 82 Eridani would certainly have caused a stir with the enclaves. I had a TODO to talk to Will about it myself, but I wasn't going to wade into that scrum. It could wait.

Marvin and Luke came over and joined Monty and me.

"Hi, Bill. Sorry to be a pest…"

"S'okay, Marv. I understand. No, still nothing from Bender. Sorry. Unless he decided to pull a Mario and head for the far reaches, I think the greatest likelihood is that something happened to him."

Marvin looked downcast, and Luke nodded and looked away. Those three were from the same cohort, so they were related in a way that was somehow one step closer than mere clonedom. It was now coming up on thirty years since Luke and Bender left Delta Eridani. The chances of an innocent explanation for Bender's silence became smaller every year.

Marvin laced his fingers together and put his forehead to them for a moment. "Victor followed Bender's departure vector. So far, nothing. He thinks Bender may have changed direction at some point. Victor's not willing to backtrack, so we're thinking of mounting an expedition."

My eyebrows rose. "Going after him? Space is pretty big. What do you think your chances are?"

Luke leaned forward, arms encircling his drink. "You know we leave a trail when we fly between systems. The gas is slightly thinner along the flight path of a Heaven vessel where we've scooped it up. It's not much, and you have to be very careful, but even if he changed course mid-flight we should be able to follow his new vector."

"Okay. You know where he was aiming when he left Eden. I guess you just start with that?"

Marvin and Luke nodded in sync.

It would take decades, if not centuries. Then I smiled. Still thinking like an ephemeral. How long it would take was irrelevant. We had forever.

# 53.  Testing

## Hal
## April 2196
## GL 877

I wasn't really what you'd call "happy" to be back. Last time I was here, I had died. Hopefully things would go better this time.

I did a quick status check on my cloud of attendants. I was surrounded by just under a hundred drones and one AMI-driven Heaven decoy vessel.

The decoy obediently matched my actions as I decelerated. The drones scattered to preassigned positions around the periphery of the star system. They would serve as an early-warning system for any comings and goings by the Others. They were designed to give as little evidence of their presence as possible. Low profile, no albedo to speak of, total radio silence, and heavily shielded reactors meant they showed very little footprint to the universe at large. And booby-trapped, of course. If the Others ever got hold of SCUT tech, we would be royally hooped.

The decoy had been constructed with all the improvements suggested by Thor: two layers of depleted uranium alternating with two layers of electrostatic shielding. We'd added redundancies for every major control system, with automatic failovers. It also had multiple independent self-destruct mechanisms and the usual booby-traps.

My new body had some improvements as well. I'd sacrificed buster storage in favor of a larger reactor and SURGE drive. At 15 G capability I could now outrun the Others, assuming that I'd seen their "A" game last time out.

Today's entertainment was in aid of testing our mods against the death asteroid. If Decoy-1 could survive a zapping, we were golden. If it couldn't... well, no one really wanted to ask that question.

I sent the activation order. Decoy-1 broke off from my vector and accelerated towards the inner system.

* * *

The SCUT connection gave me a video window into the chase. The decoy was carefully sticking to 10 G as it ran from the Others' battle-group, or squad, or whatever they called their standard collection of ships. We hadn't tried to be subtle with the sweep through the inner system, and the decoy had, predictably, picked up a tail. It looked as though we were less than an hour away from the big event.

I accepted a ping, and Mario popped into my VR. "I love car chases," he said, grinning at me.

"Especially the ones with big crashes," I replied.

I was forwarding the telemetry to Bill for the archives as well. I hadn't heard from him, but I imagined he was monitoring as time permitted. Mario got comfortable, Jeeves brought coffees, and we sat back to watch the show.

Two minutes later the death asteroid zapped the decoy, just as the decoy had finished a SUDDAR scan of its pursuers. The decoy forwarded a complete set of readings to us, then blew itself up.

Mario and I looked at each other, our eyes wide. I spoke first. "That was, uh, a little early."

"Yeah, looks like Garfield was a bit off on his estimates of the internal capabilities of the death asteroids. He's going to have to rejigger his models."

I checked the received telemetry. "Well, fortunately, we got a good scan just at the end. This should help." I took a close look at the scan of the death asteroid. "Or not. Look at that." I pointed to a section of the scan. "That looks like living area. Why the crap would they need that much living area?"

Mario thought for a moment. "Either they're really really big, or the death asteroid requires a lot of personnel to run, or they really really like each other. Like naked mole-rats or something."

"Huh. Questions and more questions. Well, we've got this much done, anyway. The decoy took a few hit points, but by and large I'd say the shielding was a success."

Mario nodded. "We'll see what Thor and Garfield have to say at the next moot." He raised his cup to me, finished his coffee in a gulp, and popped out.

I turned myself around, pointed the bow at GL 54, and headed home.

## 54.  Stuff is Happening

## Hal
## October, 2197
## En Route to GL 54

I was eighteen months into my journey when I got a message from Bill. At my current tau, any kind of real-time interaction was out of the question. I couldn't frame-jack nearly high enough to overcome the time dilation. So communications tended to wait until the end of a trip, or they came as emails, as in this case.

I grabbed the sheet and read it.

> *Hal;*
>
> *Well, the fecal matter seems to have struck the atmospheric propulsor. A squad of Others vessels was detected leaving GL 877, heading for GL 54. To be fair, scouting by other Bobs indicates that other, closer systems have already been stripped, so this isn't necessarily anything more than a normal scavenging mission. Just the same, Mario has decided to hit the road, along with every piece of equipment he has.*
>
> *We're going to leave a couple of drones behind for observation, and use one to try communicating with the Others. If they react by pointing one of the death asteroids at us, we'll blow up the drone.*

*Just thought you should know. It looks like we're heading for a formal First Contact. You may want to re-route.*
  *Bill*

Oh, fudge. May you live in interesting times. Mm, hmm.

## 55.  Contact

**Bill**
**October 2204**
**GL 54**

Mario was now in mid-trip, fleeing GL 54 for Zeta Tucanae, so it was up to me to handle the introductions when the Others arrived. I couldn't help but feel a certain level of nervousness. These were the beings that had blown up Bashful and Hal. There were a lot of ways this could go down, but I didn't think *friendly* was in the expected range.

Before he left, Mario did a little preparatory construction. He had four stealth drones set up for observation, and a non-stealth drone for making contact. With SCUT communications, I could easily control them from here in Epsilon Eridani.

The contact drone made me chuckle. The hull was shiny, the reactor leaked neutrons like a sieve, and in the radio spectrum the drone was as noisy as an unshielded electric motor. I thought he might have overdone the hee-yuk, but it was certainly a master-piece. It also had an antenna dish for tight-beaming radio telemetry to a non-existent mother-ship, which I thought was a great touch. We *wanted* the Others to underestimate us, right up to the moment we would deliver the knock-out punch.

The Others' convoy was impressive. Ten death asteroids, a

couple hundred small attendants, and twenty huge cylindrical hulks that I assumed would be cargo ships. These last units were upwards of ten kilometers in length and a kilometer in diameter. I tried to estimate the tonnage of metals that they could transport and my mind boggled at the results.

Interestingly, though, based on a rough calculation, the total cargo capacity was within an order of magnitude of what they'd need to strip this system. Either they had previously scouted the system, or they had some way to get a good estimate of available resources beforehand. Or maybe they just lucked out. They might make multiple trips if a system had enough resources to justify it.

Well, that was something for the future. I activated the communications drone, placed it right in the path of the incoming armada, and squirted a radio signal at them. For a first attempt, it was the most basic of communications: the first ten prime numbers, represented as a series of blips. Then I waited for a response. I had listed a number of possibilities while waiting for them to arrive. It might be the next ten primes, or it might be my message relayed back to me in reverse, or it might be another mathematical series. Or it might be a blast of cosmic rays.

I was *not* expecting an audio message, in Mandarin.

Fortunately I had a translation routine on file, such things having been fairly standard issue in the twenty-second century.

**We see you, food. Your time is not yet. Move aside.**

"Well, blow me down. Food, am I?" I was so flummoxed that it took me almost a half-second to come up with a response. It occurred to me during that time that I shouldn't react too quickly. If they thought I was biological, so much the better.

"We are not attempting to block you. This unit is obviously too small for that. We are trying to communicate."

**To what purpose? To beg for mercy? An interesting idea, mercy. We learned it from the cybernetic unit that we captured. We have no such concept.**

"Do you have a concept of exchange of information?"

**If it benefits us.**

Well, that was something, anyway. Based on Hal's experience, I had a couple of minutes before they were close enough to zap the drone. Assuming they were going to do so, which I figured was a pretty safe bet.

"Why are you stripping systems?"

*For resources and food. Is this not obvious?*

"Yes, but why not just colonize the star systems?"

*Another concept that we learned from the captured unit. Colonization requires splitting the hive. Splitting the hive means a new Prime. A new Prime and another hive means war. This does not benefit us. Better to simply collect resources so that the hive can grow.*

Oooookaaaaaay. A picture was forming—something insect-like. Prime was probably some equivalent to a queen.

I noted that they were coming up past the position of one of the stealth drones. These units were equipped with the new four-light-hour ultra-low-power SUDDAR units. I hoped to get a scan without alerting them.

"Can Primes not cooperate?"

*Sub-Primes can be controlled, but not over interstellar distances. We know you are using this dialog to probe for information. This amuses us. The scurrying of food as it evades the inevitable end is perhaps for us what you mean by "art."*

Okay, that was just sick.

"We seek information. Sometimes even if there is no benefit."

*That makes no sense.*

"The beings at Zeta Tucanae. You obliterated them."

*They were food. And they would have tried to prevent the harvesting.*

"Is there no way we can co-exist? The universe is a large place."

*That also makes no sense. You are food. It is not the purpose of food to co-exist.*

*We will, in time, make our way to your Sol and your Epsilon Eridani. We have seen your radio beacons. Food always thus announces itself.*

Oh, wow. Fermi paradox, resolved.

I checked my system status and noted that my drone was probably thirty seconds away from getting zapped. I decided to try and time the SUDDAR scan to coincide with that, in hopes that the zap might either command all their attention, or blind their systems for a few moments.

"You are building what we would call a Dyson Sphere. Is this for your population?"

*Yes. The construct will allow up to five hundred million times the livable area. We will not run out of space within the lifetime of the Prime.*

"And afterwards?"

*Irrelevant. That is the concern of the next Prime.*

"Isn't overpopulation a concern? Overcrowding?"

*There can never be too many of us. There can only be not enough food.*

At that moment, the stealth drone detected the outgoing zap. The Others' spokesman hadn't even bothered with a throwaway line or anything. I was absurdly irritated. You'd think I'd deserve at least "Hasta la vista."

Per instructions, the stealth drone did a quick series of snapshot scans of the Others' vessels.

Then the zap arrived, and the communications drone exploded on cue. I noted, from the point of view of the stealth drone, that a squad of Others immediately took off in the direction that the communication drone's directional antenna had been transmitting. Served them right. Let 'em waste time casting around.

I sat back and stared into space. This was big. This was going to need a moot for sure.

## 56.  Descendants

## Bob
## January 2183
## Delta Eridani

Buster grunted as he released the arrow. It flew dead true and buried itself in the target. Archimedes whooped from the sidelines, and Buster's little brother and sister yelled insults. Another universality, apparently.

Buster turned to his opponent, Arnold's son, and waggled his ears. Donald looked distinctly uncomfortable, but wasn't going to back down in front of the entire *hexghi*.

Donald released the arrow. It hit the edge of the target. Not a kill shot, but certainly crippling, if it had hit a live target. Arnold shrugged and yelled something supportive.

I took a moment to smile at the number of new faces that had grown up over the last few years. Child mortality had dropped significantly with the reduction in the gorilloid threat, and the Deltan population was up to over eleven hundred.

Archimedes' family had grown as well. Three children, and a fourth on the way. I was finally beginning to get an idea of the lifespan of the Deltans. Moses had died a few years ago, at somewhere between sixty and seventy Earth-years old. About the same or maybe even a little better than humans, given the environment.

It was a bittersweet time for me. The council had never relented in their decision to banish me. Archimedes brought it up a couple of times, but was shut down hard. His position as the tribe's premiere tool maker protected him to a certain extent, but I finally told him to drop it. I didn't want any backlash against his family.

Stories of *The Bawbe* still abounded, but I noticed that they were now being embellished. In particular, my reputation seemed to be suffering. The tone sounded a little more like Loki or Lucifer, these days. Would I end up as the devil in some far-future religious myth?

I sighed. The risks of godhood, I guess.

I sent a quick text to ask Marvin if he'd be joining today's scrub game, and got an affirmative.

## 57.   Moot

**Bill**
**October 2204**
**Epsilon Eridani**

I held the air-horn over my head and pressed the button twice. And received the usual round of boos. Gotta love tradition.

The catcalls were short-lived, though, more of a formality. The word had gotten out, and the Bobs were all business today. Even the pre-meeting session had been quiet, with a growling undertone.

"First, before we get to the main event, I'd like to introduce our newest long-range champion..." I gestured to a nearby Bob. "Bruce is from Calvin and Goku's first cohort. He is calling in from 11 Leonis Minoris, and holds the record at thirty-seven light years from Earth. Sorry, Mario."

The crowd applauded Bruce, and several people came over to talk to him. When the chatter had died down, I held the air-horn up for a moment and waited for quiet.

"I guess you've all heard by now, but I'll summarize just to make sure we haven't missed anything. We have communicated with the Others. They appear to have captured the Chinese probe at some point, and stripped its data. The good news is that they speak Mandarin, so communications were pretty straightforward.

The bad news is they know where Earth is. And thanks to my ham-handed broadcasts to every star system in sight, they know about Epsilon Eridani as well."

I waved off the yelled comments. "No, they won't get the SCUT plans. The broadcasts were encrypted, as is everything we do; and the Chinese probe wouldn't know anything about the transmission or file formats, so they wouldn't be able to separate out encrypted data from transport envelope."

I waited for any objections, then continued, "The other piece of good news is they are sufficiently arrogant that they don't feel the need to come over and squash us forthwith. Their attitude seems to be that they'll get to us when they get to us."

This produced low growls from the audience, and I grinned. "Now, we got some good scans of the armada, and we're able to observe their operations as they strip GL 54. I'm going to call up Garfield to give us a rundown in a minute. But first I want to thank Hal for successfully testing the new Heaven design against the death asteroids. At least in that area, we are ahead of the game."

There were cheers from the audience, and the usual first verse of "Bicycle Built for Two." It never got old. Hal grinned to the crowd, waved, and took a bow.

Garfield walked up onto the podium and glared at me. I laughed, held up the horn, and gave a blast.

"Okay," Garfield yelled over the boos, "I have a bit of egg on my face. My guesstimates of the power capabilities and weaponry of the death asteroid were a little off, because the Others are actually more inventive than I thought. I just hope they don't have more surprises."

Garfield waited for silence, and he got it. Every Bob in the room was now completely focused on his words.

"Power beaming via SUDDAR. It's not just for running those little ant-things they use for harvesting. It's also for charging death asteroids remotely. The death asteroids *are* capable of charging themselves without help, but it looks like it would take about a day on their own. So they have huge reactors in the cargo carriers which, in combination with the SUDDAR beaming, can run ants, drones, mining carriers, or charge up death asteroids."

"Why?" yelled someone from the crowd. "Seems unnecessarily complicated."

Garfield nodded in the general direction of the voice. "I think it's dictated by their biology. It's pretty obvious from Bill's conversation with them that they're a hive organism. A large portion of the interior of the death asteroids is living space. Far too much, in my opinion, to be justifiable just based on personnel requirements. Every vehicle they have is either automated or has the same large living space. I think they *need* to live in large groups. They may get some version of agoraphobia or something if there aren't enough of their brethren around."

"Well, it would explain their decision to build the Dyson Sphere." Hal said from the front of the audience.

"That and their comment about going to war with any splinter group," I added. "That could be phenotypical behavior as well. These beings seem to be very much driven by their biology. It may be that their reference to all other life as 'food' is more of the same. Something that drives their actions at such an instinctual level can be taken advantage of, if we can figure out how. That's one of the tasks I want you guys to take out of this meeting."

There were silent nods throughout the room. And a palpable aura of anticipation. I'd tried to keep this quiet, but somehow word had gotten out.

"And now, the moment you've all been waiting for." I grinned at the crowd. "We got images of the Others from the scans. The detail isn't great, of course. The drone was too—"

"Less talk, more show!"

I snapped my mouth shut. So much for building the drama. With a wave, I brought up the composite 3D image that we'd put together.

There were oohs and aahs from the crowd. The Other was hard to describe, simply because it was hard to get a perspective on it. The scale superimposed on the image indicated that it was about four feet tall, although it didn't really stand straight. Color shaded between an oily green-violet sheen through gray, to black.

I looked at the perplexed faces in the crowd. I understand that look. I'd worn it recently. But I'd been examining all the images since we separated them from the scans, so I had somewhat of a head start on figuring it out.

"Okay, think of the posture of a gorilla. Not quite a quadruped, but not quite upright. These things that look kind of like meaty wings are the front, er, limbs. The back limbs are more like a split tail, except that there's also a tail. Visualize a sea lion's back end with a tail tacked on. The front limbs have these big appendages that look like fat fingers, but I don't think they're for manipulating. They have suckers on them, so I think they're more for gripping their prey. The creature has what I'd have to describe as feeding fingers that fold out from here..." I pointed to the front of the thing, "... and appear to be dexterous enough to act as manipulators. They also direct food into the maw..." I switched to another image which showed the thing with its front split open in a vertical slash. "... which doesn't masticate so much as grind and strip the meal. I think it would be particularly slow and painful to be eaten by these things."

I switched images again and pointed to the front. "The head does appear to have the primary sensory apparatus, although what looks like the brain is more centrally located, here." I pointed to a spot high on the main trunk. "Vision is not great. It seems to be a large number of small eyes spaced around the dome of the head. You have to wonder why a predator would need 360-degree vision."

I switched back to the first picture. "The scan indicated they were packed into the living area with a density similar to us in this room. Except that it was like that *everywhere*. No empty rooms. No private quarters. They are probably *always* packed in like sardines."

I gestured dramatically. "Ladies, er, gentlemen, I give you— the Others."

There was dead silence for a few milliseconds, then someone said, "Should we clap?"

Everyone in the room broke up in laughter, and the tension dissolved. If I ever found out who the speaker was, I'd have to buy him a beer.

I left the image up, and closed the meeting. People broke into groups to discuss the presentation. Mario raised his chin in my direction, and I acknowledged the implied invitation with a wave.

Mario grimaced. "I had a theory that the presence of the death asteroids was proof that they don't scout a system. Otherwise they'd have known they didn't need them at GL 54."

"Mm, but if they're a communal organism, then the death asteroids are their portable community."

Mario gave me a rueful smile. "Yep. Fail."

"So how is the harvest going?"

He rolled his eyes and pulled up some images. "Thankfully there was nothing in GL 54 to get attached to, so this is nothing more than a strategic retreat to me." Pointing to one image. "The carriers go down where presumably they've detected metal. They disgorge ants, who dig down to the ore and bring it up. It's hard to tell from a distance, but based on activity, I think they use the ore to build more ants which they use to get more ore, which they use to build more ants... Eventually they reach a break-even point of some kind where the ants just haul material up. Then they harvest the excess ants and take off."

"They'd have printers specialized for making ants, then." I stroked my chin in thought. "It would have to be a cheap, quick process."

"At the current rate, I estimate they'll have the system cleaned out in a year. It's exponential behavior. They never stop, never rest." Mario rubbed his eyes. "And those cargo ships are so big, I don't think we could even make them *notice* us, let alone damage them significantly. It would be like mosquitos trying to take on tanks."

"Well, we have to come up with something before they decide Earth is next."

Mario shook his head. "There are a lot of systems closer to them than Earth. We have lots of time."

"You're *assuming* that they always do things that way. You're *assuming* that they won't suddenly decide to drive a little extra distance for some ready-made refined material." I glared at him, willing him to get the point. "I think we have to assume we *don't* have a lot of time. If we're ready early, no biggie. If we're ready late, biggie."

"Damn."

# 58. News

## Howard
## July 2198
## Interstellar Space

I was less than a third of the way to my destination when I received an email from Dexter. In a moment of weakness, I'd asked him to let me know any news about the Brodeurs.

Dexter included a bunch of other stuff in the email as well. Maybe he wanted to distract me; maybe he wanted it to seem like the message wasn't all about Bridget. Don't know, but I appreciated the effort.

In any case, it looked like things were going well, in general. Butterworth had retired—well-deserved, in my opinion. The population of the system was up around a hundred thousand people now. Human-crewed spaceships were becoming common-place, and the donuts made up an increasingly minor part of the food supply chain. Dexter apparently now had some of that formerly mythical free time, and was putting together some of Bill's asteroid movers.

New Jerusalem was now a full-fledged democracy. Seemed some incriminating videos had gotten out and Cranston had to step down. In the resulting mess, the citizenry had decided to separate Church and State once again.

I laughed as I read the details. No doubt Cranston had his suspicions, but there was no way to trace anything back to Will or myself. Speaking of, I fired off an email to Will, in case he had more juicy info.

Things were going well. If it weren't for the Others, humanity would be in a good place.

And that was it for the delaying tactics. With a sigh, I went on to the part about the Brodeurs.

Okay, not terrible. They had a son. They'd named him Howard.

I smiled, as the message became suddenly blurry. I would have to send a short thank-you note.

## 59.   Another One

**Bill**
**April 2205**
**Epsilon Eridani**

I leaned back in my chair, looked straight up, and used some words that I normally don't like to use.

Surveillance drones around GL 877 had reported that the Others had just launched another expedition. From the initial vector, it looked like they were heading for NN 4285. That wasn't too bad—it was a small M star, too dim for any chance of usable planets.

No, I corrected myself: under no circumstances should this be considered acceptable. If the Others had stuck to uninhabited systems, well, it was a big galaxy. But that wasn't their behavior. If they didn't happen to kill off a planet, it was only because there was nothing to kill off, not because of some moral reluctance. Lack of opportunity isn't the same as self-restraint. They were evil. End of story.

And if distance was an indicator, both Gamma and Delta Pavonis would probably be next, and they *were* good candidates. I checked the archives, just on the off chance. No such luck. No one had visited those systems yet, although a couple of Bobs were heading for them as part of Mario's scouting.

I got up and started pacing around my office. Then I pinged Mario, and he popped over.

"What's up?"

"Mario, the Others just moved again. This time heading for NN 4285."

"Yeah, I saw that. Not a prime system."

"Still, we have to figure out how to nip this in the bud. I'm concerned about the Pavonis candidates. Do you have an ETA for them?"

"Gamma and Delta? Claude and Jacques are heading for those. Claude will be at Gamma in about a month, and Jacques at Delta in twenty-two months or so."

"Dammit. The closest significant presence we've got is Sol, and we can't divert them from building colony ships."

"Epsilon Indi?"

"No, Epsilon Indi is too far away as well, although closer than Sol. But resources are poor, and colonists to KKP will be too busy setting up to help."

Mario nodded. He looked down at his toes for a few milliseconds, then turned and glared at me. "What is it with the Pavonis systems that's giving you a pickle up your butt, anyway?"

I sighed and stopped pacing. I favored Mario with a self-conscious smile. "Call it a premonition. Call it superstition. Call it utter faith in the power of Murphy. Based strictly on distance, those two are among the next likely targets. Based on the stars' types, they're good habitable-planet candidates. Based on our experience so far, most good systems with a planet in the right place have life. Not intelligence, necessarily, but life." I shrugged, letting Mario make the connection.

He was silent for a few moments, thinking. "On the other hand, they've just sent out an expedition to NN 4285, and the GL 54 expedition hasn't made it back to their home system. How many armadas to you suppose they have?"

"Fair point. They don't seem to have any real sense of urgency. I wonder how long a Prime lives."

"So look, Bill, why don't you build a group here and send it to the area?"

I shook my head. "Too far. I'll do it if there's no other way. We need to get an inventory of what Bobs are in what systems, so we can figure out what response is possible."

Mario gave me a nod and popped out.

I pinged Claude. His return indicated he was down to a low tau, about 0.03. That wouldn't affect communications at all, and was hardly worth adjusting frame rates for. He was open for company, so I popped in.

"Hey, Bill."

"Claude." I looked around at his VR. Not particularly anything. Tropical beach, cabana, deck chair. Could be Mexico, Hawaii, or some made-up location. I didn't have any memories of a vacation like this, so I assumed the last option.

Claude was looking at me with slightly wide eyes. He was a generation removed from me, and it was funny how the Bobiverse was becoming hierarchical like that.

I materialized a deck chair of my own at sat down. "Been following the Others, Claude?"

"Yeah, I was at the moot. And I heard about NN 4285."

"Okay, so here's the thing. With the Others taking out GL 54, there's no Bob-controlled system anywhere close to you. When you get to Gamma Pavonis, you have to assume you only have a couple of decades at most before the Others come visiting. You're going to have to mobilize for war, essentially."

Claude frowned. "A lot of assumptions in there."

"Not as many as you'd think, and the assumptions are high probability."

Claude sighed and resettled himself in his chair to face me squarely.

"Look, Bill. I get the whole thing about the Others, and they're evil, blah blah. But why here, and why now? Why this particular line in the sand?"

"I'll grant you there's nothing unique about Gamma Pavonis to the limit of our current knowledge. But we have to start somewhere. Maybe we won't be ready for them in time. Maybe they'll swoop down on you in a decade and you'll have to flee like Mario did. But at some point, we have to try. Why not here, and why not now?"

Claude gave me a wry smile. "Because here and now puts me in the crosshairs, thank you very much."

I laughed. "Well, that's why God invented backups."

\* \* \*

I popped back to my own VR, after extracting a promise from Claude that he'd get the system report on Gamma Pavonis to me on a priority basis. I checked Jacque's tau, but he was still way up there. A conversation would take days, even if he frame-jacked.

I quickly went down my list of known manufacturing centers. There weren't a lot. Most Bobs didn't bother in most systems, other than building a space station. I remembered Bart, who was the last Bob that I'd talked to in Alpha Centauri.

I sent a quick ping to him, but it looked like he was between systems. Bart's acknowledgement indicated a ridiculous tau. I'd be a few days even waiting for a response, never mind a conversation.

I queried the Alpha Centauri space station directly. The status report appeared in front of me in a window. Garfield came around and looked over my shoulder.

"No one there right now," he said. "Looks like the last group left it uninhabited."

"Well, we can't force anyone to stay and play caretaker. It's a free galaxy." I ran a hand through my hair, then stopped and looked at my hand. That was Riker's tic. I didn't need to start that. "It looks like a full-power AMI, though. If I can get it to build a replicant matrix, I can load my backup and the new me can bootstrap up from there."

"You're going to load a backup across interstellar distances, with no Bob overseeing? Wow, dude."

I shrugged. "No difference in principle. I'll checksum the hell out of it before approving it for load." I thought for another millisecond, then nodded. "I don't have a choice, anyway. We can't afford to ignore any potential source of Bobs. I'm afraid, like it or not, we're going to war."

# 60.  Arrival

## Claude
## May 2205
## Gamma Pavonis

Gamma Pavonis was an F8V class of star, which made it slightly bigger and barely hotter than Sol. The effect was a system with a comfort zone slightly farther out, but a sun that would look virtually indistinguishable from ours.

I paradoxically found myself hoping that I wouldn't find anything in the comfort zone. The whole dialog with Bill had left me freaked out and ambivalent about what I might find. I would actually feel better if there was nothing in this system worth defending.

Well, you have to know that Murphy is listening for just exactly that kind of wish, so he can give you the shaft.

The planet sat at just over a hundred million miles out. A gorgeous, shining, blue and green marble with bands and swirls of white, orbited by one larger moon and three smaller ones. Damn.

I went immediately into orbit to determine if it included intelligent life. That would be a real kick in the pants. Fortunately, the planet failed—or passed, depending on attitude—the first, obvious tests. There was no radio traffic, no web of exhaust trails in the atmosphere, no satellites, and no sprinkle of lights on the night side.

That still left pre-industrial civilization, of course, but that would require a closer look. I sent a quick email off to Bill with results so far, then deployed the exploration drones. Mario had decided that the latest-version Heaven vessels would come with enough on-board assets so that we could investigate a system quickly. This meant mining and manufacturing operations could wait for later.

The drones took up polar orbits for a couple of passes, then swooped into atmosphere to check out interesting items.

I spent five days on observation and exploration. I didn't want to screw this up. But finally, I felt confident enough to report my findings.

No intelligence. Thank God. But the ecosystem was as rich and varied as anything in Earth's history. This was a planet with everything stacked in its favor. The right size, the right distance from a sun with good solar output but relatively low UV, good-sized moons, plate tectonics active enough to ensure consistent surface recycling—the list went on and on. This was an ideal colony target, except for the part where it was on the Others' front porch.

Now I would have to move to phase 2. This system actually had a relatively low metallicity, at least according to the star's spectral lines. Perhaps that was why the Others had rejected it in favor of the slightly more distant NN 4285. But the next star out, GL 902, was over two light-years farther than this one. I doubted the Others would bypass it again.

Well, low metallicity was a relative term. I was sure I'd still find more than enough resources for my purposes, even if it took a bit of work to find.

There was a ping from Bill, then he popped in.

"Hey Claude. I've been looking over your report. Sounds like a great planet."

"And that's the problem. It is a great planet. Great system. And if you're right, due to be 'harvested' sometime in the next, what, hundred years?"

Bill looked down for a moment. "Mario has been getting reports back from Bobs hitting surrounding systems. Combined with his own observations in Zeta Tucanae and Beta Hydri, we're able to make a rough estimate of a system every ten to twenty years."

"So they've only been at this maybe a hundred years?"

"We don't know how long they were working only within their system. It might have taken them a hundred years to get started. Maybe the first out-system harvest taught them a lot. Anyway, the point is, there are a lot of unknowns before they started regularly harvesting."

Bill had popped up a star chart while he was talking, the various star systems flashing a tooltip as he mentioned them.

"Jacques will be arriving at Delta Pavonis in eighteen months. The positions of Delta Pavonis and GL 877 are about the same distance from you, so if we see the Others head your way, anything he launches from Delta will arrive here at the same time. So hopefully you'll have reinforcements."

I nodded. That was something, anyway.

## 61.  Starting Over

**Oliver**
**September 2205**
**Alpha Centauri**

*HIC71683-14. Damn. I'm not Bill anymore. Now I need a new name.*

This had happened to me once before, as one of Bob-1's first cohort, in Epsilon Eridani. Now I was a noob again, this time in Alpha Centauri.

I popped into Bill's VR. "I hate you."

Bill grinned at me. "Naw, you know the rules. New name, dude. ASAP."

"Oliver. In keeping with the Bloom County theme."

Bill nodded his approval. Oliver was a fun character and we'd liked him.

"One advantage of this arrangement, I guess, is that I know the whole plan already."

Bill laughed and nodded. "Saves time."

I stood up. "So, I'll get to it. I may set up in competition with you, though. Wanna bet I get FTL first?"

"I'd be overjoyed if you did, Oliver. Everyone wins."

I waved to Bill, and popped back home.

Both Alpha Centauri A and B had reasonable resource levels. Bart and crew had concentrated their efforts in A, but I needed to get things rolling quickly. It would be six months until my vessel was ready. At that point, I would start the autofactory in Alpha Centauri A to building Bobs on a crash basis, while I would fly over to Alpha Centauri B with another autofactory and set up there as well. At the top acceleration of a Version 4 vessel, it was less than a four-day trip.

Meanwhile, I would have to consider possible weapons against the Others. Busters could pass through the cargo ships or death asteroids multiple times and do little or no detectable damage. Nukes were effective, and the expedition to 82 Eridani had yielded some good information. We didn't have time to figure out fission weapons from scratch. I regretted, a little, not having worked on that before. But only a little.

Plasma spikes, like busters, were simply too small. Not effective against the mega monster ships we would be going up against.

I needed either a large mass, a large explosion, or a lot of energy. Heat energy, electrical energy, gravitational, or momentum. Hmm, relativistic velocities. How fast could I accelerate things?

Hands behind my back, muttering in thought, I retired to my new mad-science lab.

* * *

I really had no idea what size of force I was going to need. However, there was very little downside to overdoing it, and a lot of downside to the converse. With that thought in mind, I decided to just go for everything I could manage.

Taking a lesson from Bob-1's experience, I decided I would start by doubling my production capability. Accordingly, my first production run consisted entirely of new printers. I then assigned a couple of printers to do nothing but produce more printers, while the rest started working on drones. I was going to invest some up-front time in ramping up my capacity, which would hopefully pay off later.

It took almost two years before I was ready to start building actual Bobs. The speed at which a printer could produce an item was dependent partly on the size of the item, but also very much on the level of detail required. 3D printers delivered individual atoms using a number of tuned carbon nanotubes, each sized for specific elements. Building something like itself required the maximum level of detail and precision, as you had to place individual carbon atoms, one after another, with zero defects. This made 3D printers one of the most complex items that a 3D printer could be asked to build. Only something biological would be harder.

Anyway, finally, I was producing Bobs. After much discussion, Bill and I came up with a blueprint for a Version 5 Heaven vessel— a virtual dreadnaught compared to the original Heaven-1. I felt a little intimidated just looking at the plans.

Bill was still working on the SUDDAR cloaking from the 82 Eridani mission, but we knew enough about it to build around the requirement for now. I also put together a design for a stealth buster, very similar in overall structure to Medeiros' stealth fission bombs.

Howard had managed to extract H-bomb blueprints from Butterworth. I guess the colonel considered the Others to be enough of a threat to override military secrecy. Unbelievable that they were still even thinking in those terms, with 99.9% of the human race gone.

Three years after waking up at Alpha Centauri, I had my first cohort of battle cruisers.

# 62.  Departure

## Mulder
## November 2201
## Departure

I put my hands behind my head and stretched as I reviewed the report that I would be sending to Bill and Riker. This would be my final report from Poseidon. Tomorrow, Monty would start the return trip to Earth, empty except for some biological samples. And I would point my bow and head for a new system, leaving Marcus as Bob-in-residence here.

I pinged Monty and Marcus and invited them over. They responded immediately.

"Hey, Mulder. I'm going to miss you guys," Marcus said, looking at each of us.

"Yeah, I know," Monty replied. "I wish I could keep it down below .75 C, but we can't afford the extra transit time for a colony ship."

Marcus looked a little down, so I gestured to my report to change the subject. "Things are looking good. Three mat colonies in full operation, and two floating cities getting close to complete."

Marcus nodded. "And as of today, it's three months since the last kraken attack."

"Apparently they *can* be taught."

Marcus grinned and invoked a Coke. "And then there's this." He popped up an image.

"What the ffff…" I squinted at the graphic. "Is that actually…"

"Aerial city, as in floating in the air. Yep." He waved a hand. "Well, okay, it's a small proof-of-concept prototype, but still… I've been putting this thing together for a while. Triple redundancy, all kinds of failsafes. Theoretically we should be able to lift something as big as your floating cities and keep it in the air indefinitely."

"Unbelievable," Monty said. "When will it be ready to test?"

Marcus grimaced. "Sorry, buddy. Not for another six months. You won't be able to find out the results until you get back to Earth."

"Well, that sucks. On the other hand, by the time I'm back online, the thing might be ready for prime time. This could get interesting."

I nodded, not saying anything. This was a good argument for staying below .75, just to be able to follow the project. If this crazy idea of Marcus's actually worked, it would change the game significantly.

\* \* \*

Poseidon receded rapidly in the rear view as I accelerated out of the system. The goodbyes from Chief Draper and the friends that I'd made over the years stung more than I'd expected. It was very possible that some of those people would be dead by the time my tau dropped at the other end. Making friends with humans just didn't seem like a good idea, on balance.

Riker pinged me and I invited him in.

"Hey, Mulder. Sorry I couldn't get back to you before. It's been that kind of millennium." Will grinned at me.

"Especially the last week or so, I guess," I replied, smiling back. I summoned Jeeves and he arrived with a coffee for Will.

"So what's the status back at Sol?" I asked him.

"We have fourteen colony ships in active service now," he replied. "Colonies at or soon to be at Vulcan, Poseidon, Epsilon Indi, and 82 Eridani. Things are looking up."

"Or would be, if not for the Others."

Will sighed. "Yeah, I know. 82 Eridani and Epsilon Indi, in

particular, are close enough to be potentially in danger. We're working on it."

Yep. Just when you start to get ahead in the rat race, the universe delivers bigger rats.

# 63.  The Pav

## Jacques
## February 2207
## Delta Pavonis

I looked down from orbit at the sprinkles of light decorating the dark side of Delta Pavonis 4, realizing that there was a good chance these beings would be dead soon.

The, uh… well, *Deltans* was taken. Pavonians? No, that sucked. *Pav* for now, I guess. The Pav appeared to be well into their industrial age, probably equivalent to the Victorian era on Earth. They were pumping smoke into the atmosphere at a prodigious rate, setting the earliest stages for global warming. I sincerely hoped that in the fullness of time, they'd have the opportunity to get all bent out of shape about environmentalism.

I finished my initial survey, packaged up the results, and fired it off to Bill.

It took about ten minutes before I got a ping, and Bill appeared in my VR.

"Well, this sucks."

I nodded. "Remember the days when we thought finding intelligence would be a *good* thing?" I leaned forward and put my head in my hands. "And I could end up being witness to the massacre of an entire species."

Bill materialized an Adirondack chair—a little anachronistic in my VR, but whatever—and sat down. He sat in silence for a few milliseconds before replying. "Jacques, it's very likely that Gamma will get hit first. That's a full planetary ecology, but at least Claude hasn't found any sentient life. And if the Others head that way, you'll be able to help. Meanwhile, you need to start working the system and concentrate on building a bunch of Oliver's dread-naughts."

I looked at him and shook my head. "No. Well, yes, but also no. I'll build dreadnaughts, and I'll be ready to help Claude, but I'm also going to try to build a couple of colony ships, using Riker's design. With the experience he's gained, I should be able to complete them in half the time. If the Others come a'knocking, I want to get some Pav off-planet. I'm not going to sit by while an entire race gets blown away."

Bill stared at me, frowning, for several milliseconds. Then a smile slowly formed. "I can't decide if you're brilliant or a moron. I'll think about it. It's definitely a noble idea, Jacques, but maybe not doable. I think we're due for a moot. Maybe we should run it through the group consciousness."

I shrugged. The group could talk all they wanted. I knew what I had to do. Bill nodded to me and vanished.

* * *

Regardless of whether I went with Bill's plan or mine, the first step was the same. Find resources, build autofactory. This system was metal-heavy, so I didn't anticipate any kind of problem.

I turned to Guppy, who was waiting at parade rest, as usual. Funny, even several generations and versions away from Heaven-1, Guppy really hadn't changed. Same fish-headed, deadpan, taciturn sidekick. But he got the job done.

"Guppy, we need autofactories, and soon. Send out everything we have to look for locations. Top priority, and don't be subtle."

Guppy nodded and went into command fugue. The ship shuddered as a cloud of scouts and drones took off in all directions. I was glad we were past the days when I'd have to personally fly the system with SUDDAR ranging in all directions. The improvements to SUDDAR and to the AMIs meant that even that part of the process could be delegated.

The order hadn't included the planetary exploration scouts, as those would be useless for that task. And they were already planetside, anyway. I began to draw out a plan for concerted and organized accrual of information about the Pav.

* * *

The Pav looked for all the world like giant meerkats. They stood six feet tall or so when upright. They could walk bipedally, but for any kind of distance, they went down on all fours. I was having a little trouble getting used to the sight. Apparently, I'm a bipedalism bigot. Who knew?

The Pav wore clothing, but seemingly less for protection or modesty than for decoration and pockets, except in very cold climates. They were organized into countries or states, and seemed to use forms of government very similar to what humanity had come up with. Even their societies looked familiar. About the only real difference was the almost complete absence of monogamy. Pav seemed to organize into families of up to eight adults, generally evenly divided between genders. This created a somewhat different standard design for residences, but otherwise didn't seem to have a large effect on society as a whole.

I picked one of the countries that resembled early America, selected one of the larger cities, and settled in for some dedicated research.

The absence of electronic media made for a bit of an inconvenience. However, I did find several bookstores. I managed to sneak in a couple of roamers, late in the evening. They took up positions in the shadows of the rafters and waited for closing time.

Then they started going through books. There wasn't anything like a children's section, but there were books for beginning readers, with illustrated alphabets. It took two nights to go through the entire contents of the stores.

Because a significant portion of the population was still illiterate, there were clubs set up where a Pav would read aloud from a book, while patrons ate or drank. Seemed like a very civilized idea to me. I stationed drones in the shadows of every reading club I could find, and made a point of scanning the books that were read at my earliest opportunity.

Within a month, I had a working vocabulary of the language of this country. The inhabitants, who called themselves *Zjentfen*, spoke a language that they called *Tinozj*.

Meanwhile, the mining scouts found more than enough resources to get going. As expected, this was a rich system. As with many star systems, an asteroid belt sat to the inside of the first Jovian, and the pickings were beyond easy. I set the printers to producing more printers first. I think we'd all learned a lesson from Bob—early reproduction of printers paid off in the long term.

I would wait for the Bob-moot, and hope that they'd have good suggestions for manufacturing allocations. But if their suggestions didn't include colony ships to get some Pav off-planet, well, they could go jump.

# 64. Moot

## Bill
## March 2207
## Epsilon Eridani

The airhorn's blast brought the usual expressions of appreciation. I couldn't bring myself to grin at the antics, though. This was going to be a tough meeting. The looks on everyone's faces showed that they understood this.

"Okay, guys. Let's summarize. The Others have kicked Mario out of GL 54 and they're busily stripping the resources. They've launched another expedition heading for NN 4285. I've expressed concern that Gamma and Delta Pavonis are going to be next. And oh, look, there's a habitable planet in one system and a civilization in the other."

I looked at the sea of faces. Everyone was totally focused on my words. "Oliver in Alpha Centauri has come up with a latest and greatest battle-wagon design. He's too far away to help Jacques and Claude, though, unless the Others hold off a lot longer than I really expect. Jacques is prepared to send reinforcements for Claude if it comes to that."

"Or the other way around, if necessary."

I looked for the owner of that comment. It was Jacques. I raised my eyebrow at him in an invitation to continue.

"Delta's farther away from GL 877, so from that point of view, Gamma is a more likely target. Except that Delta has *way* higher metallicity, as can be seen plainly in the spectral lines. Maybe the Others will skip the closer system for the better system. They already bypassed Gamma once."

I closed my eyes for a moment. An undercurrent of muttering passed through the room.

"It's a point, Jacques. We won't know until they move. We have full coverage around GL 877 now, so we can see *any* departures." I motioned to Garfield, who was standing to one side of the podium. "Garfield will give us a rundown on weapons capability."

Garfield stepped forward and gave an aborted wave to the crowd. He wasn't in the mood, either.

"We have fission bombs, thanks to Medeiros. We have fusion bombs, or at least the plans, thanks to the USE and Colonel Butterworth. We've been able to size up the plasma spikes somewhat, but there's a practical limit to the size of the magnetic containment. We've probably reached that. It's enough for the smaller Others' vessels, but not enough to seriously harm the death asteroids or cargo vessels."

Garfield popped up a diagram. "We've got the basic concepts of the cloaking figured out, but we weren't able to salvage enough hardware to see how the Brazilians were actually doing it. Which means we're starting from scratch. This appears to have been another one of those accidental discoveries, so it's not just a matter of hours thrown at the problem. We're going to need some breakthroughs."

Someone at the front commented, "Without the cloaking, we can't get the bombs close enough to be effective. They'll just zap them or shoot them down. I think it's safe to assume the Others have things like missiles as well."

"We can get the items close enough," someone else responded, "if we transport them in the cargo hold of a battle-wagon."

There was silence as everyone looked at each other. We all knew what that meant. The battle-wagon would be destroyed in the explosion as well.

"We could put AMIs in some battle-wagons and make them suicide bombers."

I felt my eyebrows climb up my forehead. That was actually not completely idiotic. We'd have to think about how many dreadnaughts we'd staff with AMIs, though.

"Or SCUT-based remotes."

I looked around. "Okay, who is that? Those are some good ideas. Maybe you should be on the committee."

Someone stepped forward. It was Elmer. "No thanks. I'm just trying to spare my hide." He grinned around at the audience and we finally got some laughter.

"There's also relativistic ramming," another voice interjected.

I shook my head. "We thought about that. It would have to be busters, or something that could be directed. And even so, you'd have to launch weeks before the encounter, and you'd have to plan it to intercept the enemy at the right place and the right time. Chances of getting it right are too low. Plus they'll see the approach from a light-hour out with SUDDAR and they just have to dodge. The busters would have a ridiculous tau and wouldn't be able to react quickly enough. If we forget about relativistic speeds and just stick to our normal ramming, they won't even feel it. Or they'll just zap ship-busters a couple dozen at a time with those big zappers."

There was a short silence as everyone digested this.

We knocked around the weapons issue for a while, but soon realized we were all rehashing the same information. I ended the meeting, and we broke into groups. Technically, this was the social part of the get-together, but we've always been a workaholic. Each small crowd turned into a single-issue discussion group.

In one group, Jacques was doing an informal presentation on the Pav. I found Bob, Bob-1 that is, in the audience. I stepped up beside him; he nodded an acknowledgement and turned back to the presentation.

I wanted to say something to him about the Deltans—to commiserate, or express sympathy, see how he was doing, *something.* He was effectively banished from their society. He'd pretty much adopted the tribe as his family, and to be cast out like that couldn't be easy.

But, you know, we are Bob. Smart, driven, and socially inept. I focused my attention on the presentation.

The Pav seemed, in many ways, to be very human. Okay, they were furry, had group marriages, and ran around on all fours. But other than that...

The Pav tended to a sort of natural socialism. They had social institutions for the less fortunate, but those seemed to be supported by private funding. And well supported, too. Pav governments, even the types that, on Earth, would have been heavily interventionist, tended to be lean and hands-off. On the other hand, the Pav were, by human standards, about as organized as a basket of puppies. I wondered what effect introducing Robert's Rules of Order would have on them.

Jacques finished his presentation, got a round of applause, then the questions started. I grinned, nodded to Bob, and wandered off.

So many Bobs. So much intelligence in this room, if I did say so myself. So much control of resources, spread over a sphere that might be approaching a hundred light-years in diameter. And we couldn't put together a plan to protect a single planet. With a grimace of self-loathing, I popped back to my own VR.

# 65.  Grandpa

**Bob**
**January 2195**
**Delta Eridani**

Archimedes hovered like a nervous father as Belinda cleaned up her new pup. Buster smiled at him, but I could see an edge of irritation as well.

*It's the sacred duty of every parent to drive their kids crazy. Especially when they become grandparents.* I grinned at the thought of my mother and father as grandparents, doing their best to make Andrea and Alaina insane. Then I had to wipe my eyes as the thought brought back a cascade of family memories. A quick frame-jack allowed me to get it together without missing anything.

Belinda handed the pup to her mother-in-law and started cleaning herself. Diana rocked the baby for a few moments—very likely another universal—then smiled at Archimedes.

It was a picture-postcard moment, if you could ignore the bat-ears and pig snouts and fur. And I wanted, more than anything I'd wanted in a long time, to be able to share in it. Archimedes and Buster would have been fine, but Diana would go screeching to the elders at the first sign of a drone. Damn, I disliked her.

In his forties, now, Archimedes still showed exceptional good health. He was, of course, the first generation of Deltans to grow up with the improved nutrition that *The Bawbe*'s inventions had brought to the tribe. But even so, he seemed to be aging slowly for a Deltan.

I thought of pestering Bill again about the androids, but he had so many projects on the go, not the least of which was the terraforming of Ragnarök. Bill was good-natured about it, but I had to believe that I was being a bit of a pain.

Just the same, he said he was close. A decade or two at most. It just wasn't a priority. I suppose I could offer to help out, but realistically the Deltans and the armaments project still occupied most of my time. And anyway, no one likes a kibitzer.

I pulled out of the surveillance drone, and picked another that was spying on Caerleon, the new Deltan village. Caerleon was situated in another of the old abandoned village sites—not surprising, since whatever made it a good location the first time would still hold true. With the reduction in gorilloid populations and alteration in gorilloid behavior, the village was a good deal safer now. I smiled sadly at the thought. That was the result of my efforts, and they couldn't take that away from me.

Caerleon sat at the top of a rise, barely classifiable as a hill. But the thin soil prevented trees from growing there, resulting in a nice open space. Good for living, and easy to defend.

I found myself constantly worried, though, about relations between Caerleon and Camelot. The establishment of the second village had been peaceful in that no one got stabbed on the way out. But the acrimony had been strong, and tensions still ran high between the two villages. It boggled my mind that so soon after almost becoming extinct, the Deltans had managed to develop into some kind of cold war mentality. The real problem seemed to be that most of the residents of Caerleon were in the adolescent age range, and apparently felt a need to prove something.

The antagonism of the Caerleon Deltans concerned me enough, in fact, that I'd set up a surveillance system that would warn me if a significant number of them started a march on Camelot. I was probably just being paranoid, though. I hoped.

# 66. It's Happening

## Bill
## January 2208
## Epsilon Eridani

[Others convoy detected]

Not good. This was probably it. The Others would be heading for Gamma Pavonis to strip it down, leaving a dead planet and an empty system.

"Okay, Guppy. Details?"

[Convoy is twice the size of the GL 54 convoy. Projected destination is Delta Pavonis]

*Delta Pavonis? That can't be right.* "Confirm that, please, Guppy."

[Convoy trajectory is pointed directly at Delta Pavonis. Barring an unexpected course correction, certainty is 100%]

"Son of a bitch. The Pav." I sent a quick email to Jacques in Delta Pavonis and Claude in Gamma Pavonis, explaining the situation. I followed up with messages to Oliver and Mario. Everyone else would get the announcement on the Current Events RSS feed.

Within seconds, several people popped into my VR.

"This is not according to plan," Claude said.

Jacques shrugged. "I mentioned this possibility at a moot a

while back. Delta is a richer target. A couple of extra years may be a small price to pay for double the payoff. And they know it, seeing the size of the convoy they're sending."

"Any chance that's because of us?"

"Not a chance, Claude," I said. "They don't know we're in that system in the first place. And anyway, it's not like we've done more than buzz around them like a gnat. We *are* irrelevant."

"And we will be assimilated." Oliver gave us a lopsided grin. We all chuckled dutifully, at the attempt at levity more than anything.

"Getting down to business, how is our troop buildup?" I looked at each person in turn.

Jacques spoke first. "I've got twenty dreadnaughts, each of which has five fission bombs and the usual complement of busters for defense. I've been working on some fusion bombs, but haven't gotten them far enough along. And now we're out of time."

Claude jumped in as soon as Jacques was done. "I've got fifteen dreadnaughts, but I've managed to make a total of six fusion bombs to replace some of the fission weapons."

I looked at Oliver, who shrugged. "I'm building like crazy, old man, but I'm too far away to do any good. I'll send out what I have, and maybe they'll be useful for when the Others hit Gamma. Assuming they go there next."

I looked around at everyone, then shook my head. "Another year or two, and we'd have had the cloaking cracked. I'm sure of it. As it is, do what you can. We'll have a moot over the next couple of days, but other than moral support, you guys are on your own."

\* \* \*

The moot was held within a day. It was a somber affair. When I ascended the podium, all conversation ceased. No air horn, no boos. A sea of faces looked back at me, all wearing the same downcast expression.

"You all know the situation. Anyone have any ideas?"

"I don't suppose your asteroid mover could move Pav..."

I looked at Thor. It probably hadn't been a serious suggestion. "Sorry, buddy. In theory, the system can move anything, but right now I'd have trouble getting something the size of a planet to budge. Maybe someday..."

"If we don't mind the inhabitants freezing to death about midway through the move."

I nodded at Ben, one of the new batch of dreadnaughts. "True. The trip would still take a year or two subjective, and all that time spent without a sun. No bueno for sure. I think we're stuck with the situation as it is. It's going to come down to a toe-to-toe punch-up, and unfortunately before we're ready. The only advantage we have is that we know it's going to happen and they don't."

* * *

I looked over my reports. Claude had launched all of his new dreadnaughts to Delta Pavonis. With their better acceleration, they'd arrive before the Others, but only just barely. Any strategies would have to be worked out while they were in transit.

Between Claude's group and Jacques', we had thirty-five dreadnaughts. Jacques would probably get that total up to about sixty by the time Claude's group arrived. It sounded like a lot until you looked at the size of the Others' force. Twenty death asteroids, forty cargo vessels, and several hundred attendants. The attendants could be considered equivalent to busters. They were almost certainly AMI-controlled, and could be depended upon to ram an enemy if required. The cargo vessels would be difficult to destroy simply because of their size, but I didn't expect a lot of offensive capability there.

The death asteroids would be the big unknown. We were pretty confident that we could withstand their death-rays, but we really didn't know what other weaponry they might have in reserve. It was a safe bet that the Others had thought of the possibility of running into another species capable of fighting back.

I mentioned this to Garfield, and was surprised when he didn't agree with me.

"I think we've visited pretty much every system that the Others have been to, Bill." He waved a hand casually at the star map he'd popped up. "And they haven't run into anything like that. So they've never had their butts kicked. Even when we've run up against them, the worst we've done is blow ourselves up. They're arrogant. Borg-level arrogant and maybe even beyond. We're not even assimilation targets to them, we're just food."

I thought about this. "So you think they may be overconfident."
I grinned. "Or maybe just appropriately confident."

Garfield responded with a rueful chuckle. "Yeah, whatever. The point is, though, they may not have a plan B."

## 67.  Bad News

# Howard
# December 2210
# HIP 14101

HIP 14101 was a bit of a bust. Nice sun, nice spectral lines, but nothing orbiting it worth talking about. A Jovian had managed to set up shop at the outer edge of the comfort zone, leaving no space for any terrestroid planets.

I was having a good time investigating it, though. According to WikiBob, no one had yet given a gas giant anything more than the standard cursory once-over. Okay, granted, they're hard to colonize. But still.

Adapting the drones to operate inside the atmosphere of the Jovian was a constant headache—a game of Whack-a-Mole, as Original Bob would have said. I would get a little deeper in with each new prototype, but I was losing about one in three. But there was lots of metal in this system, and I had all the time in the world.

I was relaxing out on the patio when a *ding* indicated an incoming message. I popped it up and started to read.

It was another update from Dexter. More about the colonies, several new cities, population up over a million, space industries, yadda yadda.

Oh.

Stéphane was dying. Haliburton's Encephalopathy had been identified within a decade of landing on Vulcan, and appeared to be one of the few diseases that found Terran life compatible. There was no treatment yet, and it was fatal within six months. I felt my stomach drop away. Stéphane had been my friend for a long time, and the thing with Bridget hadn't changed that. Not really. But it reminded me that I called humans ephemerals for a reason.

I'd been lounging around in this system for too long. First, I wrote an email to Bridget and Stéphane, and asked when I could arrange a call.

Then, there would be other calls to make.

\* \* \*

I pinged Bill, then popped in when I got an acknowledgement. Garfield was there as well, sitting and drinking a coffee. Diagrams and notes covered all the walls. Just your basic, normal, mad-scientist lab.

Both of them looked down in the dumps. All the Bobs were preparing for the Others' arrival in Delta Pavonis. Bill and Garfield no doubt felt pressure to produce new weapons, but you could only do what you could do. Well, I sympathized, but I had immediate concerns.

"Hey, guys," I said, motioning to the decorations. "What's the project?"

"Couple of different ones," Garfield answered. "But most of this wall is the Android Project. That's what you called about, right?"

I nodded, and examined my shoes for a few moments before looking up. "How close are you guys to a more-or-less human-equivalent android? I'm going to have a funeral to attend soon."

Bill and Garfield looked at each other, then back at me. "Pretty far along, actually. We've got a prototype. It looks like a mannequin, and you wouldn't want to go dancing, but for walking around, I think it's ready."

"Could I make one in three months?"

Bill thought for a few moments. "Right now it's all prototypes and one-offs, with manual assembly. We'd have to put together formal printer plans, but once we have those done, yes."

I nodded. It would be in time. You never knew for sure with medical predictions, of course. But one could hope. "Send the plans to Dexter at Vulcan when they're ready, okay?"

* * *

I'd received an email from Dexter that the android was ready. It was time to arrange a visit. I took a deep breath and placed a phone call.

After a few rings, Bridget answered the phone. "Howard?"

"Hi Bridge. How's Stéphane doing?"

Bridget hesitated. She looked terrible. Stéphane's illness was taking its toll on her as well. Her eyes were red, her hair was gray. Her *skin* was grey. I wanted to take her in my arms and make it all go away. And, I realized with a start, this was the first time that I had articulated my feelings about her so clearly.

"Stéphane won't last much longer. Another couple of weeks is the most the doctors will commit to."

"I'm so sorry, Bridget. How's he taking it?"

"He's mostly not lucid any more, Howard. We knew that was coming, and we've said our goodbyes." She blinked back tears as she spoke. Brave words, but the pain behind them shone through.

I endured a momentary wave of grief as I realized I wouldn't be able to say goodbye to my friend. I looked at Bridget without saying anything, and she nodded, understanding completely.

I tried to say the usual inane words of encouragement. I would have stayed on the line as long as she wanted. But she was tired, physically and emotionally, and she soon begged off.

I hung up the phone and put my face in my hands. It took several milliseconds to get myself under control, then I pinged Dexter.

"Hi Howard. Checking up on Manny?"

"Yep." I looked around Dexter's VR. It was a basic library sort of thing. I'd begun to notice less and less effort by the Bobs, especially the later generations, to put together an interesting VR. I made a mental note to discuss the shift in attitudes with Dexter if the opportunity ever came up.

He nodded and popped up a video and some report summaries. The video showed Manny the android in his support cradle. He looked complete. I leaned forward and looked closely at the summary windows.

"All tests completed successfully," Dexter said. "I figured you'd want to do the first activation."

"Thanks, Dex."

Bill's android project had been going on and off for sixty-five years now, and this was the latest version. Manny consisted of a carbon-fiber-matrix skeleton, designed and articulated to replicate the human version as closely as possible. Memory plastics that contracted when a voltage was applied stood in for muscles. The artificial musculature was laid down over the skeleton in the same layout as human musculature. The result was something that should be able to move, behave, and appear realistic. And neural feedback from the android would ensure a realistic experience for the operator.

Unfortunately, human-appearing skin and hair were low on the priority list. Right now, Manny did indeed resemble a mannequin more than anything else. No hair, pale plastic-texture skin, and gray, staring eyes. According to the specs, facial muscle control was still a little spotty. I had a quick glance at the Deficiencies List.

Well, Bill had said it was a prototype.

# 68.  Recording

## Jacques
## September 2212
## Delta Pavonis

Guppy popped into VR. **[New memory core is online]**
"Good. It was getting a little tight. Have the drones resume the full program."

Guppy nodded and disappeared.

I had implemented a plan to record as much of the planet as I could before the Others got here. Not just Pav civilization, either. Plants, animals, scenery, geology, anything and everything I could think of. I built a standalone set of stasis chambers well in advance of the colony ships, and now I was slowly stocking it with genetic material from every species that I could get a needle into. A very informal and ad hoc genetic diversity vault, in essence. I had no overall organization, as I'd had no time to catalog and categorize the life on Delta Pavonis 4 into any kind of system. I was, in effect, stealing a strategy from Noah and treating everything as a "kind". The recordings would help with identifying species and such later. If there was a later.

I was also recording Pav societies, cultures, and languages. Between all the spying and recording, my data storage requirements were massive. Guppy had just done the third upgrade since

I'd started the project. I estimated there was at least one more upgrade coming.

I had played with the idea of contacting some Pav on the sly, perhaps to get a personal account of life. But Bill had convinced me that it would be cruel at best, and at worst, ghoulish.

Instead, I operated as a passive observer. Our technology was much better than the Victorian-era Pav sciences, but even so, things didn't always go perfectly. There'd been a couple of sightings, and Pav society now had their own version of conspiracy theorists and flying-saucer nuts.

It made me wonder if the human equivalents had been based on some kind of reality. I tried to imagine some alien version of replicants hanging around Earth and kidnapping people. Mmm, nope. Especially with the anal probe thing. Just, no.

\* \* \*

Since the plan involved kidnapping twenty thousand Pav, I wanted to have a pre-selected target group. Running around, grabbing people until I hit my quota, just didn't strike me as efficient. I spent some time doing a census of small towns until I had found two that came in just under ten thousand souls each. I could, if necessary, top up the numbers from what appeared to be nearby military bases. The two towns, Mheijrkva and Aizzilkva, were like small-town USA—rural, residential, stable population, family-oriented.

I wanted to document and understand Pav society at the grass-roots level. On the other hand, I didn't want to go down the road of Bob-1 and end up getting attached to individuals. I had a bad feeling, though, that we Bobs had a shared weakness of some kind—some need for attachment. It would require a delicate balancing act.

I picked a house at random in the town of Mheijrkva and set up surveillance. Gnat-sized roamers installed cameras and microphones in the house. I felt dirty, like some kind of voyeur, but reminded myself that I was preserving the record of a culture that would likely not exist in another decade.

\* \* \*

The Los family group seemed fairly average, as Pav families went. Six adults, split evenly between the genders, plus nine children at various ages. The Pav didn't have a large need for privacy, so bedroom organization was based mostly on available space. Furniture tended to move around on a daily basis, depending on mood.

Meals were held at specific times, simply because of the logistics of preparing food for that many people. But there was no organization that I could see. My best metaphor was a birthday party attended by two-year-olds—a total free-for-all.

The adults held an assortment of jobs. The Pav didn't seem to care about stratification of social classes. The matriarch of the house, Da Hazjiar Los, was on Mheirkva's town council. She seemed intelligent and, for a Pav, very level-headed. I made a point of tagging her for special handling, if and when.

I settled in for some long-term spying on people's lives.

# 69. Wake

**Howard**
**January 2211**
**Vulcan**

*Okay, here goes.* This was the third time I'd said that, but I still hadn't opened the cargo bay door. Stage fright, for sure.

Manny would never be mistaken for human. He was a giant step down from Mr. Data, in fact. But I had told Bridget I would be there, and I was going to keep my promise.

I took a deep breath—Manny performed the motion, not that he needed oxygen—and commanded the door to open. I stepped out and looked around.

I had landed the cargo drone in the parking lot of the funeral home. A small crowd of people was gathered in front of the building entrance, watching. I guess they'd been waiting for me. I activated magnification for a moment and recognized several people, including Butterworth.

I walked toward the group, concentrating on not falling flat on my face. I'd practiced beforehand, but this was my first physical public appearance in almost two hundred years. *Nervous* didn't even begin to cover it.

Butterworth nodded to me. "Not bad, Howard. I'm sure you'll continue to improve the product."

I nodded back. There wasn't enough facial control to smile, yet, and I didn't trust my voice right at that moment.

We stepped into the building, where Bridget was waiting. She smiled, and my heart was almost wrenched out of my chest at the sadness there. She'd been with Stéphane for eighteen years. She stepped up to me and said, "Howard. I'm glad you came. Can I hug you?"

"Yes, of course. Manny has full sensory input. It'll be my first real hug since I, uh…" Died. Wow. Almost a total foot-in-mouth moment. "…since I became a replicant."

She wrapped her arms around me and hugged, and I could feel every bit of it, from her head against my cheek, to her breasts against my chest, to her arms around my back. The moment lasted an eternity, and a fraction of a second. Bridget stepped back and looked into my eyes, and I tried to re-engage my brain.

I finally managed, "It's good to see you." A small, panicked corner of my mind wondered if Manny had faithfully rendered my imitation of a fish trying to breathe. I hoped not.

I looked towards the coffin. "I guess replication wasn't an option?"

"Catholic, remember?" Bridget gave me a wan smile. "I don't think the Archbishop would approve."

I wanted to ask if she would reconsider it for herself, but this wasn't the time or place.

This was the memorial. The funeral mass had already been held, and I hadn't actually forgotten that Stéphane was Catholic. I would have been a distraction, to put it mildly. Bridget had been careful with who she invited to this event, to prevent any kind of awkwardness with yours truly.

We stood around and talked, compared memories. I met Bridget's children, Rosie, Lianne, and Howard, who answered to Howie. He would have just turned thirteen by the old Earth calendar, and seemed uncomfortable with his height, as if he'd just been through a growth spurt.

Howie bombarded me with questions, while the two girls stood behind him and looked on with wide eyes. Turned out Stéphane had told stories about me.

I told Howie a few stories about his father. As I did, memories of our early days on Vulcan flooded back. Stéphane had always accepted me as just a guy he talked to on the phone a lot. There'd never been any awkwardness, any reserve. It hit me that he was the best friend I'd had since well before I died. I scheduled a good cry for later, when I was alone.

Bridget came over to stand beside me, a plate of food in her hand. I looked down at it: the usual mix of hors d'oeuvres, meat slices, and crackers. Bridget saw my glance and asked, "Can you eat?"

"Not yet. Bill's going to engineer Manny to be as human-like as possible, eventually. He's been distracted with the Others thing, though. I'll eat something in VR."

Bridget looked at her children, at her plate, everywhere but at me. I knew the conversation we'd had before I left Vulcan was still hanging there, between us. I sighed, and experienced a moment of panic when I realized that the sigh was audible.

"We'll talk some other time. You're not leaving right after the memorial, are you?" Bridget had a small smile on her face.

"Uh, well, physically I'm about nineteen light-years away, Bridget. SCUT remote capability is making distance mostly irrelevant. Manny will go into storage when I'm done with him. So there's no *leaving* as such. I'll always be around, whether by phone or in person. So to speak."

I looked around. The two girls had wandered off, but Howie was glued to our conversation.

\* \* \*

"How'd it go?" Bill's posture reminded me of Bridget, the day we introduced our product to Butterworth.

I guess I should have expected it. This was a potentially watershed moment for the Bobs. Real physical contact would change all of our interactions.

Bill and Garfield had both popped in as soon as I came back to VR. Dexter was there, as resident Bob. And Bob-1 had shown up as well. I gathered from conversation that he'd been harassing Bill for years about the androids.

"It worked," I said. "It was a controlled environment, and everyone there was expecting me, of course. I don't know about going out in public."

"But it's a start. And a successful one." Bob was nodding his head repeatedly. I wondered for a second if his avatar had gotten stuck in a loop. But no, that was just excitement.

I accepted the inevitable, and settled into my chair for the debriefing.

"But how did it *feel?*" Bill fairly glared at me with the intensity of his question.

I had a momentary image of him reaching down my throat and ripping the answer out of me. I snickered, which got me a couple of concerned looks. "Uh, compared to VR?" I looked up for a moment, organizing my thoughts. "It's an order of magnitude more real. I don't know how much of that is psychological, just from knowing that it *is* real. But I think the VR only provides the sensations we've programmed it to provide, while Manny gives us everything, expected or not, relevant or not, and not under our control. Think of it as the difference between trying to tickle yourself versus being tickled by someone else. It's an entirely different, far more intense experience."

"Yeah," Bill responded. "I tried to get some of that back with the baseball games, but I think it still falls short."

"Don't get me wrong, Bill. It's not like I expect us to all fall over and go crackers. The VR saved Bob-1, and it's saved all of us. We all agree on that." I shrugged. "But it's not the full-on experience. We've forgotten what that's like. Today just reminded me."

I looked at Bob, who had finally gotten the head-bobbing under control but was now bouncing on his toes. An arched eyebrow made him blush and stop the motion.

"I think the Android Project should be bumped up in priority," Bob said.

Bill rolled his eyes. "There's a surprise. You willing to help? You have the free time, right?"

Bob looked abashed, and Bill winced at the unintentional cheap shot. "Sorry, buddy. Didn't mean that the way it came out."

Bob shrugged. "I get it. And yeah, I do have a lot of free time these days. Maybe this will help."

Bill popped up the project notes and schematics, probably rushing to change the subject. Garfield moved in, and the conversation went all technoid.

I sighed, stood and waved to everyone, then popped back to my VR. I had some thinking of my own to do.

# 70. Conversation

## Howard
## May 2211
## HIP 14101

Bridget's voice sounded tired. She was looking better, though, at least over the phone. Her color was coming back, she was starting to take care of herself again. I ached to say something, to take her hand, to—okay, I needed to cut off that train of thought. I silently chanted *ephemeral* a half-dozen times. It didn't help.

"But it wouldn't be me, would it, really?" Bridget's image in the video window smiled.

Her sad smile was a pale ghost of the high-wattage grin that I remembered from better days. I swallowed and, after a false start or two, replied, "That's a philosophical argument that I freely admit I'm not able to be objective about. I'm not Original Bob. I'm not even Bob-1 or Will or Charles. But I'm me, and I feel just as alive as Original Bob did."

I stood up and began to pace around my apartment. The image that Bridget's phone displayed to her would, of course, stay centered on me. "It would be you in very real ways, Bridget. I don't know from souls, but in every other way, you would live on."

"I mentioned the idea casually," Bridget said after a moment of silence. "The girls looked horrified. Even Howie looked unsure. And you know he's all about you and the other Bobs."

I smiled in response. Bridget's son was certainly my biggest fan.

I hesitated before continuing. "Look, Bridget, it's not like any decision is irrevocable. Except the one that's in force if and when. I checked with Benning. All you need to do is have her record a video call where you state your wishes. It counts as a codicil. You can record a new one any time."

"I know, Howard. And for the moment, at least, I'll have to pass."

I sighed, defeated. "Okay, Bridget. But I'm still going to build the equipment. At least we don't have to behead and freeze you nowadays—the stasis pods will do a much better job of preservation. And the scanners are pretty straightforward. Plus, it's not necessarily just you. We could—" I stopped abruptly as a thought hit me. I queued it for consideration after the call.

Bridget looked at me with an arched eyebrow, but I didn't explain, so she dropped it. "I hope you won't be upset at me for this, Howard. I still want you to visit and all."

"Of course not. It's your decision, Bridget, and I'll respect that. And yes, I'll visit when I can." I gave her an apologetic shrug. "Manny is getting a makeover right now. Bob-1 is insanely OCD when he's motivated—no surprise to anyone—and he's been improving the android tech at a furious pace." I chuckled. "Bill admitted to me that he's a bit embarrassed. He worked on the project for decades, and Bob's leaving him in the dust in a timespan of months."

"So Manny will be a little more human next time I see you?"

"Actually, Manny will look like Original Bob, from what I'm told. Believable hair and skin, and so forth. And he'll be able to eat. Although he won't—uh, never mind." TMI. She really didn't need to know the ultimate fate of the meal.

Bridget laughed. She knew exactly where my mind had gone. Just one of many things I loved about her.

"So we can finally have dinner together?"

I smiled and nodded. Finally, a real date.

* * *

"Butterworth?" Bill stared at me, eyebrows climbing his forehead.

"Well, granted, Riker will probably have a cow, which will be ironic. But Butterworth has got to be in his eighties now, if not more. The guy's like an Egyptian mummy. He just gets drier and more leathery."

"Maybe he's a Pak Protector." Bill grinned at me.

I rolled my eyes. Honestly, sometimes the early-generation Bobs were a bit weird. "Yeah, anyway, he's military. Or ex-military, whatever. Maybe he can help with the war."

"Interesting thought, Howard. I'm not against it, by any means. We should run it through a moot before bringing it up with Butterworth, though."

I nodded, unfazed. Moots were held weekly, these days, because of the Others' threat. I wouldn't have to wait long.

\* \* \*

I'd never seen Butterworth actually speechless before. I'd seen him trying not to explode, I'd seen him explode, I'd *listened* to him explode. This was new.

Butterworth stared into the video window, his jaw hanging slightly open. Finally, he found his voice. "You want to *replicate* me?"

"Well, eventually. Not like this week. The process can't be done on a living person, not if you want to be left with a living person afterwards. But I'm building the equipment for—er, for any such circumstance, and it occurred to me that you would be valuable for the war effort."

Butterworth looked down at his desk in silence. Then he looked up and smiled. "Sure, why not?"

*Well, that was easy.* "Um, okay. I'll send you a file with some information. You'll need to update your will."

Butterworth nodded and ended the call.

# 71.  Charlie

## Bob
## June 2213
## Delta Eridani

Charlie hung in the rack, powered down and looking boneless. The Deltan android looked utterly convincing—I had put a lot of effort into getting the fur right, both in texture and layout. I didn't want Charlie to come across like all the bad ape and werewolf costumes from twentieth century movies. This needed to be believable.

I realized that I was stalling. The android had been checked out every which way, and it was now time to put up or shut up.

Sighing, I ordered the cargo drone to open the hangar door, while I activated Charlie.

I turned my head and looked out the cargo bay doors. It took a moment for my eyes to adjust to the bright daylight outside. I undraped myself from the support rack and, staggering a little, walked to the doors. I stood for a moment, looking around at the forest. I'd seen all of this many times, of course, from the various drones, but there was something viscerally different this time. I was *here* in some undefinable way. It might be as simple as the feeling of the breeze lightly ruffling my fur, or the smell of the damp leaf layer that formed the floor of the forest. I spared a moment to grin with unconstrained joy, which the autonomic interface converted to a spread-eared, wide-eyed expression appropriate to a Deltan.

Stepping out onto the surface of Eden, I looked down at the ground, feeling the slightly slimy texture as the decaying leaf fragments squished between my clawed toes. Dappled sunlight flickered as the tree branches and leaves moved in the breeze. With an effort, I brought myself back on task. I triggered the heads-up display and pulled up a local map. The image hovering in my line of sight showed my location, and the location of Archimedes relative to me. I turned to line him up, and began to walk.

* * *

I spotted Archimedes through the underbrush, the observation drone hovering near his shoulder. He casually worked a small flint core as he waited. It appeared I was far more nervous about this meeting than he was. Or maybe that was his way of coping.

Well, whatever. Showtime. I walked towards him, and said his name as soon as I was within conversational distance. He looked up, and his eyes went wide. Springing to his feet, he squeaked, "Bawbe?"

I grinned at him as I approached. I opened my mouth to respond, but stopped in surprise when he jerked back and exclaimed, "Woof! Wow!"

"Problem?"

"Sorry, Bawbe. You smell. Kind of like the drones, especially when a new one is delivered. And also a bit like the ashes from a cold fire. You definitely won't fool anyone."

"Aw crap." I rolled my eyes in frustration. "I didn't think of that. Deltans depend much more on the sense of smell than humans do. Is it really bad?"

"Not as long as I'm upwind, no." He grinned at me.

"Gotcha. Okay, I'll go work on it. How about the rest? Does it look okay?"

Archimedes cocked his head one way, then the other. "You move in a sort of jerky way. Like a pup when he's learning to walk, but maybe that'll go away. What's more weird is that your fur pattern is exactly the same on both sides of your body. No one is like that. It stands out."

Of course. I'd made Charlie completely symmetrical. I would have to fix that. And the odor. I needed to smell like a Deltan, and more importantly like an individual. I took a deep lungful of Archimedes, cataloguing his odor and the lingering essence of what had to be Diana. It wasn't insurmountable, thank the universe. Just chemistry.

"Got it. Okay, Archimedes. I'll go away and fix this stuff. I can see you trying to stay upwind of me, even though you're being polite about it." I chuckled. "Having been downwind of a couple of people who needed showers, in a former life, I can relate."

Archimedes looked slightly confused, but nodded. I waved goodbye and turned to walk back to the cargo drone.

\* \* \*

Charlie the android, Take 2. I walked up to Archimedes and spread my arms, palms forward, in a *Well?* gesture.

He took a deep sniff, cocked his head, and nodded. "You're walking better, as well. I guess that's just practice, like with children. And your fur pattern is better. It's very simple, but I know a few people like that. You'll just be forgettable." He grinned at me.

I laughed in response. "Well, that's fine. The last thing I want is to attract attention. Now, will I be questioned if I enter Camelot?"

"No, I don't think so." Archimedes turned and gestured towards the village, and we began walking. I silently ordered the drone to return to standby.

"Camelot is so big, now," he continued, "and Caerleon is growing as well. Even with the tension between us and them, a certain number of people still move back and forth. It's not like there are rules about it." He gave me a sideways glance and a knowing grin.

I pantomimed silent laughter at him.

Archimedes and I had talked about many things over the decades. I think he now understood that I wasn't some kind of supernatural being, just someone with more knowledge than him. In a society where very little changed from generation to generation, it was easy to think of The Way Things Are as some kind of natural state. But Archimedes had seen enough new knowledge in his lifetime to understand that when you went from not knowing something to knowing something, it changed the way you lived.

With the loss of that awe had come a much deeper friendship, and a better understanding between us. Archimedes thought a lot of the things humans took for granted were hilarious. Like the idea of rules for everything. Deltans simply wouldn't stand for such regimentation of their lives.

I found myself coming around to his point of view, more and more.

In short order we arrived at Camelot. With an effort of will, I suppressed the Monty Python skit from my mind.

As we walked across the land bridge, I looked ahead at the village proper. It was a sea of Deltans, in groups around the central fires, and smaller groups around individual fire-pits. I could see Archimedes' point. No one would be able to keep track of this many people. Really, based on the old definition of a village where everyone knew everyone else, this could be thought of as an unhealthy development. Caerleon wasn't much better. I wondered if the Deltans had a higher tolerance for crowding, or if they had developed a reluctance to split off villages because of the gorilloid and hippogriff threats. I resolved to bring it up with Archimedes when time permitted.

We moved toward Archimedes' *hexghi*. There I saw Diana, Buster, Belinda, and a couple of generations of children around the fire. Buster's siblings had long since moved on to their own firepits, but Buster had stayed close with his father. I was glad of that.

So, Diana. I was unreasonably nervous. Really, how could she associate me with *The Bawbe*? I appeared to be some random Deltan. Just the same, I couldn't shake it.

We sat down at the fire, and Archimedes introduced me to the adults using a common Deltan name, which I instructed the translation routine to render as *Robert*. I performed the proper ear-waggle greeting to each. Diana didn't even twitch, and I relaxed.

I noted that Diana was looking old and frail. It confirmed my feeling that Archimedes was aging more slowly than average. Probably the same gene responsible for his increased intelligence was affecting his lifespan. I felt a moment of relief that she might be gone soon, then a spike of shame at the thought. I might not like her, but she was Archimedes' life mate, and he was my friend.

The kids—I realized with a shock that these were Buster's *grandchildren*—had started a game of tag while the adults talked, and one of them barreled into me. There was a moment of tense silence, then I laughed and poked the child with a finger. The tension dissolved and Diana passed around some jerky.

Just family.

## 72.   Battle

**Bill**
**February 2217**
**Delta Pavonis**

> *All warfare is based on deception.*
> *-- Sun Tzu, Art of War*

The defensive crews were less than a week away from Delta Pavonis, and their tau was now down to the point where it was worthwhile having a conversation. Rather than asking them to jack up to our time rate, we would be slowing down to theirs. Because of the numbers, I was hosting the meeting in the moot VR.

"First and most significant," I said, "is that we've cracked the cloaking tech. It took a lot longer than I expected, so Jacques has only been able to retrofit about half of his nukes. There's no time for you to do anything, so all the non-stealthed hardware—including Bobs—is going to be considered decoys."

I looked around the room at a sea of somber faces. We'd all gone into this with the attitude that it was probably a suicide mission. With remote backups, suicide missions weren't as final as they used to be, but still... the person restored from a backup was not the person who created the backup. It was some comfort to know that your memories would go on, but it didn't feel that it would be *personal* in some way.

I glanced at the status window that I had put up. It showed the Others' armada only two days farther out. We had very little time to deploy a defense.

"How are we doing this, then?" asked Andrew, one of the squad leaders.

I nodded to him, acknowledging the question. "I've discussed strategy with Butterworth. Unfortunately, most space battle strategy is theoretical, since there's only been one space war. But I discussed options extensively with him, and the colonel did have some suggestions about deployment. He can't be personally involved, of course, since he operates on biological time. For what it's worth, I'll be acting as his proxy."

There were silent nods around the circle. I added arrows and icons to the status window. "Your group is coming in from this side, and Jacques' group will be coming in from *here* and *here*. We'll hit in three waves, staggered so we're not taking each other out. Hopefully the Others can't redeploy defenses quickly enough and will have to split their assets into three groups instead." The animation in the window played out a visual of my description.

"While the Others are fending us off, the stealth bombs will come straight in. We hope that they will be able to get in close and do some significant damage."

I sat back, chin in hand, and studied the graphic. There was no subtlety at all. On the other hand, it was nice and simple, with few unknowns.

\* \* \*

The first attack group was five minutes out when the Others registered their presence. The group's trajectory brought them in at thirty degrees off of their approach line. I could see in the SUDDAR window that the Others were deploying drones to act as a first wave of defenders. There wasn't enough detail at that distance to be able to tell, but we assumed they were rotating the death asteroids to target us as well.

There was very little conversation as we approached. Each Bob presumably took the time to make peace with his own thoughts. Or update his backup. Either or.

At about three minutes distance, there was a whoop from one of the dreadnaughts. "Just took a hit from a death ray," he announced. "I got sparks, but no significant damage."

I smiled but didn't comment. At this distance, even a version-3 Heaven vessel would have survived. We had to assume they were either massively overconfident, or that had been just a probe of some kind. At least one death asteroid was now discharged. It was unlikely it would be able to recharge in time to participate further in this battle.

At one minute, I activated the general channel. "Time to rock, boys. Deploy all busters and nukes. Let's light up the sky!"

The Bobs did as ordered. Seventy-five ships became almost four hundred signatures. Now the Others would have to react. Death zaps would simply not be an option for taking us down.

And sure enough, SUDDAR indicated a massive rearrangement of vessels. We had a couple hundred drones to deal with. Statistically, we should be able to get through the defenders with about half of our units, but that wouldn't be enough to take the Others' main vessels down. I was sure the Others must be smiling—or whatever they did—with glee at our pathetic showing.

And finally, contact. Andrew's group was the first to pass through the Others' armada. At the speeds they were travelling, there was no chance of any actual visual contact. *Star Wars* notwithstanding, ships didn't buzz around each other like World War II fighter planes. Everything happened in microseconds, and showed up only in status windows.

Results from the first pass showed we'd lost about half of our busters and bombs, and eight dreadnaughts, but we'd taken out about twice as many of them. That was pretty good, and should wipe the smile-equivalents off of the Others' face-equivalents.

Apparently the Others agreed, because half of the death asteroids released zaps at our armada.

"Report," I ordered on the general channel.

Responses came back. No further Bob casualties, although a couple of the dreadnaughts were doing emergency repairs. They must have been caught square in the middle of a beam.

However, the bombs and busters weren't particularly shielded, and any unit caught anywhere in one of the death-rays was dead. We had made a decision, based on this likelihood, to equip these units with regular radio comms only. No advanced SUDDAR, no SCUT, and no chance of giving anything away to the enemy.

The second wave came in right away, not giving the Others time to regroup. They approached from thirty degrees off the Others' flight line as well, coming in from a vector at 120 degrees of rotation. I watched in the status window transmitted by the group leader.

The second wave passed through the Others' armada as quickly as we had, but with much less organized resistance from the Others. We were able to put several nukes into a couple of big cargo carriers, and even into one of the death asteroids. The nuke must have hit a charged accumulator of some kind, because the pyrotechnics were truly epic—far more than could be accounted for by a low-yield fission bomb. Twin jets of white-hot plasma, glowing right into the x-ray band, shot out of the vessel in opposite directions. The surface of the death asteroid peeled back, then it completely disintegrated, spewing pieces in all directions. Cheers went up from all the video windows.

The Others responded with a volley of something—possibly drones, possibly missiles—aimed at the receding attack group. The bogeys displayed truly incredible acceleration, in the hundreds of G's. It took only moments for us to find out what they were.

Fusion bombs.

The second battle group had been clustered together—no reason to scatter, as far as they knew. Now they were melted slag. We'd lost twenty-five dreadnaughts and a couple hundred drones. Bobs looked at each other, stunned.

But our third battle group was coming in, and we had no time to mourn. I sent a quick IM to the group leader, instructing them to scatter at the end of their pass.

The Others started moving their defenses to the point a further 120 degrees around, where they expected us to come in, given a symmetrical series of assaults.

Exactly what Butterworth had suggested they'd do.

Our third group came in only ten degrees off the first group's path, 130 degrees away from where the defenses were forming, completely blindsiding them. The dreadnaughts and drones tore through the defenders like tissue paper. Lobbed fission weapons took out two cargo vessels and another death asteroid.

As the battle group exited the theater on the far side, they scattered. The Others launched another volley of fusion drones in pursuit. The Bobs had a massive head start, but the pursuers had that ridiculous level of acceleration. It was a footrace we couldn't win.

Everyone was intent on the developing drama, which left the door open for Butterworth's next suggestion. A trio of lonely nukes, on ballistic trajectories, with virtually no emissions, now sailed in from the vector from which the Others had been expecting the third attack. Three flashes, and two more cargo vessels were drifting, offline.

I imagine, somewhere in one of the death asteroids, some Others general was screaming invective at his subordinates while veins pulsed on his neck and forehead. Or some equivalent. In any case, the Others apparently decided to finally take us seriously. A massive series of SUDDAR pings emanated from their fleet, swamping our receivers. The transmission power was truly incredible, and my jaw dropped at the readings. I looked at one of the other Bobs. The sheer power behind that broadcast said, better than anything else they'd done, that we were gnats.

And more to the point, it lit up every vessel and drone in the immediate area. Whether it would reveal our last surprise or not, well, we'd know in a few moments.

It did.

The Others launched a dozen fusion drones straight forward along their flight line, where several cloaked fusion bombs were approaching. This would have been our coup de grâce. Instead, it would be little more than a parting shot.

I instructed the incoming nukes to begin evasive maneuvers. The Others might not be able to maintain a continuous bead on the cloaked units.

The Others' fusion drones deployed into a defensive grid, and detonated simultaneously.

"Not bad..." Charlie said. "They estimated that pretty well."

I checked status. "They took out two of ours. The last one still looks operational. I don't think they have time to do anything about it. It's also interesting that they haven't broadcast another ping like the last one..."

"Like the gamma-ray blasts, it probably requires a recharge."

I nodded distractedly while I guided the last cloaked fusion weapon. Right into one of the death asteroids. It detonated perfectly. When the flash cleared, there was nothing left but scattered debris.

We were done. We'd used up everything we had. Our battle groups, what was left, were heading away from the Others' fleet at far too high a velocity to be able to turn around in any reasonable interval. By the time we could get back in the game, the Others would be at the Pav home planet.

Eight death asteroids and eleven cargo carriers were still under power. If they decided to continue on and rebuild in the system, there would be nothing we could do. We held our breath, as the seconds ticked by.

No change.

I sat, stunned, as the Others continued on towards Delta Pavonis, and the Pavs.

We'd failed.

**[Incoming message. In Mandarin]**

I was almost doubled over with nausea, but it was logical to find out what they had to say. "Put it on, Guppy."

*You have proven to be more than food. You are pests. We will harvest this system, despite your pathetic attempts at defense. Then we will harvest your Sol and Epsilon Eridani systems. And your species will end its existence in our larders.*

Fuck.

I tried to open a chat with Jacques, but got nothing. I pinged Andrew instead.

"Hey Andrew. Any idea where Jacques is?"

"Hey, Bill. Sorry, Jacques was killed during his group's attack. We have a differential up to the last few minutes, so we'll be restoring him as soon as we have a new vessel."

"Crap." I rubbed my forehead. We had some spare matrices, but it could still be days before we were able to get that done.

Andrew interrupted my train of thought. "Did he ever follow through on that plan to kidnap some Pav?"

"Yeah. Kind of a worst-case response. I've triggered implementation already. We'll get twenty thousand Pav off-planet before the Others get there. We're not going to be gentle about it, though. We can't afford to have a discussion and ask for volunteers."

The Pav were now an endangered species. I just hoped that Jacques had taken plant and animal specimens and such.

# 73.  Collection

## Phineas
## February 2217
## Delta Pavonis

I closed the connection with Bill, and turned to Ferb. The defense of Delta Pavonis had failed, and we now had to compound the karmic deficit by ripping up to twenty thousand people from their homes by force.

Jacques had put a lot of thought into the problem, and Ferb and I had expanded on the plan once we'd come online. It wasn't going to be pretty. But there simply wasn't time for explanation and debate. It should have helped that the people we were going to snatch would otherwise die. It didn't.

Jacques had selected two towns of the right size, in different parts of the target country, to maximize genetic diversity while still retaining community. We carried specialist drones in our holds, ready to do the deed.

I hovered over my town, Mheijr, in the dead of night. If this was Earth, it would be about 3 a.m. A dog barked—well, the local equivalent of a dog did the equivalent of barking—but otherwise, there was no movement. Without an electrical grid, most places still went totally dark once everyone went to bed.

I sent out the first wave of drones. These were equipped with canisters of a heavy, odorless gas that we'd developed. It would render the victims unconscious for up to four hours. By then, hopefully, we'd have them all in stasis.

The drones performed their task, then headed back to the cargo hold, and the second wave of drones exited to collect bodies. Each drone could hold two adult Pav. It would take about fifty trips per drone to collect the full ten thousand people.

I hoped that we would come up under ten thousand in total rather than have to leave people behind. I dreaded what anyone would have to go through, waking up to find that almost everyone in their town had disappeared. It would be devastating, even without the inevitable suspicion that would fall on them.

The operation completed flawlessly.

Some comments over the SCUT from Ferb indicated that his end wasn't going quite so swimmingly. I smiled, thinking of the ribbing I'd give him. Then I lost the smile when I realized neither of us would be in the mood.

I'd emptied the town, with a count of 9,273. I checked with Ferb, to see what his head count would be like. His town was coming in under as well, so I implemented one of our contingency plans. There were a number of bases within a few hundred miles that housed either standing armies or perhaps some version of peacekeeping forces. I raided three of them, and brought my total up to within a hundred of my maximum capacity. Some military personnel would be worth having.

The gas we had used would biodegrade within hours. By the time investigators were brought in, there wouldn't even be an odor. Assuming they had time to do that before the Others got here.

I pinged Ferb. "Ready to go?"

He didn't answer for a few milliseconds. I was just opening my mouth to repeat the question when he responded.

"Yeah, looks like it. Woo hoo…"

I nodded to myself. Yeah, woo hoo, indeed.

## 74.  Observing the Process

## Bill
## May 2217
## Delta Pavonis

The Others ignored us.

I wasn't sure if they knew we had nothing left, or if they were simply not interested unless we attacked again. But either way, they didn't chase us out of the system or attempt to sweep it for drones.

We had a dozen or so stealth drones still in service, so we deployed them to record the harvesting process. This would be the hardest thing I'd ever done, but we needed as much information as possible.

The Others took a week to set up around Delta Pavonis 4. Then the death asteroids started a series of sweeps that eventually covered the entire planet. We couldn't get close enough for a visual, but we knew what was happening. Up to a billion sentient beings were being slaughtered, to serve as food and to clear the way for efficient mining operations.

Over the next several weeks the Others deployed massive printer operations. It was too early to tell for sure, but it looked like at least some of them would be building new cargo vessels.

I closed the windows and instructed Guppy to let me know if

anything needed my attention. I pinged Jacques, and received an invitation to visit.

Jacques had had ten years to prepare for the arrival of the Others, and he'd planned accordingly. He had built two colony ships adapted for Pav passengers. They now contained twenty thousand Pav in stasis. We could keep them in that state for as long as necessary. Eventually, the Others would leave. We would attempt to restart the ecology, then we'd decant the Pav. I didn't look forward to that conversation.

Jacques had also built several spare matrices and housed them in the colony ships, ready for any casualties of the attack. He probably hadn't counted on being one of those. Now he was a passenger, with no ship of his own.

Still, with the state of our VR tech and SCUT communications, it wasn't a huge disability. More of an inconvenience.

I popped in. "Hi Jacques. How's the life of a passenger?"

He shrugged. "Meh. I'm more of an administrator right now. Trying to clean up and organize the surviving Bobs and equipment, and do inventory. Nothing unaccounted for, so we don't have to worry about the Others getting SCUT or something similar."

I waved that away. "I already checked up on that. I'm more worried about the Pav. Should we consider moving them to another system?"

"I know what you mean, Bill. Here, they'll be going back to a dead planet. Psychologically, that's going to be devastating. I've got enough seed stock and such to rebuild a basic ecology, but ninety percent of the planetary diversity is gone for good."

"So, why not another system? Besides the psychological issues, by the time the Others are done with it, there'll be no metal left."

"Erm, the Others aren't *that* thorough. They take like 95% of it, but they don't scrabble for every last gram. Still, it will be a problem if the Pav want to rebuild an industrial society. Could we bring in resources from out-system?"

I sighed and shook my head. "Theoretically, sure. But then we've got another race depending on us. Another *client* race. Do you really want to become an overlord?"

"Crap." Jacques sat back and rubbed his forehead. "Whatever happened to heading off into the cosmos and exploring? I distinctly remember that was the plan when Bob-1 was heading for Epsilon Eridani in the first place."

"I know. No one to answer to, no responsibility except to ourself. Maybe we'll get back to that eventually. Right now, though, we've got all these problems, and we can't just walk away."

"Yeah, yeah." Jacques gave me a wry look, with one eyebrow raised. "Still, Pacino just keeps looking smarter and smarter."

"Mm. Look, all this is on the agenda for the next moot. It's not going to be a fun meeting."

\* \* \*

It was not a fun meeting.

We had just witnessed the death of somewhere between half a billion and a billion people. We Bobs are generally upbeat and optimistic, but this had really kicked the stuffing out of us.

"I keep telling myself that this isn't the first species that they've wiped out," Howard said, to the room in general. "But it doesn't help."

"This is the first one that we've witnessed," Tony responded. "It's just more real, somehow."

There were nods, followed by a long silence.

From the back, a voice muttered, "They need to be exterminated."

The crowd muttered agreement. I looked in the general direction of the voice. "That's a significant decision. Nevertheless, I'm not inclined to argue. Let's wait a couple of days to let our emotions die down, then take a vote."

"Leaving outstanding," Thor said, "the small detail of exactly how we're going to do that."

This comment produced another long silence. No one was really in the mood for deep thought. We'd save this subject for another day.

\* \* \*

I orbited over Ragnarök, watching listlessly through my forward camera as the planet turned beneath me. After the moot, I'd had some idea of working on my current android, but I couldn't even get up the energy to do that. Funny, since Bob-1 had woken up in New Handeltown all those years ago, we'd always seemed to be on top of things. Yeah, there were dangers, there were scary times. I remembered being unsure of whether I'd come out alive in the encounter with Medeiros. And I also remembered being almost unsurprised when he went down.

This was the first time that we had completely, unutterably failed at something. This was a total rout. There was no way to wring a moral victory out of it. And worse, I didn't see any way to turn it around.

I watched Bullseye slide across my view as I passed that section of the planet. The crater was now a freshwater sea, with a central island. Okay, that was kind of a failure, too.

The Others had brushed us aside like fleas. They'd stated their intention to hit Earth, and if we tried to stop that, they'd probably just brush us aside again. There was no way that Will was going to be able to get everyone off Earth before the Others arrived. Not even a significant fraction.

We might, if we threw everything into it, be able to get a couple million out of the way. But no more. And that would only delay the inevitable. The Others were coming, and coming to *all* the possible homes of humanity. We were an endangered species, as long as they continued to exist.

Garfield popped in, and we exchanged a few words. He wasn't in any better mood. There would be no cheering up happening here today, not by anyone. He sat and watched the video window with me.

The time passed, almost unfelt. Eventually, Bullseye came around and slid across my view again, mocking me with this visible reminder of my fallibility. Nothing like a couple hundred thousand tons of ice to make a dent in a planet.

Nothing like a couple hundred thousand tons... I sat up, abruptly, frowning. Garfield glanced sideways at my unexpected movement. Maybe we'd been looking at this all wrong.

# 75. Reunion

## Howard
## January 2216
## HIP 14101

Wow, and I thought the stage-fright was bad *last* time. I'd been staring at the inside of the cargo door for what felt like forever. By this time, Bridget would have given up and gone to bed.

I checked the time. Three seconds elapsed. *Oh, for—*

With a feeling akin to resignation, I ordered the door to open, and walked out of the cargo bay.

Bridget stood on her porch, waiting. She gave me a smile and a small, aborted wave as I turned in her direction. I walked toward the patio, cataloguing all the sensations I was receiving from Manny—the cool evening breeze, the slight unevenness of the front walkway, the brush of my clothing as I moved. And the disappearance of every inch of distance as I approached her. Like falling down a gravity well.

Finally, after a million years or so, I walked up the two wooden steps, stopped in front of her, and held out my hands. She took them and said, "You're looking good, Howard."

I smiled—I'd checked in the mirror a few dozen times, and the smile looked normal—and replied, "It's nice to see you again." Bridget would be 57 by now, physically. She'd stopped dyeing her hair and was showing her natural gray. She had crow's feet around her eyes, and an incipient double-chin.

I quite literally couldn't have cared less.

# 76.  Funeral

## Bob
## November 2220
## Delta Eridani

I stood to one side as Archimedes hugged with Buster and his siblings, Rosa and Pete. Diana had died overnight. Peacefully, thank the Universe. Deltans didn't cry as such, but their equivalent was just as heart-wrenching.

Diana was laid carefully into the grave, then Archimedes and his children each placed one white flower in her arms. As they stepped out of the way, the long line-up of descendants filed past and added more flowers.

Diana and Archimedes had done quite well with spreading their genes. When the line-up was finished, thirty-one flowers formed a large bouquet in her embrace. The family filled in the grave, then placed several large stone slabs over it to protect it from scavengers.

When it was done, everyone but Archimedes stepped back. He slowly sank to his knees, leaned forward, and hugged himself. Uttering a low keening, Archimedes rocked slowly back and forth.

I popped into VR, shaking and taking deep breaths. Charlie would be fine for a few moments on autonomous control, and I was very close to losing it. I rubbed my eyes savagely, muttered a few curses, then popped back into Charlie.

The crowd was slowly dispersing, leaving Archimedes and his children to their mourning. I took the opportunity to look Archimedes over. I had only an estimate of his age from when I first showed up, of course, but I put him at about seventy, which put him slightly older than Moses when he passed away. And Moses had been considered ancient.

All of which meant that I would probably be attending another funeral soon. I vowed it would be my last.

## 77. Completion

## Bill
## April 2221
## Delta Pavonis

It took a little over four years for the Others to strip Delta Pavonis.

It was an impressive speed, until you realized that exponential behavior was involved. They brought a huge complement of autofactories, which they used to produce equipment, which mined resources for the production of more equipment. At some point, they stopped building equipment and started loading the cargo vessels. Finally, they harvested most of the equipment they'd built. The fleet that left the system consisted of only cargo vessels and death asteroids.

Once they were gone, we moved in to examine the damage. The asteroid belt and any small moons in the system had been stripped, of course. What really hurt was the state of Delta Pavonis 4.

The Others hadn't been concerned with ecological damage, obviously. They'd left the planet a dirty ball of mud. All the green had long since faded to a dull brown. The blue of the oceans was replaced by a mottled grey, and the ice caps had either melted or been coated with dust and soot.

Every major city had been demolished. The lack of corpses was, in a way, a blessing. But it left a ghostly, empty tableau that would have been completely appropriate to any of a hundred post-apocalyptic movies.

I took it as long as I could, then I turned off the video feeds, put my face in my hands, and wept.

* * *

Jacques agreed that rehabilitation of DP-4 would take a long time, but he quite correctly pointed out that flying the Pavs to another system far enough away from the Others to be safe would possibly take just as long. We had a reasonable candidate—a wandering Bob had found a suitable colonization target at HIP 84051. At more than 40 light years from Sol, it didn't even rate a name. Just a minor designation in the constellation Ara.

I popped over to visit Will. "Hey guy. How are you holding up?"

Riker still wore a haunted look. Homer's suicide had affected him more than anyone would have thought possible. With the perfect memory that being a replicant brought with it, things didn't fade with time. The vengeance that he had extracted had helped some, but there would always be a hole in the Bobiverse.

He gave me a small smile. "Holding steady, Bill. You here about HIP 84051-2?"

At my nod, he continued, "It was on the discussion agenda, and when I brought up the circumstances, the UN voted to make it available to the Pav refugees. Honestly, I think it's a little too far from Sol to be really attractive, anyway."

I sat down and materialized a coffee, and took a moment to look around. Will had long since given up the *Star Trek* motif, and he was going by his first name—um, I guess Number One's first name, anyway—most of the time, now. That was the name that our relatives knew him by, anyway.

The VR resembled a housing unit on Vulcan, although I recognized some décor and paraphernalia from Original Bob's apartment. I smiled to see the Limited Edition Spock plaque, signed by Leonard Nimoy, hanging on the wall.

"Life just keeps getting more complicated, doesn't it?" I raised the coffee in salute.

"Suppose so." Will stretched, then materialized a coffee of his own. "I'm beginning to think Bob-1 has the right idea. He's been talking about going out again, once Archimedes is gone. Just point the ship and accelerate for a while."

I sighed and nodded. We were, what, eight to ten generations deep in Bobs, now? Bob-1 had achieved a kind of legendary status. He rarely showed up at moots any more, and when he did, it was like a Shatner sighting. I felt a deep sympathy for him. He was the first of us to get emotionally involved with ephemerals, and until Jacques and the Pavs, his had had the worst outcome.

"I understand you're going to wake some Pav and put the question to them," Will said.

"Mm, yeah. Jacques has an unreasonable attachment to the idea of recolonizing DP-4, in my opinion. But he's rational enough to see it."

Will returned one of his rare full-on smiles. "Well, *Bob*, right?"

We laughed together, and I continued, "So we'll give them the choice—attempt to recolonize DP-4, or head for a new world with an already-established ecosystem. And a compatible one, as seems to be the norm." I chuckled. "I sure wish I could go back and talk to Dr. Carlisle. I bet he'd be tickled that his theories have been so emphatically vindicated."

Will nodded but didn't comment. I sat back, and we sipped our coffees in silence, simply enjoying the company and the momentary pause in existence.

\* \* \*

The Pav huddled in a corner, whimpering. I'd expected a certain level of fear, but the Pav's reaction bordered on xenophobia.

But I doubted the, uh, *recruitment* had involved a lot of discussion and consent. Kidnapping was a pretty accurate description. The specimen in front of us was probably still traumatized.

At that moment, the door to the chamber opened and three more Pav staggered in. They were still suffering from post-stasis confusion, but they reacted in instinctive Pav pack fashion, by huddling in a pile with our first candidate. The presence of company seemed to calm her significantly.

Over the next few hours, we brought in several more Pav, until we had eight of them in the room. The number was arbitrary, but Jacques' investigation of the species had indicated a general maximum of eight adults to a family group. We hoped that it was a significant number for them.

When they appeared outwardly calm and had started to compare notes with each other, I decided it was time for official first contact.

"Hello."

All eight Pav went into alert posture. The resemblance to meerkats was even more pronounced than usual, and in better circumstances I would have chuckled at the tableau.

"Who are you? Where are we?"

This was not going to be easy. "My name is Bill. I'm part of BobNet." The translation routine rendered proper names phonetically, but the sounds wouldn't mean anything to them. "Who we are is a very long story. Where you are and why, is a shorter and very unpleasant story."

I described the Others to them, and explained their habit of raiding systems and killing off planets. A monitor on one wall displayed images of Others, the aftermath of Zeta Tucanae, and finally the destruction of Delta Pavonis 4.

As the images of dead cities, oceans and forests flashed on the screen, the Pav began to keen. Sitting through that was one of the hardest things I'd done, but I had a moral obligation to stick with it.

It took a few hours, but we finally got through the whole story. The group seemed perplexed.

"You want us to decide? To return to Aszjan or settle a different world?"

"That is correct."

The Pac huddled and argued in low voices for several minutes.

Hazjiar, who seemed to have taken on the role of spokesperson, said, "Why?"

"Because we don't know you well enough to know what would work best for you."

"Why not?"

"Because we haven't been studying you for long enough."

"Why not?"

*Oh, holy...* "That's not important. We will make the decision if you don't want to, but we wanted to give you the option first."

"And there are twenty thousand of us? Why not more?"

"That's how many will fit into the two ships that we were able to build."

"Why?"

*What're you, a four-year-old?* I would have to nip this in the bud, before I blew a transistor or something. "Again, not important now. Are you willing and able to make that decision? If not, let us know and we'll take care of it."

"We will discuss this. Is there food?"

"You mean at the new planet? Oh, you mean now. Sorry. I'll get some."

Fortunately, Jacques had thought of stocking up on standard Pav food and drink. I decanted a small supply and delivered it. The Pav laid in as if they hadn't eaten in a week.

I stared in shock at the free-for-all. So far no one seemed to have lost a limb, but that could just be luck.

Jacques chuckled at the expression on my face. "No, that's pretty much normal feeding behavior. Miss Manners would never catch on with these people."

I shook my head. "Count them after they're done, okay? Make sure there are still eight."

\* \* \*

At Hazjiar's request, we provided images of the proposed colony planet. It possessed a marginally heavier gravity, with correspondingly thicker atmosphere, but was similar enough to Aszjan that adaptation wouldn't be an issue. The flora and fauna would be completely unfamiliar to them, of course, but it didn't include anything too large to deal with.

We promised the Pav any help they needed, regardless of their decision. They seemed heartened by that, and I privately sighed in exasperation. Again, we were going to be responsible for another client race. If Jacques wanted to be involved, fine, but I resolved to keep my distance.

\* \* \*

"We will choose the new world." Hazjiar stood tall and spoke with confidence. I knew that the decision hadn't been easy, or unanimous, but I was impressed at their willingness to even make a decision.

She looked down, then continued in a softer voice. "We do not like the idea of all resources being supplied by you. No offence, but we do not know you."

I grinned at Jacques, who smiled back and shrugged.

"That's fine, Hazjiar. We'll get started right away. It will be necessary to put you back to sleep. But we'll be gentler, this time."

Hazjiar nodded. By coincidence, a nod meant the same thing to the Pav as it did to us. "When we awake, we will be there?"

"That's correct. And we will have set up an encampment for you to live in until you can build something for yourselves."

Hazjiar cocked her head slightly. "I am curious. Why do you do this? Who is paying you? Or do you expect us to pay you?"

I chuckled, which the translation routine converted to the Pav expression of humor. And a good thing—who knew how a human chuckle would come across.

"We don't use money, Hazjiar. We have no need for it."

This statement produced a look of shock. Apparently capitalism was alive and well in Pav culture. After staring at the monitor for a few more seconds, Hazjiar turned away, while muttering something that sounded like "*Dozhagriyl.*" The routine translated it as "critters with broken brains."

The Pav seemed reluctant to return to the stasis chambers, and generally acted like a bunch of kids trying to delay bedtime. Eventually, though, we managed to cajole them all through the door and into the prep room. Within an hour, they were all squared away.

"Well, Bill, I guess this is it."

"Not quite yet, Jacques. A couple of the guys did some scavenging. We've managed to retrieve enough resources to put together a couple of version-3's for you and the other Bobs who are bodiless right now. It'll take few months, but at least then you'll be able to ride escort instead of supercargo."

Jacques nodded. "Thanks, Bill. Let's do that."

* * *

Finally, departure day. The two refugee ships, officially named REFUGE-1 and -2, brought their SURGE drives up to full power and turned their bows to aim for HIP 84051. I watched their departure from the forward camera of one of the Bobs that was still in-system.

With the departure of the refugee ships, there was no longer any reason to maintain a presence in this system. It represented our greatest failure, and several Bobs had complained that it felt as though it was full of ghosts. Everyone who didn't have a reason to stay had long since left, and now most of the rest of us would be departing. A couple of eighth-generation Bobs had volunteered to stay behind and do a post-invasion survey.

I looked at Andrew across the table, waiting for him to speak. Finally, he took a deep breath and leaned forward to put his elbows on the table. "Everyone is gathering at Gamma Pavonis. Threats or no, the Others still have a Dyson Sphere to build. They won't halt everything while they march off to Sol. We want to be ready next time."

I stared into space, nodding. "Meanwhile, Riker has started building dreadnaughts at Sol, and I'm building a fleet in Epsilon Eridani. Ditto Oliver in Alpha Centauri. We have the cloaking nailed now, so we'll be able to give them a harder time of it. The root problem, though, is still to produce enough ordnance to make a dent in the Others' armada. The size problem is still overwhelming."

"This is all just a delaying action." Andrew shook his head morosely. "As long as the Others are always making the first move, we can never defeat them. All they have to do is huddle for a decade or two, rebuild, and we're back to square one. We have to take the fight to them."

"This is true, and you know damned well it's been the subject of many a moot." I glared at Andrew. "I have an idea that I'm working on that might form a final solution, but I'm not sure yet if it's even feasible. And even if it turns out to be workable, it's a long game. Meanwhile, we're also trying to gear up to an invasion fleet. Maybe we can drop in on the Others and pay our respects."

Andrew's only answer was a predatory smile.

## END BOOK 2

# Appendices

# List of Terms

AMI — Artificial Machine Intelligence

ETHER — Estimated Time of Habitable Earth Remaining

FAITH — Free American Independent Theocratic Hegemony

GUPPI — General Unit Primary Peripheral Interface

HEAVEN — Habitable Earths Abiogenic Vessel Exploration Network

SCUT — Subspace Communications Universal Transceiver

SUDDAR — Subspace Deformation Detection And Ranging

SURGE — Subspace Reactionless Geotactic Emulation

VEHEMENT — Voluntary Extinction of Human Existence Means Earth's Natural Transformation

# Cast of Characters

In alphabetical order

| Archimedes | Deltan native that Bob befriends. |
|---|---|
| Arnold | Large Deltan warrior. |
| Arthur | One of Riker's clones. Dies in a salvaging accident. |
| Bart | Calvin's clone. Resident Bob in Alpha Centauri for a short time. |
| Bashful | One of Mario's clones. Part of the group that works to identify the Others' range. |
| Belinda | Buster's mate. |
| Bender | One of Bob's clones in Delta Eridani |
| Bill | One of Bob's first cohort of clones. Sets up a Skunk Works in Epsilon Eridani and acts as the central clearing house for news and information. |
| Bob Johansson | An engineer and business owner, who gets killed in a traffic accident and wakes up as a computer program. As Bob-1, the first Heaven vessel. |
| Stéphane Brodeur | Security Chief on Vulcan, and Howard's best friend. |
| Bullwinkle | Bill's name for his experimental android. |
| Buster | Archimedes' eldest son. Deltan Native. |
| Colonel George Butterworth | Leader of the USE post-war enclave, and of the USE Vulcan colony. |
| Calvin | One of Bill's clones. Calvin and Goku battle and defeat Medeiros in Alpha Centauri. |
| Charles | One of Riker's early clones. |
| Charlie | Bob's Deltan-configured android. |
| Minister Michael Cranston | Leader of the FAITH post-war enclave, and of the FAITH Romulus colony. |
| Cruella | Deltan medicine woman. |
| Dexter | One of Charles' clones, who takes over for Howard at Omicron$^2$ Eridani. |
| Diana | Archimedes' mate. Deltan native. |
| Donald | Arnold's son. Deltan native. |
| Dopey | One of Mario's clones, part of the group who work to establish the Others' range. |
| Minister Sharma | UN rep for the Maldives on post-war Earth. |
| Garfield | Bill's first clone, and his assistant in Epsilon Eridani. |

| | |
|---|---|
| Goku | One of Bill's clones. He and Calvin battle and defeat Medeiros in Alpha Centauri. |
| Guppy | Bob's personification of the GUPPI interface. Various Bobs give Guppy different levels of system resources, resulting in slightly different behavior. |
| Hal | One of Mario's clones, part of the group who work to establish the Others' range. |
| Hoffa | Deltan native, council leader in Camelot. |
| Homer | Riker's first clone, assists in the Battle of Sol and invents the Farm Donuts. |
| Howard | One of Charles' clones. He accompanies the first two colony ships to Omicron$^2$ Eridani and stays to act as the resident replicant. |
| Howie | Bridget and Stephane's son, named after Howard. |
| Hungry | One of Mario's clones, and part of the group that works to establish the Other's range. |
| Linus | One of Bill's clones. He goes to Epsilon Indi and discovers Henry Roberts, the Australian probe replicant. |
| Luke | One of Bob's clones in Delta Eridani. |
| Manny | The first anthromorphic android, used by Howard on Vulcan. |
| Mario | One of Bob's first clones. Mario is somewhat misanthropic and takes off for GL 54, where he discovers evidence of the Others, and sets up a program to determine their range. |
| Marvin | One of Bob's clones in Delta Eridani. Marvin hangs around and assists Bob. |
| Major Ernesto Medeiros | The Brazilian Empire replicant. Brazil sends out a number of copies, which keep popping up to bedevil the Bobs. |
| Milo | One of Bob's first cohort of clones in Epsilon Eridani. Milo goes to Epsilon$^2$ Eridani, where he discovers the double planets which he names Vulcan and Romulus. He then goes to 82 Eridani where he runs into Medeiros. |
| Moses | Deltan Native. An elder who teaches Archimedes how to work flint. |
| Oliver | Bill's clone, who sets up in Alpha Centauri after Bart's departure. |
| Riker | One of Bob's first cohort of clones in Epsilon Eridani. Riker takes on the task of going back to Sol to find out what happened, and ends up |

| | |
|---|---|
| | in charge of the Earth's emigration effort. |
| Henry Roberts | The Australian replicant |
| Rocky | Garfield's attempt at a flying android. |
| Sam | Exodus-3 controlling replicant. |
| Bridget Sheehan | Senior Biologist in the Vulcan colony and Howard's eventual love interest. |
| Sleepy | One of Mario's clones, and part of the effort to determine the Others' range. |
| Surly | One of Bill's clones and part of the second expedition to 82 Eridani to oust Medeiros. |
| Gudmund Valter | The Spitsbergen enclave leader on post-war Earth. |
| Verne | One of Bill's clones and part of the second expedition to 82 Eridani to oust Medeiros |
| Bertram Vickers | Head of VEHEMENT |
| Victor | One of Bob's later clones in Delta Eridani. Takes off after Bender to find out what happened to him. |

# Genealogy

**<u>Bob</u>**
- **_<u>Bill</u>_**
  - _<u>Garfield</u>_
  - _<u>Calvin</u>_
    - <u>Bart</u>
    - <u>Thor</u>
  - _<u>Goku</u>_
  - _<u>Linus</u>_
  - _<u>Mulder</u>_
    - <u>Jonny</u>
    - <u>Skinner</u>
  - _<u>Oliver</u>_
  - _<u>Khan</u>_
  - _<u>Elmer</u>_
  - _<u>Hannibal</u>_
  - _<u>Tom</u>_
  - _<u>Barney</u>_
  - _<u>Fred</u>_
  - _<u>Kyle</u>_
  - _<u>Ned</u>_
- **_<u>Mario</u>_**
  - _<u>Bashful</u>_
  - _<u>Dopey</u>_
  - _<u>Sleepy</u>_
  - _<u>Hungry</u>_
  - _<u>Hal</u>_
  - _<u>Claude</u>_
  - _<u>Jacques</u>_
    - <u>Phineas</u>
    - <u>Ferb</u>
- **_<u>Riker</u>_**
  - _<u>Homer</u>_
  - _<u>Ralph</u>_
  - _<u>Charles</u>_
    - <u>Howard</u>
    - <u>Dexter</u>
  - _<u>Rudy</u>_
  - _<u>Edwin</u>_
  - _<u>Arthur</u>_
  - _<u>Bert</u>_
  - _<u>Ernie</u>_
- **_<u>Milo</u>_**
- **_<u>Luke</u>_**
- **_<u>Bender</u>_**
- **_<u>Victor</u>_**

Printed in Poland
by Amazon Fulfillment
Poland Sp. z o.o., Wrocław

60585706R00181